Ensign Pinson Goes to Flight School

a novel by James N. Dozier

1. Navy - Fiction 2. Flight School - Fiction

ISBN: 978-0-578-80828-4

First Edition
10 9 8 7 6 5 4 3 2 1

Contents

FOREWORD

Ensign Pinson is a distant cousin to Ensign Benson, an iconic character who is used for illustrations being taught in Naval officer schools. Benson is used sometimes to illustrate things being done the wrong way.

Our Ensign Pinson doesn't always do things the conventional way either, but despite occasional missteps, he usually lands on his feet. The standard path to Navy flight school with a goal of earning the "Wings of Gold" normally travels through ROTC programs in college or through the United States Naval Academy. Other programs are the AOC program for college graduates who come to Pensacola to get their commissions as they begin working to get their wings. The parallel program at Pensacola is to bring in candidates with two years of college (NavCads, MarCads) who undergo a longer program to become commissioned than AOCs, but also are working to get their "Wings of Gold." That program lasts almost two years. Some, but not many, come from the fleet after qualifying for flight school by taking tests and physicals at local Naval Air Stations. The "Needs of the Navy" is the ultimate filter for the number of candidates flowing through Pensacola.

Another factor affecting flow and scheduling is the number of foreign pilots being trained by the Navy. The United States sells numerous military airplanes to foreign countries and agrees to train their pilots as part of the deal. These pilot trainees do not usually land on aircraft carriers and waive that part of the training syllabus. They generally waive the survival at sea training, as well as the escape and evasion. Their own military operations determine the level of proficiency they require. That level is nowhere near the level of proficiency our own pilots achieve. Our Navy washes out a very high number of candidates for a variety of reasons. They pride themselves on the pressure they exert on the candidates, starting with the academics of ground school. The swimming and survival programs are also no piece of cake.

Our Ensign Pinson has qualified for flight school by applying from the fleet and passing physical and aptitude tests. Normally, the blessings of one's commanding officer are recommended, but are not always gained. Sometimes, the commanding officer doesn't want to lose a vital member of the staff and would prefer to reject a transfer request. The "Needs of the Navy" always prevail.

Ensign Pinson achieves orders to flight school and separates from his ship, the USS Neptune, in Barbados. Again, not the usual way to get to Pensacola. Ensign Pinson takes a very circuitous route to his destination, stumbling through a few landmines along the way.

FAREWELL NEPTUNE

As I was piped off the USS Neptune, I took a look back, saluted the ensign flag, drew a deep breath and wondered to myself—what have I done?

I shouldered my duffel bag and hailed the only taxi in sight. We headed to the Grantley International Airport in Christ Church, Barbados. As we drove through town, I smiled as we passed the cat house where all the chaos happened two nights ago. We arrived to the sound of steel drums reverberating near the ticket counter. Did I really want to be leaving the security of a Navy ship to enter uncharted waters? Well, it was too late now—the die had been cast. Besides, my position on the USS Neptune may have been compromised. Better to get out while the getting's good.

I chuckled to myself at the thought of the Phantom's revenge. If Captain Tuna figured out what I had done, I would be in the brig with all of my deck division sailors. I felt a twang of remorse as I left my shipmates behind—they were actually beginning to grow on me. Oh well, I can still keep in touch.

My plane tickets showed me on CaribeAir to San Juan, Pan American to Miami, and National Airlines to Pensacola. This was the first time I had been able to wear my dress whites in a long time. I loved the stares of the other passengers in the terminal. Orders to Navy Flight School were an unbelievable turn of events after a year on a Navy workship. Rags to riches, I think. The kicker, however, is I don't have a clue how to fly an airplane. What will I do when I actually sign in—tell them I am a fraud who just wanted a change of duty station?

I checked in with a smiling agent. She had a beautiful Bahamian accent. "Senor, we're happy to have you fly with us today. I must tell you that you'll have some interesting co-passengers today."

"Will you give me a hint?" I asked.

"No, I would like it to be a surprise," she informed me with a pleasant smile.

The aircraft was a DC-3, an older airplane which had been in service for many years. It was a tri-cycle gear tail dragger, which has two main landing gear forward and a tailwheel in back. The cockpit was the highest point and the back of the airplane the lowest while sitting at rest on the ground. The entrance was in the rear and the incline was very noticeable.

There was a single stewardess who met me at the door, as I boarded from the back.

"Hello, Senor Pinson, I am Constantina. You are the only passenger today, so you will have a few seats to yourself. I'll be serving a meal to you of huevos rancheros."

"I understood there would be co-passengers today."

"Yes, there are, come on in."

Sitting up in the first-class section were thirty-six crates of some types of fowl, like chickens.

"What the heck is that?" I called to Constantina.

"Those are prized fighting cocks specially raised here in Barbados. They'll be sent to San Juan for entertainment. Barbados is proud of this source—best in the world. We had to take out all of the first-class seats."

This is just dandy, I thought. The birds screeched and emitted an awful smell. "Is the air conditioning on?" I asked.

"Sorry, there is no air conditioning on DC-3s."

"How long is the flight?"

"About four hours," she said.

Crap! I thought. Maybe I would have been better off to go by boat.

I threw my duffel bag into the overhead and took the back seat, farthest from the birds. I took out my officer record folder which contained my fitness report. This report is generated by your current or previous commanding officer and is essentially your performance grade—life or death for advancement in the Navy. I was hesitant to look, but the chicken was in the pot now so I might as well take a peek. I'm on the way to flight school, so I can't be stopped. (I don't think.)

The performance grades were to be expected. "Average" across the board. The Navy had a great need for pilots, so Captain Tuna couldn't afford to blackball me. He would be called in for obstructing our war effort. Quite ironic, "Average" coming from a Captain who had just run aground in Bermuda.

Everything happened so quickly. There I was, deck division officer on the USS Neptune, managing sixty men from the boatswain mate division, the working division of the ship. These men did the most menial jobs, including deck swabbing and other similar duties. My chief petty officer was the real boss, and I tried to stay out of his way.

Before my demotion to engine room watches while at sea, I was a proud officer of the deck while underway. Upon getting orders to flight school, Captain Tuna decided I needed a change of watch schedules and assigned me to midnight engine room watches from Bermuda to Barbados. I'll admit it was a very creative form of punishment.

All that is now history, and I strapped on my seat belt as the DC-3 started cranking the engines. The sound of the engines infuriated the birds and they sounded their displeasure. Four more hours, I disgustingly surmised.

"Do you have ear plugs, clothes pins, and blinders?" I pleaded to Constantina.

"No, Senor Pinson, but it will be better when we're airborne. The airflow will be calming to them, I think."

"Don't you have sedatives for fighting cocks?"

"No, they are on a corn diet. I'll feed them after we're airborne."

"What are the chances of feeding them after we get to San Juan?"

"Sorry," she laughed. "I have my orders. Their tickets cost more than yours."

Captain Cortez alerted us on the PA when we were ready for takeoff. "Constantina, make sure the birds are strapped in good . . . also, don't forget the passenger."

The DC-3 struggled into the air and we did a flyby over the Neptune. I could see some of the deck apes waving to me. They had no idea about my flying conditions.

As we settled into the cruise phase of flight, the ride became bumpier. Constantina came to my seat and informed me the pilots had a report of some bad weather coming into San Juan.

Constantina served me the "huevos rancheros" which I scarfed down. Then she proceeded to feed the birds. The birds quieted somewhat during the feeding. After about three hours the air got really bumpy. The birds reacted as you might imagine, and the smell became intolerable. I barely beat Captain Cortez to the toilet.

Co-pilot Roberto Rodriguez announced to us a tropical storm was forming around San Juan. El Nino was acting up again.

My last few airplane rides had been disastrous. The T-28 ride at Breezy Point resulted in air sickness. The landing in Hamburg resulted in the evacuation of Ole Shaky. I'd already lost my breakfast today and a storm was brewing in San Juan. Maybe flying is not the road I should travel.

"Constantina," Captain Cortez announced on the PA. "We're going to an alternate instead of San Juan. The winds are too high for our crosswind limitations. The winds are over forty knots and increasing. We'll head up into the Bahamas and stay ahead of the storm. Make sure the birds are strapped down."

I wondered why the Captain was so worried about the fighting cocks? He doesn't seem that worried about me.

The next hour the ride got extremely bumpy. Constantina and the co-pilot also made trips to the toilet. The birds were trying to fly out of their cages. We went into the clouds and couldn't see the water anymore. We finally broke out of the clouds and started our descent. Suddenly the left engine began to sputter.

Constantina ran up to the cockpit. She came back shortly and looked white as a sheet. "Senor Pinson, we're getting short on fuel and Captain Cortez decided to use the remaining fuel on the right engine. We're hoping to make it to Nassau. It is in doubt, I think."

Why me, Lord? I could be back in my cozy ship stateroom, having a nice meal with my shipmates, getting ready to watch a movie, and yet here I am in a DC-3 without enough fuel to make landfall. I've just about had enough of this aviation bunk.

The left engine stopped completely, and the airplane yawed left then right. We were in the clear and you could see an island off to the right. Captain Cortez turned the airplane abruptly toward the island and started a sharp descent. Rodriguez shouted over the PA that we were planning to make a water landing.

A water landing—this is no seaplane! I said to myself.

Constantina checked my seat belt latch and told me how to brace for the landing. I must have been born under the wrong star.

Captain Cortez made a smooth touchdown on the water. The fighting cocks barely changed their chorus of screeching. After the initial impact, we became a floating object, like a boat. The engines stopped, and there was no electricity or lights.

Captain Cortez jumped out of his seat and started back down the aisle, carefully checking to see if the fighting chickens were strapped in place. He then worked his way back to check on Constantina and me.

"Man, I hate this," he said. "We almost made it. The company has been sending us out real tight on fuel lately. The good news is these airplanes are known for their floating capability. Sometimes you have to shoot them to sink them."

That made me feel really good. I guess we'll have a casual lunch now, if I don't faint.

Captain Cortez continued. "I got a call out on 'guard frequency,' which is monitored by just about everybody with a radio, so we should get help before too long. Feel free to get up and walk around as long as you don't make the plane list. I'm going to open the cockpit window just to make sure there's enough air for the birds."

Boy, this crew is sure casual. You have to wonder if this happens to them all the time.

"Where are we, Captain? I saw an island off to the right as we came down."

"You know, I'm not sure. I was getting a signal from Nassau, but I think we're way short of it. All these islands look just alike."

After about two hours of floating, Roberto yelled out there was a high-speed yacht approaching from the port side. We all looked out the port windows and observed a beautiful, sleek cutter bearing down on us.

"Hallelujah, our plight is about to change!" I exclaimed. "I can see myself riding on a yacht like that."

The big boat slowed and began to prepare a small boat to come alongside. I pulled my duffel bag down and planned to disembark. Constantina opened the main cabin door which was about two feet above the water line. The ocean was calm which was a real bonus. Two crewmen tied the small boat up to the door and came aboard.

"Buenos dias, folks, are you all okay?" The first crewman inquired.

"Si," said Cortez. "I made a perfect landing."

Pedro, the second of the two, stated, "Our instructions are to take the birds off first. There is a festival in San Juan and the birds are a high priority. If you don't mind, maybe we could form a conga line and pass the birds back and onto the small boat. It'll take three trips to get all of the crates to the yacht."

I guessed it wouldn't hurt to help out which would expedite our departure. We all lined up and began to pass the crates out. The smell was awful, and my pretty white uniform and shoes were getting soiled terribly. After the last crate was passed out, Pedro untied the rope and pushed off from the gently rocking DC-3.

We all gathered up our belongings and moved toward the back door. I looked up just as the small boat was raised onto the yacht.

"Hey!" yelled Captain Cortez. "What are you doing?"

"Sorry," Pedro answered. "We must rush the birds for a flight to San Juan. We will notify the Coast Guard where you are located. Have a nice day!"

"You can't run off and leave us!" Rodriguez shouted. "What's wrong with you people?"

Our only response was the sound of the twin engines roaring as the boat sped away, leaving spinning waves in its wake. In a matter of minutes, it had completely disappeared, leaving us in silence and dismay.

"Well, folks," sighed Captain Cortez, "I believe we just got sucker punched. The plane seems to be floating pretty well, and I think we have a couple of hours before sunset. Let's keep our life jackets on and hope our mayday call was picked up by someone other than the chicken fighter handlers. I never should have trusted that bunch of crooks. We have two life rafts on here, but I won't count on them working. The company has been cutting a lot of corners. We aren't very far from Nassau and I think Eleuthera is within a few miles. We could swim it if we had to. I don't think the sharks are that bad in these waters. Let's go ahead and get one of the life rafts inflated. The second will be inflated later, if needed."

Rodriguez pulled down a yellow raft, inflated it and then launched it out the main cabin door.

I just don't get it. I have tried all my life to do things right and bad things keep happening to me. I must admit I took advantage of a few things along the way. What would Suzie or the German girls say if they saw me now, adrift on a floating airplane in the Caribbean Sea.

"Captain, did you say we were close to Eleuthera, the island?"

"Yeah, what about it?"

"I have a friend in the Navy who is stationed there. What are the chances of us drifting that way?"

"I don't know anything about currents here, but the trade winds blow from the east predominantly. It might take a day or two to drift there, but it is possible. I hope we get rescued first."

"What if the airplane sinks during the night? Which way do we swim?" I asked.

"We have a couple of more hours of daylight. Look out over the right wing. That is Eleuthera. That is the closest point of land. After dark, let's keep an eye out for the light pattern of Eleuthera in case we have to swim for it. I want us to pair up as buddies, so no one is alone. Mister Pinson, you and Constantina will buddy up and Rodriguez and I will be the last to abandon the airplane."

Nightfall came quickly, and now we were floating in the dark. We gradually started picking up the lights of Eleuthera. We had plenty of liquids, but no food was left. The huevos rancheros was the last of the food except for some peanuts. The sea was getting rough, and we could hear the lapping of the waves on the fuselage. The adrenaline was pumping in all of us, and there was no possible way to get any sleep.

Around 0500 Captain Cortez announced, "We are beginning to take on some water. Constantina, you and Pinson take the #1 raft and get set to disembark. Roberto and I will stay a while longer. I would like you to get clear of the fuselage. We will hang around as long as she is floating. Leave your bags behind. I don't want you to drown thinking about personal belongings."

We did as we were instructed and entered the rubber raft already floating in the water. We broke out the paddles and pushed away from the airplane. Daylight was beginning to break, and we could make out an island in the distance. The sea had become rough, and the winds were gusty. A light rain was falling.

Constantina proved to be very adept at rowing, and we gradually closed in on the island. As the sun came up above the horizon, we observed a boat of some kind to starboard. It was moving slowly, maybe a fisherman trolling for lunch. Its course looked to bring us close aboard.

In a few minutes it was close enough to start waving. He obviously saw us and slowly closed in.

"What can I do for you?" one of the two asked with a thick Bahamian accent.

"We have unfortunately crashed our plane at sea and need to get ashore as soon as possible. Could you give us a tow?"

"Maybe in awhile after our fishing, we could tow you to shore. We're catching some nice stripes presently. We should be finished in a few hours."

Constantina chimed in. "I have three nice bottles of rum in my purse if you could take us in right now."

"What kind?" he asked.

"John Watlings," she responded.

"Well, they really weren't biting that good. I'll throw you a line. My name's Jean, and this is George."

We hooked up to the fishing boat and headed in.

"Are we going to Eleuthera?" I asked.

"Where in hell else would we be going?" Jean responded curtly.

We looked back toward the plane and it was still floating.

"Do you think they'll be okay?" I yelled to Constantina above the roar of the outboard motor.

"Sure, they'll be fine. Let's go enjoy the vacation. I should be on flight pay for all this. Maybe even overtime pay."

"Where'd you get the rum?"

"You didn't think I'd let it go down with the ship, did you?"

"You stewardesses think of everything," I said with a grin.

We slowed and Jean threw out a rope and pulled the little lifeboat in. He tied us up to a piling and we stepped out onto a small pier.

"Do you guys want this little rubber boat?" Jean asked.

"Naw, we don't have any use for it," I said. "Take it."

"Now that you're here, where do you want to go?" George asked.

"Do you know where the US Naval station is?"

"Sure, It's about $50.00 from here."

"How about $25.00?" I offered.

"Farther than that."

"Okay, $35.00."

"Oh, all right. But you'll have to ride in the back of the truck."

We arrived at the front gate of US Naval Facility, Eleuthera in about twenty-five minutes. The gate was guarded by a sharply dressed Marine with a carbine close by. He stopped us and asked us about our business.

I jumped out of the back of the truck, and the Marine quickly grabbed his rifle.

"Halt," he yelled at me. "Sailor, you're out of uniform. You're not wearing a hat. Are you trying to impersonate an officer? Where is your identification?"

"My officer records and identification are back on the airplane."

"What airplane? I don't see no airplane."

"It's out in the ocean floating."

"Sailor, I don't know what you've been drinking or smoking, but you and your floozie are going to the brig. You stay right here."

"Wait, wait, let me explain. Our plane crashed into the sea."

"Don't try to shit me. I saw you come up in that pickup truck. You two come into the guard house. You're under arrest."

The gun he was pointing at us looked very big and we obediently followed him into the guard house. The only way things could get worse is for him to shoot us. Constantina was looking very frightened. Trying to explain was not going to work. He frisked me for weapons but thankfully left Constantina alone.

We were put in a small holding room and the door was locked. The Marine guard made a phone call and soon a chief petty officer arrived. We could hear them talking about us in mumbled words.

"Chief Dyas, they claim they came from a floating plane. They have no identification. They jumped out of the back of a pickup truck. I think they are on drugs. Maybe they were at a costume party. I didn't get the tag number on the pickup truck. I recommend we keep them overnight to sober up."

The chief petty officer opened the door to the little room and cautiously crept in, his hand close to his holstered pistol. "So, you came from a floating plane?" he smirked.

"Yes, sir," Constantina blurted out. "We were left behind on the plane because the boat took the fighting cocks and left us."

"So, the boat took off with the fighting cocks and left you behind." The chief produced a sarcastic grin.

"That's right," I said.

"Did this plane have marijuana aboard?" The chief said with a straight face.

"Of course not, chief. It was a commercial plane."

"I see," said the chief. "This must be a commercial seaplane, carrying fighting cocks, right?"

"No, no, no," I said. "We ran out of fuel dodging the storm in Puerto Rico."

"Just tell me the truth, folks. Were you over at the Blue Moon Club? If so, maybe I can go easy on you. I have been there myself. In the meantime, just relax, and we'll let the base C.O. hear your story tomorrow, then he'll decide what to do."

He turned to Constantina. "Don't you work over at Blue

Moon? I'm certain I've seen you there."

"Absolutely not. I'm a stewardess."

"That's a good one." He laughed.

"I have a Navy serial number you can check out," I volunteered.

"Give it to me and I'll see what I can find out."

"670013."

"In the meantime, you two ain't going anywhere."

Constantina and I settled into the holding room which consisted of two recliner/bunks, two lamps and a small table in the middle. There was also an adjoining head with shower.

A few minutes later, Chief Dyas returned. "I've got some bad news for you, whoever you are. Whoever you're impersonating is on a ship at sea. Nice try though."

"No, no, that would be me. I've separated from my ship and now I'm on the way to flight school."

"Boy, you're full of it today, aren't you, pal? I can't wait to tell my buddies at the chief's club what I dragged in today."

Constantina blurted out. "You idiot, can't you understand anything? Our plane ran out of gas and we floated all night. The two of us came in on a raft."

"Well, that is even more special." The chief smiled. "I had no idea airplanes could crash and float. Your raft sure looked a lot like a pickup truck to the Marine on duty. Could he be mistaken?"

"Yes, yes, two fishermen brought us in the back of their pickup truck," Constantina pleaded.

"Okay, okay, I've had enough of this tale. Try to be cleaned up when the command duty officer comes in tomorrow morning. Perhaps he'll show some leniency. We'll send you dinner from the enlisted mess tonight. Enjoy your night." The chief turned on his heel and strode out.

"The chief invited us to enjoy the night. Guess we better make the best of it," I said with a grin.

"Why not?" Constantina smiled.

WHERE IS ENSIGN PINSON?

Constantina and I awoke from the sunlight entering our small room in the guard shack of Naval Station Eleuthera. How did we end up in such a dilemma? Hopefully, things would get better.

A knock on the door and a different Marine sentry entered carrying coffee and donuts.

"Good morning, kids, feeling a little better today?"

"I don't know yet, seems bad things keep happening to us. Are you going to spring us?"

"No, not yet. You get to tell your story to the command duty officer in a few minutes. I've brought you a copy of the *Nassau News*, our bi-weekly rag."

I picked up the newspaper and frowned at the headline:

CARIBEAIR FLIGHT 711 DITCHES SHORT OF NASSAU

Lady luck was riding with CaribeAir 711 Monday when it ditched in the sea forty miles south of Nassau while escaping tropical storm Alexa located over Puerto Rico. The plane floated for almost twelve hours before taking on water and sinking. Fortunately, thirty-six crates of fighting cocks were saved and sent to San Juan for the festival beginning today. In addition, the pilot and co-pilot were rescued by helicopter. There was no report of passengers or crew. The fighting cocks were especially important since the cock fighting is the highlight each night of the carnival festival. Mayor Juan Disanto sent a personal thanks to the brave responders who risked their lives to save the fighting cocks. The search plane had no sightings of the yellow life rafts so it is assumed there are no survivors.

The article continued without a mention of Constantina and me. Don't they give a damn about us?

An hour or so after the sun had risen, we could hear the sound of a jeep screeching to a halt. The door of the guard house slammed open and the voice of a person in charge could be heard.

"What have we got here, Sergeant?"

"Just a couple of partygoers trying to slip on base without credentials," the Marine guard answered.

"Okay, I'll take care of them. Could they be dangerous? Were they armed?"

"No, they seem pretty harmless."

"Stay close by in case I need you."

"Aye, sir."

Ensign Tom Tucker slowly unlocked the door and peered inside. I looked at him and almost fainted. He looked at me and let out a burst of laughter that caused the Marine guard in the background to freeze.

"Peter, am I seeing a ghost? You're the last person in the world I'd expect to see here. Give me a minute to collect my senses before I ask what you're doing here. Who is your friend? You both look like hell."

"This is Constantina. Just get us out of here. Trust me, we're not criminals. Just a little misunderstanding."

"Of course, gather up your things and follow me."

"We don't have any things—they were left on the airplane."

"Say that again."

"I told you to trust me."

"Okay, okay, we'll sort it out later. I think I need a drink but can't because I'm the command duty officer until noon."

I hadn't seen Tom since our graduation at OCS over a year ago and now I run into him in the brig at Eleuthera. Or, I guess he runs into me. I took the newspaper with us while Tom was signing for custody of us in the activities' logbook.

I said good day to the Marine guard, and he didn't know if he should slug me or salute me. He sure had a puzzled look on his face.

"Get in the jeep and I'll take you to my pad over by the Cotton Bay Club. You can clean up and I'll find some clothes for you. Sorry about your overnight quarters. You can both use a shower."

We left the base and arrived at a small bungalow adjoining a beautiful, well-groomed golf course. It was a typical Bahamian abode, highly colorful, nicely landscaped and very homey looking. It overlooked a golf course green surrounded by several sand traps.

"How in the devil can you have a place like this on Navy wages?" I asked.

"I'll tell you when I get back. I'm still on duty till noon, and I'll be back then. I've got some shorts and golf shirts for you and some girl's clothes for Constantina. Ophelia, my girlfriend, comes down every weekend and has plenty of clothes for Constantina."

"Okay, take this newspaper with you and it will explain some things."

Tom drove off and I turned to Constantina. "Tom and I go back to college days when we were roommates and became best friends. We went into the Navy together and got our commissions at OCS in Newport, Rhode Island. He bid shore duty and I bid auxiliary ships, and we've been split up until now. I'm on the way to Navy flight school in Pensacola, Florida, and as you can see, he's living it up here on Eleuthera. He was always luckier than me. Constantina, when did you start flying with CaribeAir?"

"A couple of years ago. I just wanted to see the world a bit before I go to med school. I finished college in San Juan, but I'm from Tortola, British Virgin Islands. I may fly one more year, maybe less, if we keep on crashing."

"Do you need to hurry back to work?"

"No, I'm in no hurry. I'm on the clock so I can stay here awhile. How about you?"

"I'm like you. No hurry to get back. I get paid by the month, so I'll get paid while here. I've been lost from the Navy before, so maybe I'll let them find me. No sense in hurrying away from paradise. From the newspaper article from Nassau, it doesn't seem like they're looking too hard. I believe we can get Tom to host us awhile till they find us. Let's call the folks so they won't worry. What is your favorite thing to do here?"

"A loaded question, but I want to go sailing. Get a little beach time in, snorkeling, maybe try some fishing, and maybe even some golf."

"Good, we can work from those options. To tell you the

truth, I'm about to get cold feet from this crashing. I had to evacuate from an Air Force plane after a hard landing in Hamburg, Germany. I'm not sure I want to be a pilot. Wonder what the chances are of the Navy switching me to duty here?"

She burst out laughing. "You know the answer to that."

"Yeah, but you wouldn't believe some of the screwups in Washington. I was sent to the wrong ship one time. A ship in Germany instead of Virginia."

Tom was back right at noon. "I see you two have adjusted to the surroundings. I read the *Nassau News*. So, you two are the missing passenger and stewardess."

"Yeah, can you believe it? Saving the fighting cocks was their main priority. I'm amazed they came back to get the pilots. Constantina and I are in no hurry to leave. Think you can shield us for a few days until someone finds us? I went missing in Germany on my original orders and they like to have never found me. Two German girls saved my life. As for Constantina, she is on hourly flight pay so we can stay a while."

"Okay, I'll play dumb and just say you and Constantina dropped in for a weekend visit without any advance notice, which is true. Let's go over to the Club for lunch and we'll sort out what the hell you're doing here. I get a Navy housing and food allowance because of insufficient officer quarters since the base is so small. I elected to join the Cotton Bay Club. Not bad, huh? You and Constantina are okay to wear shorts and sports shirts to this club. Very informal."

We entered the club and were seated at a table overlooking the pool. The sounds of the "Beach Boys" were heard playing loudly in the background.

"Tom, I don't know how you get away with it. I've been on a cable layer ship for the last year going through all kinds of traumas and you're down here living at a country club. You must feel awful about it."

"Well, you do have to be in shape for all of the activities. This afternoon, we'll just start by playing nine holes of golf. Do you play, Constantina?"

"No, but I'll try if you will put up with me."

"That won't be a problem." Tom chuckled.

"I'm off tomorrow and I was interested in getting into a local sailboat race, but I don't have a crew. Would you two want to give it a try?"

"Sure, I'm off tomorrow as well," I said straight faced.

"Me, too." Constantina grinned.

"I've been taking sailing lessons and have become quite good," Tom proudly stated. "I've primarily been working as a crewman on a Morgan out-island sailboat the Navy recreation department owns. I'm allowed to check it out as captain and can't wait to get in this race tomorrow. I can tell you two how to help me. The first-place prize is a thousand bucks. Entry fee is $100. Are you game?"

"You bet. I guess I can get on a little boat for a change. I was Officer of the Deck on a 350-foot Navy ship, you know."

"Yeah, but this is a lot tougher. All you did was tell some sailor what course to steer. I will teach you the art of sailing."

"This oughta be good."

Tom gave us a tour of the base that afternoon. "The Naval Facility controls a beautiful stretch of beach for our operations. We listen to sounds of ships at sea through our cable pickups."

"How ironic," I stated. "We were the ones who laid the cables for your sound pickups. I had no idea how the system worked. I've got to admit, you out-bid me for duty assignments. You should be ashamed."

"You had the same choices, podner. You shouldn't have listened to an upperclassman who didn't know jack about the real Navy."

"I know, I know, but I've made the best of some bad situations. Look who I'm travelling with now."

"Touche, my friend, I compliment you." Tom laughed. "After our tour, we'll head over to the club for dinner. They're having a lobster special tonight."

"I'm for that," Constantina said emphatically.

"I'll get something else. I only eat lobsters from Argentia," I smirked.

"What a snob!" Tom quipped.

"When I have time, I'll tell you how I became lobster control officer of Argentia."

The sun came up early and Tom dragged us out for a sailing briefing.

"I'll teach you all you need to know. I'll handle the steering and I'll advise you how to set the sails for best efficiency. The wind will be from the east and I'll let you know when we need to come about. We'll sail north to the number 6 'nun' buoy just south of Abaco Island, and then come back to the number 17 'can' buoy here. Any questions?"

"No, not yet, we'll trust your expertise," I replied and rolled my eyes.

We arrived at the north end of the island at the Queenstown Marina at Dunmore Town. Ten sailboats were signed up for the race, all being thirty-five feet or longer. Two Naval Facility sailors had been bribed to bring our boat over to Dunmore, and they had her ready to sail.

Tom coughed up the hundred-dollar entrance fee, and we hopped aboard.

"I'll man the wheel and you two will be handling the lines and sheets on my commands. Peter, throw off the forward lines. Constantina, you bring in the aft lines. Stow them neatly in a coil on the deck. We can't have any fouled lines. Okay?"

"Aye, captain, we're ready."

Not surprisingly, Constantina had her lines on board and coiled up before me. Stewardesses were trained for handling ropes on emergency life rafts.

The gun sounded and eleven sailboats raised their sails. Being our first time sailing together, we were slightly behind most of the boats. Luckily, Constantina raised her sail very quickly. I thought I might need to help her, but that was not the case.

The Morgan is not built for speed, more of a stable boat. Tom inadvertently turned the wheel to leeward while he was instructing us, and we quickly lost all our wind. He quickly corrected, but we lost more ground. We came about and began to tack to try to catch up.

"Why are we heading downwind while the other boats are steering upwind?" I hollered above the sound of the wind.

"Don't worry. We've got them where we want them."

Constantina suddenly jumped up and grabbed the wheel.

"Get out of the way, you two clowns. I'm taking the wheel."

"What is this, a mutiny?" Tom yelled back.

"Hell, yes!" She said. "I've seen enough. I'll show you how to sail this thing. Did you forget I grew up in Tortola, B.V.I., the sailing capital of the world? My folks owned the Moorings. Have you heard of it?"

"Sure, everybody has heard of it. Okay, you can give it a try. If you can't hack it, I'll take back over."

"I can hack it. Just shut up and do what I say. Crank up the diesel engine."

"Is that legal?"

"Yes, dummy, everything is legal on the high seas. We're so far behind already nobody can see us."

Constantina began yelling commands to us. She obviously knew what she was doing, and it was equally obvious Tom was just a pretender. I reset the sails while Tom cranked the 39-horsepower diesel engine. Our Morgan started to move faster and for the first time we began to close on the cluster of boats ahead. When we closed to four boat lengths of the trailing boat, Constantina ordered Tom to shut off the diesel engine.

"These amateurs ahead must not have noticed the ground rules, which didn't mention not using the aux motors. We won't need them anymore, anyway. Just trust me."

Tom looked at me and smiled. "I think you've brought in a ringer."

"Yeah, let's just smell the roses."

In the next half hour, we moved up to fifth place. The looks on the faces of sailors on the boats we passed were priceless. Nobody gave our boat a chance. By the time we approached the #6 "can" buoy just south of Abaco, we were in third place.

"Okay, boys, we're going to make a risky turn inside the other two boats ahead of us on the 180 degree turn at the buoy. You're going to need to be sharp or else we might hit somebody. They're going to be pissed when we cut them out, but it's our best chance to get the lead. One screw up and we might have to buy somebody's boat."

We tensed up as Constantina made the daring cut. The winds suddenly shifted, and Tom yelled out. "We're headed for the wrong side of the buoy!"

"Keep your shirt on, big boy. Let out a little on the jib for me."

Tom complied and we cleared the buoy with inches to spare.

"Boy, that was close!" I yelled.

Constantina turned toward us and gave a big wink. "I could have cut it closer."

Coming out of the turn we opened up a two-boat length lead.

"You boys just pay attention and we'll show them our dust. We've got to really kick it now. Some of them may figure out to turn on their auxes. It won't matter because we're mostly downwind now. Put up the spinnaker."

The Morgan held on to the lead and we passed the "can" buoy #17 leading by three lengths. Constantina insisted that Tom take over the steering wheel so no one would be able to identify her as the missing stewardess. With sunglasses and a big hat no one seemed the wiser. Tom made a big show of being the seasoned racing captain. Constantina and I slipped into the shadows and stayed away from cameras that might capture us and be placed in the *Nassau News*. We waited in Tom's car while he took the bows and had his picture made for the local news. The reporters wanted to find out about his mysterious crewmembers, but Tom portrayed us as just a couple of shipmates who still needed more training.

After a few more days of snorkeling, fishing, golf, and tennis, Constantina and I decided to give ourselves up. We notified the *Nassau News* that we were almost recuperated from the harrowing ordeal and would be going our respective ways. CaribeAir was rerouting a flight through Eleuthera to pick her up, and I was scheduled out on a Pan American flight headed for Miami.

"Tom, I'll give you credit. You outbid me in getting this shore duty in paradise. I may want to drop out of Navy flight school to try to get duty back here. Would you write me a letter to Bureau of Personnel stating you need another ensign down here?"

"I will, but I don't think it will make a difference. You just need to buckle down and learn to be a fly boy. That'll be a lot more fun than watching for submarines down here. I guess we do have a few fringe benefits."

"I'll say. Thanks for the hospitality. Let Constantina and me know when you have another sailing race. We'll come and give you another win."

"Constantina, maybe. I don't know how much you're needed."

"Okay, okay. Rub it in."

"I'll be ready when needed." Constantina grinned.

PARADISE BEHIND

We had a great run during our "tragedy" in Eleuthera. My golf game was still awful, but the fishing, sailing, spearfishing, and beach time was pretty special. The seafood and local hangouts warrant coming back down before long. I wouldn't be surprised to see Tom retire here.

Constantina and I informed all of the appropriate people and now must go back to regular lives. The *Nassau News* ran a front page spread about the odds for betting on the fighting cocks in the San Juan Carnival. "Chanticleer" was a 5-1 favorite. "Cocky Rocky" was the next favorite at 7-2. News of finding the two missing persons from the crash were listed in a paragraph on the page after the betting odds.

CaribeAir would be picking up Constantina on a daily flight. Pan American Airlines had a commuter flight into Eleuthera on weekends. It was no coincidence that the CEO owned almost half of the island. I will fly to Miami and change to a National flight over to Pensacola. The Secretary of the Navy sent a congratulatory letter on our survival, as well as plane tickets for me to Pensacola. I considered asking for more "recovery time" but decided at this point I was ready to get to flight training.

"Constantina, you're always welcome in Eleuthera." Tom smiled.

"Same goes for Pensacola," I countered. "Prettier beaches."

"Easier to get here," Tom responded.

"More things to do in Pensacola," I offered.

"Okay, okay, boys, I know where I can vacation now, if I still have a job. Losing an airplane may cost a few jobs. I'm not real senior."

The crew of CaribeAir were gleeful to see Constantina alive.

"We had already planned your services," Chiquita, the tall brunette stewardess laughingly said.

"It was a harrowing experience, especially the recovery here," Constantina said with a straight face. "I was lucky to have such great survival facilities on this island. Do you think my flight pay has been running for the last ten days?"

"I doubt it. CaribeAir is so tight they may have docked you for not finishing your last trip. You may owe them vacation money," Chiquita quipped.

"That would figure," Constantina said and turned to me and Tom. "Thank you, boys, for aiding in my recovery. Next time you need a deckhand, let me know."

She waved goodbye through the window as the DC-3 taxied out. Soon the silver airplane was roaring down the runway with both engines humming at full power. The DC-3 rotated slowly and soon disappeared from sight. There were no fighting cocks on the plane this time.

My outbound Pan Am flight landed shortly thereafter. As it taxied in, a long, white limousine pulled out onto the tarmac. The door of the Boeing 727 opened, and the first man off was a distinguished-looking man in a Palm Beach suit and tie. Several airline officials rushed up to greet him.

"Who's that?" I asked Tom.

"That's Mr. Trippe. He owns most of Pan Am and a lot of this island. He's the reason we get this good jet service to Eleuthera. You played golf on his golf course."

"Well, Tom, looks like you got me beat on duty station orders. I'm told if I wash out of flight school, I'll probably get shore duty. You may not have seen the last of me."

"That's fine. There's room enough for the two of us. Good luck in the flight school. Don't kill yourself."

"I'll be careful. The only thing I worry about are the takeoffs and landings."

The Secretary of the Navy leaked the story to the media without our knowledge. I didn't crave the publicity, but he sent information out to all the major networks, including the *Navy Times* weekly newsletter. I would have preferred anonymity, but I knew it wasn't to be.

Upon boarding the Pan Am airplane, the pilot and stewardess met me at the door. Captain Merrill offered his hand and said, "It's an honor to welcome you aboard, Mr. Pinson. What an amazing story of survival. How many days were you at sea in the life raft?"

"Oh, it wasn't that long, though I can't remember exactly. My companion in the raft made it seem to pass quickly. She was a good sport and very well trained. I believe we could have survived a few more days."

"I can see you've lost a lot of weight and have a deep sunburn," Miss Phillips, the stewardess added, observing my baggy uniform.

"Yeah, I guess so." I decided not to tell them this was Tom's uniform. I should have used more suntan lotion the last few days.

"The Navy only paid for you a coach seat. But we've pulled strings and have you upgraded to first class all the way to Pensacola. Is that okay?"

"Certainly. I'll try to endure it," I smiled.

The short flight to Miami went smoothly, one of my few normal flights. I'd change to a bigger airplane in Miami for the flight to Pensacola.

A Naval Flight Officer met my flight at Miami International Airport. "Mr. Pinson, I'm Ltjg. Don Johnson, media relations officer for Miami. I'm here to guide you over to your National Airlines flight to Pensacola and insulate you from the media. Do you have baggage?"

"Are you kidding me? Everything I owned is somewhere out in the Carribean Sea. You're looking at my net worth."

"Sorry about that. I didn't know."

"That's okay. We really roughed it for awhile."

"Stay close to me. I see some reporters lurking nearby."

We weren't quick enough, and several reporters hemmed us in.

"Tell us what happened at the crash," one yelled out.

"Did you think you were about to die?" another shouted out.

Ltjg. Johnson held up his big hand for silence. "I'll give you five minutes with Mr. Pinson, and then we've got to make another flight."

I chose my words carefully. "Thanks for your interest, fellas. It was quite an ordeal. The high sea state, the brutal sun and wind, the tiny life raft, the freezing water, all was fretful. Constantina and I held each other tight so as not to fall overboard. I was lucky to be aboard with such a professional stewardess. I hope her airline gives her a big promotion. We spent a few days of rehab in Eleuthera trying to get over the ordeal. You can see by my uniform how much weight I have lost. I got sunburned from the predicament as you can see. Thanks, guys, see you later."

We sprinted over to National Airlines at a distant gate. We received another warm welcome from the National crew. Captain Lovvorn ushered me to a seat in first class. "Welcome, Mr. Pinson. We have a nice, big steak for you on this flight. I can see you've lost a lot of weight from your ordeal."

"Yeah, but I'm catching up fast."

"Miss Morrisette is your first-class stewardess. She will help with your lost weight problem."

PENSACOLA AT LAST

The flight to Pensacola was uneventful. The food was excellent, and Miss Morrisette tried to over-serve me and succeeded. I deplaned the steps rather clumsily at the Pensacola City Airport. I didn't expect a reception. The mainstream media had been alerted and cameramen and reporters were everywhere. The Navy sent a PR man to meet me, a fellow ensign named Henry Cain.

"Mr. Pinson, we're so glad to see you here. You'd been given up for dead. Everybody calls me Hank. Do you want to speak to the media today?"

"Sure, let's get it over with. Sorry about my looks. It's not my uniform and I have been over-served on the flight over."

"That's okay, it emphasizes the torture you have endured in your survival."

"It wasn't as bad as it sounds."

"You weren't exactly in a country club setting."

"Actually, I was."

"Sorry, but I don't believe you."

"I don't blame you."

The first reporter from the *Pensacola Times-Union* shouted out. "Ensign Pinson, how were you able to survive in such adverse conditions?"

"Just good luck, and my very well-trained stewardess companion. The lifeboat was very cramped, but we weren't that far from land."

"You appear to be very sunburned. Was it extremely hot?"

"Yes, the Bahamas are extremely hot, and we were in the sun every day."

"I can see you lost a lot of weight by the looks of your baggy uniform."

"Not really. We ate a lot of fresh-caught fish. We had to eat what was available. There are lots of fish, even lobsters, in the Bahamas."

"Was it cold in the raft at night?"

"Yes, we had to rely on body warmth."

"Did you see the rescue planes and get frustrated?"

"We never saw the rescue planes. They were probably looking in the wrong place."

"Don't you need some time off for R and R?"

"No, I'm ready to get to flight school and get to work."

"Were you in fear of dying?"

"No, but I wasn't in shape for this type of survival."

"What is the shape of the stewardess?"

"Pretty fantastic, well above average."

"Do you have any flight experience?"

"Only as a passenger. I've had an emergency evacuation on an Air Force C-124 and now an evacuation at sea on a DC-3, as well as surviving my former ship running aground. Perhaps the Navy will waive my emergency training."

Hank pulled me away from the press.

"Mr. Pinson is obviously exhausted from his ordeal. Perhaps we can schedule a press conference for later."

We jumped into a Navy vehicle and headed for NAS Pensacola field.

The Marine gate guard snapped to attention as he recognized Hank's official vehicle. We arrived at the Bachelor Officers Quarters and Hank escorted me to the check-in desk. A steward mate petty officer first class was in charge of the sign in.

Hank explained the situation. "Mr. Pinson has no paperwork yet because it has been destroyed enroute to Pensacola. So, you can give him temporary services under authority of Admiral Gay, Commander Naval Air Training, Atlantic Fleet."

"Aye, sir, we've been expecting him."

"Hank, can you loan me five bucks? My checking account needs to be activated after being at sea for awhile. I need uniforms and other necessities."

"Sure, I can get you started."

I thanked Hank for his help and immediately went to the commissary. After losing my duffel bag and orders, I had to start a new life from scratch. My first real need was a new car. I sold my car before the cruise on the USS Neptune. I checked into my new quarters and met my roommate, an ensign from the Coast Guard.

"Hi, I'm Frank Hammer," he cheerily said as he popped up

from his standard issue desk brimming with flight manuals. "Your celebrity precedes you."

"Totally inaccurate," I said, smiling at the suggestion. "I'll give you the straight skinny later on. The media writes what they want to believe."

"Okay, I can't wait to hear your story."

Frank was short, stocky, dark-haired and energetic with an outgoing personality. He was pumped to be going through flight school, even though it was controlled by the Navy. His future airplanes would be very dissimilar from the Navy and Marine aircraft. Seaplanes and helicopters are their staples.

"Frank, my only assets are savings in the credit union. I have no car or uniforms. I have saved up a considerable amount of money by being at sea for six months and it's in the credit union. Think you could give me a lift for a few days till I get squared away?"

"Sure, I'm almost finished with ground school and have a couple of days off. Where to?"

"Let's start with the credit union."

Frank was driving a beautiful Baltic Blue Buick convertible.

"The Coast Guard must be paying better than the Navy, huh, Frank?"

"Don't think so." Frank laughed as he hit the passing gear shoving my head back against the headrest. "I've kept her below a hundred so far. You should see some of the cars the pilot candidates are driving—particularly the ones who are already commissioned."

The Navy Federal Credit Union is the best bank ever. They know your job is secured by the government so an officer is a safe risk. A car loan is a no brainer.

"I've always wanted a Corvette," I said as Frank slowed back to the speed limit.

"You've got to be careful on the base. The shore patrol loves to make examples of the zoomies. They know we're only pretenders so far. The washout rate is sky high."

"I'm going to try for a Corvette. They can't do anything but turn me down."

"Well, you won't be unique. Seems like every other Tom,

Dick, and Harry on the base has one. The local dealer is by far the number one seller in the country. You'll have to get a pink one if you want to be unique."

The Credit Union was in an approving mode, so we left the base looking for Corvettes. As we left the main gate, I observed a wrecked car left out as a static display as an example to be seen by Navy personnel. It was a Corvette.

"Don't pay any attention to that wreck. The safety officer is just being dramatic."

"It does make quite a statement."

"Let's go to Honest Bob's used car lot first. He gets a lot of turnovers when the NavCads (noncommissioned cadets) can't make payments and he repossesses the car."

Frank's convertible had hardly rolled to a stop when two attractive girls in short shorts mobbed me. They weren't particularly civil to each other.

"Hello, boys," the quicker of the two bellowed out. "How about a cold beer?"

"I'm actually here to see a salesman, maybe later on the beer."

"I'm Fannie Mae Ham, and I'm your salesperson."

"Oh, sorry, I didn't expect service this good."

"Listen, flyboy, I'll have you know I was salesman of the month last month. I know my stuff."

I could see why she was salesman of the month. I won't let her intimidate me into an easy sale. I know how to drive a tough bargain.

"What are you looking for?"

"What kind of good deals do you have for me today?"

"We have a nice deal on a two-year-old station wagon. I think you would look good in it."

Who does she think I am? I'm not interested in any station wagon.

"I think you may have misjudged me, Fannie. I was thinking of something a little sportier."

"Well, I have some Corvettes, but you don't seem the type. They are high performance and can be dangerous to the inexperienced. How about a four-door Buick?"

My blood was beginning to boil. Can't she tell I'm a pilot candidate? I can handle a Corvette.

"I've got a really great deal on a two-door Dodge. A schoolteacher took real good care of her—only 15,000 miles. A beautiful lime-green! It's a steal."

Trying to keep my cool I said, "I'll take that beer now."

"Okay, I'll get you a cold one. You can be looking around."

I tried not to be too eager. I am going to get a Corvette whether she likes it or not. I sauntered over to where three Corvettes were parked. One black, one red, and one yellow.

Fannie hurriedly brought out a nice cold beer. "Listen, sailor, I know how much money you boys make. I'm trying to do you a favor and put you in some affordable wheels. I hate to see all these repossessions."

"Let me just drive the yellow one around the block."

"Okay, you can take it out for awhile. I'll need the odometer reading. Don't drive it over forty. You'd better not get a scratch on it and have her back in thirty minutes. I'll keep Frank as collateral."

"Of course." I left Frank having a beer and drove straight to the base. I was going directly to the credit union to get a loan on this baby, no matter what the payments. I drove into the gate and was stopped by the Marine guard.

"I need to see your ID, sir." I had forgotten to get an ID.

"I'm awaiting a new ID, sergeant. You may have heard of me and my situation."

"Sorry, sir, I don't know you. Would you step out of the car and show the registration for the car."

"I can explain everything."

"Just get out and keep your hands where I can see them."

"It's not my car."

"Then it's stolen?"

"No. I'm just checking it out."

"Mister, you are wearing a uniform which is obviously not yours, driving a car which is not yours, you have no ID, do you have a driver's license?"

"No, but I will get one tomorrow."

The Master Sergeant in charge heard the commotion and emerged from his office.

"Mister, you come with me. I'm putting the cuffs on you," the sergeant boomed at me.

"I can explain."

"You'll get your chance. I suppose you don't know this very same car was used to try to penetrate the base last week by a Russian spy."

"I don't know what the hell you're talking about."

"You're under arrest under suspicion of espionage."

"My lord, this is ridiculous."

"Just calm down, the base security officer is on the way. He will read you your rights."

"I want to call Admiral Gay!"

"I'm sure you do. Just shut up or I'll do it for you."

This can't be happening, I thought. *What have I got myself into? There must be an easy way out of this.*

"Can I make a call to Honest Bob's used car lot?"

"In due time. Maybe you might want to contact your lawyer first. Honest Bob sure as hell can't help you."

"I don't need a lawyer. I just need to make a few phone calls."

Abruptly a black military vehicle pulled up and a Lieutenant Commander stepped out.

"Commander Staton, we have a possible base incursion by an imposter. He has no driver's license, no ID, a stolen uniform, and is driving the car which attempted an incursion last week."

"Wow, this is serious. Is he restrained?"

"Yes, sir, he is in the holding room."

"Okay, I'll talk with him. Come in with me. Are you armed?"

"Yes, sir."

The Commander and the burly sergeant entered the room with frowns on their faces, the sergeant with his hand on his gun. "What's your name and what's your game, mister?"

"Thanks for asking. It's Peter Pinson, US Navy, reporting for flight school. I can explain everything."

Commander Staton suddenly had a shocked look on his face. He looked as if he was about to faint.

"Come outside with me, sergeant. We have made a terrible

mistake. This is the ensign who was rescued in Eleuthera after his plane crashed in the Caribbean. His picture was in all the papers. He's here to begin flight school. Your sentry is to be commended for taking the prudent approach. He certainly could have been mistaken for a terrorist. I will handle the damage control. Keep this down home, if you get what I mean."

"Yes, sir, I get what you're saying."

The Marine gate sentry suddenly entered the room. "Sir, the Pensacola police are here and looking for a stolen yellow Corvette. What do I say?"

"Tell them the car is here and will be returned. There has been a mistake. Get the name of the owner and tell them the car will be returned shortly."

"They also want to know if an Ensign Hammer, who was held as collateral, can be released from their custody."

"Tell them to let him go. I'll call them shortly. Ask them to keep this out of the papers, if possible."

Commander Staton quickly stepped back into the room where I had been moved.

"Mister Pinson, I would like to personally welcome you to Pensacola. We apologize for the mistake here and hope you can forgive us. Security has been tight after some terrorist incursions against our military worldwide. You've already been through a lot and we will try to make it up. I presume you are interested in buying this Corvette. It was unfortunately involved in the breach attempt last week and was repossessed to Honest Bob's car lot where it was put back up for sale. I don't suppose the salesman told you about it."

"No, sir, actually, it was a sales *lady*."

"It wasn't by chance Fannie Mae Ham, was it?

"Yes, it was."

"I've heard she is quite a salesman. Majored in marketing up at Tallahassee. I'll have a car follow you to security right now to get your ID card and picture. Then he'll take you to the credit union to work on a credit application for the Corvette if you still want it. Then you can take the car back to Honest Bob's to work on a possible deal. Far as I know, it doesn't have any damage reports on it. Good luck in flight school."

Wow, what a close call, I thought. *I almost got locked in the brig again. I've got to get a lower profile.*

I went back by my room and found Frank with a stern look on his face.

"Roomie, you really hung me out to dry. I was in custody of the sales lady all afternoon without a clue where you were. We were getting worried. I tried to talk her out of calling the police. I was pretty sure you hadn't hightailed it off with her car. She said to tell you to come back and she'd make you a great deal."

"It was all a perfect storm—baggy uniform, no ID, hot car, needing a haircut, deep suntan. I could have passed as a terrorist, I guess. I'm heading back to Honest Bob's now. I'll call you if the deal doesn't work out."

"Okay, but I've a gut feeling you're going to make a deal."

I drove slowly into Honest Bob's lot. Fannie came out with a frown on her face.

"Thought I told you to bring her back in thirty minutes."

"I know, I know," I said with a defiant tone. "Things happened beyond my control."

"Sorry about the police but I don't know you from Adam's house cat. You had good collateral. I could have made a pretty penny on Frank's convertible." She laughed and motioned me to come inside. "That's the first time I've had a customer get locked up on me."

Fannie proved tougher than I thought, but I felt good about beating her down $100. I drove the Corvette out with the top down and took a brief tour of Pensacola—a beautiful city with a lot of history. I passed several Corvettes, but none were yellow like mine. At least my color is unique. I drove through the main gate and this time the Marine guard gave me a nice salute and a big smile.

"Welcome back, sir." He grinned.

Upon entering my room, Frank handed me an envelope. I opened it and had a stunned look on my face.

"You okay, Peter?"

"Yeah, it's from Admiral Gay. He wants to see me in his office on Monday morning at 0900. Frank, why can't I just have a normal ensign's life?"

ORIENTATION

I woke up Monday morning in a cold sweat. I have met an admiral (Harris) before, but under different circumstances. I had been in high demand as the lobster control officer of Argentia, and I had been able to send Admiral Harris some fresh lobsters down on a regular basis. This is different. I don't know if I'm on the doo-doo list or not. Suppose Admiral Gay found out I took a little longer than prudent in surfacing in Eleuthera. Suppose he got a message from the Captain of the USS Neptune exposing my chicanery in the engine room regarding the air conditioning prank on the senior officers? Suppose my fitness report from the Neptune was deficient? Suppose the incident with the union longshoreman was going to court? Suppose the time spent in Germany was being re-visited. Suppose the incident at the gate involving the Corvette needed to be explained?

All of these things swirled through my head as I showered and shaved. The worst thing that could happen would be to go to the brig or be sent to the Great Lakes Training Center—or maybe be sent back to the Neptune. What a horrible thought! On the other hand, maybe I will get kicked out of flight school and sent to Hawaii. Now that's a better thought.

I slowly drove the shiny new Corvette over to the administration building where Admiral Gay's offices were located. The offices overlooked Sherman Field, the airport the Blue Angels called home. The atmosphere was electrifying as the jets took off with tremendous sounds and lifted quickly into the sky.

I checked in at the front desk with a second-class yeoman's mate, a Miss Sweatland. She offered me coffee and had me seated in a leather chair. Much better than the rocking chair the recruiter used. My palms were sweaty—hopefully, the admiral won't notice.

At 0930, I was called into the admiral's office. "Sit down, Mr. Pinson. I was going over your personnel jacket and noticed you had been recommended by Admiral Harris in Norfolk. I decided to call him and catch up a bit since he was the one who recommended you. He is a good friend, and we were at the Naval Academy together. He gave you high marks as being a very innovative young officer. That's a good thing since you didn't get a recommendation one way or the other from the skipper of your last ship. That's not unusual because there's a bit of jealousy between the black shoes and brown shoes. You have certainly had a lot of interesting things happen to you in your year and a half in the Navy. The lobster control officer takes the cake. Well, you've got a clean slate here. I look forward to your becoming a Naval aviator. I trust you got squared away with the Marines at the gate?"

"Yes, sir, we just had a small understanding. Everything worked out fine."

"I understand you bought a Corvette. Be careful with those things."

"Aye, sir, I plan to keep her in the speed limits."

"Good, I don't expect to see you again until I pin your wings on next year."

That was a close call. I have no idea what the Marines at the gate reported. Admiral Harris saved the day.

I spent the rest of the day checking in, getting uniform parts, and registering my (almost) new Corvette. Frank had been in the BOQ for a month and was already a commissioned officer like me. This is a huge advantage over the cadets (Navy and Marine), who are going through officer training as well as pilot training. We have steward mates taking care of our room and other services which the cadets don't have. We eat at general officers' mess which is a cut better than the plebes. The cadets all have to salute us. They are getting up at 0500 and suffering through the chiefs' and sergeants' initiation techniques, at the same time learning how to fly airplanes the Navy way. Officer's life at the BOQ ain't half bad.

Orientation classes were on the agenda for me now. I hadn't had much time to think about what I'm here for. I didn't know beans about airplanes, much less about being a pilot. I was now changing my whole thought process.

I reported for my first ground school indoctrination class at the Mustin Training center. I was wearing my new khaki uniform which fit perfectly for a change. I felt a little sheepish driving up in my yellow Corvette while the MarCads and NavCads were marching up in formation. We gathered in an auditorium which included Navy, Marine, and Coast Guard officers, enlisted cadets studying to become officers and pilots, and some foreign pilot trainees which included Vietnamese and Saudi Arabian students.

A snappy-looking lieutenant entered the room and took the podium. He was dressed in greens, the uniform restricted to aviation officers only. Brown shoes went with this uniform. This difference in uniforms caused a natural competition internally between the two Navy branches. You might be called a brown shoe or black shoe depending on your branch.

"Gentlemen," the suave young officer announced, "I am Lieutenant Cassidy, your administrative liaison officer. I will start you off with the basics of the program today. I will be available in my office here in this building to help you along the way. The program you have signed up for and been approved for, is a difficult and demanding assignment which won't be an easy one for most of you. We put extreme pressure on you from day one, and many of you will wash out or drop on request (DOR). The ones who finish will achieve the 'Wings of Gold,'which you wear upon your chest with pride. I won't sugar coat it. We are trying to wash you out. It's up to you to prove to us that you belong here. Does anyone want to leave right now?"

I had a fleeting thought of getting up now. Maybe this would be a chance to put in a request to transfer to Hawaii. Somehow, I don't think it would be that easy. You could see by the looks on everyone's face that this was a different set of determined young men.

Lieutenant Cassidy continued with a serious look on his face. "It'll take fixed wing pilots approximately a year and a half to get your wings. Those pilots should be ready for carrier quals in about nine months. Foreign pilots, NFO's (naval flight officers,) and Coast Guard pilots won't go through carrier quals. All of you will attend ground school at this time followed by swimming, survival at sea, parachuting, escape and evasion, obstacle training and then the infamous Dilbert Dunker.

Anybody ever heard of it?"

Every hand shot up.

"Officers and enlisted will mix equally for quizzing and check rides. Enlisted will respect all traditions of the military as to recognizing the seniority protocols of all military services. You must respect and be cognizant of all officer and enlisted ranks as to Navy, Marine, Coast Guard, Army and Air Force. Cadets are junior to everyone except garbage cans."

This prompted a series of groans and boos among the cadets.

"Some of you have previous flight time from various sources. That doesn't mean diddly crap to us. We start everyone from scratch here and teach you the Navy way. Anyone who tells an instructor you did it a different way in your previous life can kiss his ass goodbye. Our instructors are specifically hired for this program so pay attention or be gone. Crying will not be tolerated. Any questions so far?"

A baby-faced naval cadet (NavCad) raised his hand. "I have twenty-five hours in a Cessna 180. Will this waive some flight time in the basic trainer?"

"Actually, it'll put you at a disadvantage. We'll have to un-train you before we train you the Navy way.

"There will be separate ground schools for Polish, Italian, French, and Vietnamese student pilots. There will be interpreters available as necessary. American Navy, Marine, and Coast Guard pilots will go through the same ground and survival classes. Can anybody here not swim?"

Half the foreign students' hands went up.

"Oh, my gosh." Lt. Cassidy grimaced when he saw the results. Most of the hands belonged to non-Americans. "In that case we will have separate classes for non-swimmers. This is, after all, a Navy facility, you know.

"Everyone here will start together in ground school, which consists of aerodynamics, power plants, navigation, water and land survival and rules of the road and air. Basic instruments will also be introduced. Celestial navigation will be introduced at a later date. Strict attention must be observed, absolutely no cheating, with the exception of foreign students who have their own standards. We encourage DOR's from student pilots who are struggling or don't think they can make it through the curriculum. I am guessing that one out of five of you will make it all the way. It is no disgrace to drop out before actual carrier quals which you'll perform solo. If you wash out, you will be reassigned to a variety of naval facilities, from Hawaii to the Great Lakes Training Center. It gets very cold up there in winter."

I sat there mulling over the situation. I wondered if there was a fifty-fifty chance of getting orders to Hawaii. I had no idea if I could make it through this program. Didn't sound like good odds.

Lt. Cassidy continued, "The only ones of you who will undergo carrier quals are Navy and Marines. Coast Guard and foreign students will not.

"A word about survival school. This will be done over at Fort Walton Beach at Eglin Air Force base. You'll be given an extensive snake identification course in case you are bitten. It happens far too often. Try to hold and identify the snake if you are bitten so the instructors can decide on the course of action. We must get poisonous victims to medical assistance immediately."

With that, a hand shot up on the second row. "Do you have a question, cadet?"

"I would like to DOR, sir."

"Right now?"

"Yes, sir, I would not make it through the program. If I saw a snake in survival, I might have a heart attack."

"Okay, you can meet me in my office later. You're dismissed.

"Now, I would like to say a few things about our swimming and survival program. I presume all of you Navy and Marine pilots can swim. Is that correct?"

One Navy ensign raised his hand. "I'm a fair swimmer. How good do I need to be?"

"Do you think you can swim a mile in a flight suit and boots?"

"No sir, I need to DOR."

"Okay, wait for me in my office. You're dismissed.

"Now, let's talk about carrier operations since we've culled out a few wimps. You will be trained to proficiency in landings by what we call field carrier landing practice, or FCLP. It is done on land and simulates the speed and configurations of a carrier landing and is almost identical to the carrier except there are no cables to restrain you on landing. You'll be solo on your first carrier flights. You leave a land base, here or Mayport, and rendezvous with the carrier at sea."

"Did you say it would be solo?" a young MarCad sheepishly asked.

"Yes, of course."

"I want to DOR. I had no idea you had to do it solo."

"You can join the line waiting in my office.

"Now that we are left with the brave, I want to show you a video of the Dilbert Dunker. This is one of the favorite devices of flight school. It is a simulated cockpit on a set of rails in a huge swimming pool and is designed to simulate a crash in the ocean. We had some deaths in the past, but the frogmen are better trained now, and things have run smoother as of late."

The video was awesome, but the demonstration person was obviously struggling to get out from under the sinking cockpit. The frogmen swooped in and unbuckled his parachute harness and the cadet came up spitting and coughing. The narrator of the video emphasized that you must keep trying until you become proficient in this maneuver. I wondered if the video was designed to frighten us. If so, it succeeded. The fifty-fifty odds of going to Hawaii are looking better every minute.

At the end of the video two more hands shot up.

"You two can head over to my office with the rest." Lt. Cassidy shook his head disgustedly.

"Okay, that's all for today. I can't afford to lose any more pilot candidates before you get to make your first flight. After I finish processing the DOR's, you may come by my office to get your individual syllabus. Mr. Pinson, I need to have a word with you now."

I cautiously approached the speaker's stand as the others filed out. "Mr. Pinson, your situation has put you in an unusual situation. You're a bit of celebrity because of your unusual survival. You'll be treated a little differently from the cadets, but you won't receive any favoritism. In fact, you'll be treated a little harder in order to set a higher example since so many cadets will be looking for you in a leadership role. Do you get my drift?"

"Yes, sir, I understand. But you realize I have no aviation background whatsoever."

"We do, so you will have to work harder. This is a challenging program. I'm here to help if needed."

"One more thing. If I wash out, where would I be sent?"

"The last one went to Hawaii, but you never know. I'm not supposed to tell people that."

OCEAN SURVIVAL

"Frank, did you have any trouble with ground school?"

"Naw, it was all a piece of cake. I majored in aeronautical engineering and got my commission in ROTC at Oregon State University. My dad was a pilot in World War Two. I grew up around airplanes. I have over four hundred hours of flight time. The swimming training was the most difficult for me. Wait till you go to Eglin and go through survival in the jungle. I've heard the snakes are bad this year, especially cottonmouth moccasins. Do not pick them up."

"Are you kidding? I'll be going the other way. There were two DORs today when Lt. Cassidy started talking about snakes. I almost DOR'd myself."

"Don't do that. You may get sent back to the Neptune."

"That would be awful. I would be permanently below decks in the engine room."

Frank and I took breakfast together in the Officer's mess. The officers were in a much-preferred situation than the cadets who won't become officers until a few months in the program. The cadets become officers after six months. They receive their wings after about a year and a half.

"Frank, does the Coast Guard have any carriers?"

"No, just you 'swabbies' and 'grunts' do that stuff. We have fixed wing seaplanes and choppers mostly. A few Lear Jets. Choppers are the backbone of the coast guard. Seaplanes are on the way out."

I left the BOQ for an 0800 class in orientation. I had a little exposure in college when I took Air Force ROTC. We were required to take some form of military service for credits, so I picked the one with the least work and best chance for a good grade, Air Force. Naval ROTC was a four-year curriculum and required too much effort and spit and polish. It's ironic that I decided to go to Navy OCS in Newport after graduation. Who knew Vietnam would come into the picture for every young man eligible for the draft? The Army ROTC cadets were required to carry a rifle and perform at inspections and other arduous drills. Air Force was the answer—no guns to clean or drills in the hot sun. In addition, the Air Force honorary "angels" were knockout girls from some of the sororities on campus—icing on the cake.

Lt. Bennett introduced himself to our power plants class of thirty-five. Included were 18 NavCads, 4 Marine MarCads, 3 Navy Officers, 1 Marine Officer, 4 Coast Guard Officers, 1 Saudi Prince and 4 Vietnamese cadets.

"How many of you have previous flight time?" Lt. Bennett asked.

Everybody except the foreign students and I shot up their hands.

"You folks will have a slight disadvantage but not much. We're going to train you the Navy way, so forget all the techniques you may have learned. We'll be flying high performance airplanes, landing on carriers with pitching decks at night, probably getting shot at, navigating at sea and in foreign countries, operating at all hours of the night and day.

"Those of you pansies who aren't making carrier landings will have an easier syllabus but don't think you won't get yelled at. We have some professional yellers here, so I don't want to hear of any of you crying after an instructor jumps you. That goes for you cadets who aren't officers yet. Those of you who are already officers and senior to the instructor will get respect from the instructor although you may be called a dumb shit on many occasions. You may not hold the instructor responsible while in the airplane. You don't want to have a bad reputation among the instructors. Do you officers get my drift?"

We all nodded in unison.

"All of you will go through power plant schools the first week. Also, you will be attending survival swimming in the afternoons. Any non-swimmers will have special classes. If you are hopeless, you will be dropped from the program, and we recommend you try the Air Force or Army. Any questions?"

"How about foreign students?" the Saudi student pilot queried.

"Sorry, I forgot about you. I guess there's no swimming required in the desert. You are secured for now. All of you will start power plant training in Building 1 at 1000 tomorrow. Good luck, gentlemen."

We arrived at Building 16 for afternoon swimming. There were various pools which were configured for various activities such as parachuting into the ocean. Our first activity was based on survival at sea.

"Good afternoon, gentlemen." A fit, muscular lieutenant motioned for us to fall into ranks by a generic looking pool. Officers were required to be in the front. After roll call, Lt. Williams came over and stood directly in front of me.

"So, you are Ensign Pinson?" he scowled.

"Yes, sir," I reluctantly responded.

"Well, I'm so happy to see you," he said in a very sarcastic tone.

"You see, I had a commanding officer by the name of Pinson, Captain R.P. Pinson. Boy, what a son of a bitch he was. I would still be in the fleet if it weren't for him. I would also be a lieutenant commander. I'll bet you are kin to him. Are you?"

"No, sir, I don't think so," I stammered.

"Well I'm going to find out for sure. You'd better not be, or your ass is grass. By the way, are you the ensign who was on vacation from the Navy in the Caribbean for a few weeks?"

"Sir, it wasn't vacation. I was almost lost at sea. It was a nightmare."

"Whole thing sounds suspicious to me. Especially the part about your survival partner. Especially her. What did she look like?" he said with a cynical smile.

"I can't remember much about her. It was such an ordeal." I had a hard time getting the words out.

"Your suntan looks like you've been to the beach. Didn't you have clothes on to protect you from the sun while in the raft?"

"We stripped down at times to wet our clothes. Guess it doesn't take much to get a suntan."

"Since you have so much survival at sea time, I guess you won't mind doing the demos for our class. We'll start today with drownproofing. I want you to enter the water in the deep end and dog paddle while I give you instructions."

"Aye, sir." I jumped in and immediately began to cough.

"What I want you to do is ball up with your arms around your knees. Take a breath and stick your head underwater for a minute. The air in your lungs will cause you to float and bob. Then you come up and take another breath and repeat the maneuver. You should be able to float for hours until you get picked up by the helicopter. You can start now."

I knew I wasn't quite ready to start but I tried to get a good breath. I was under about ten seconds before I came back up for air.

"Damn it, Mr. Pinson. That wasn't a minute. Try it again."

The results were about the same. I came up snorting and coughing.

"You get one more try, Pinson. Get your breath for a minute. We've got others to train if you can't make it."

The third time was better, but I think I'd rather just drown.

"Men, you've just seen a good demonstration about how not to do it.

Are there any college swimmers among you?"

The blond-headed ensign I had just met raised his hand.

"Your name and school?"

"Dick Callahan. I went to Auburn and swam the sprints. National champs three years. I was a breast and back stroker."

"Okay, go to it. Show Mr. Pinson how to do it."

Callahan dove in and commenced to do the maneuver perfectly.

One by one, the class all jumped in. Performances were mixed. Callahan was the best by far.

"Mr. Pinson, ready to try again?"

"Sure." I jumped in and started all over. While inhaling, I noticed him looking at some other class members. I felt for the bottom with my long legs and could just feel it. I determined I could use it for lift on occasions to help with the drown proofing. I somehow lasted a good five minutes.

"Okay, sailors. That's all for today. We have three more days allotted to get you qualified. Same time tomorrow. You will need to last thirty minutes to qualify. You're dismissed. Mr. Pinson, I don't think you're gonna make it."

I felt bad for the cadets who lined up to march to the mess hall while I was riding in my Corvette. I decided it would look better if I walked back to the BOQ.

Frank was two weeks ahead of me in the program. He will be a great help to keep me informed on what to expect in the coming days. Every bit helps.

"How was your swim?"

"I didn't have such good luck in the pool."

"What happened?"

"I was the guinea pig today. A jerk instructor linked me to a former Navy commander he despised. He decided to take it out on me. I had to demo 'drownproofing' and almost drowned myself."

"Yeah, I had a little trouble with that myself. Supposedly, your lungs have enough air to keep you buoyed for hours, but you feel claustrophobic with your head underwater for so long."

"I hope the rescue helicopters will be punctual in pickup."

"You can count on the Coast Guard," Frank smirked. "I don't know about the Navy!"

"Yeah, maybe. You'll probably all be on the golf course!"

A knock on the door and two of our new classmates appeared.

"Hey, guys, I'm Rufus Baxley and this is Joe Francis."

"A pleasure, I'm Peter Pinson and this is Frank Hammer. He's a Coastie. Where are you guys from?"

"I'm from Wyoming and Bax's a Georgia boy," Joe chipped in. "I was a Wyoming Cowboy. Toughest football team in the west. I couldn't make the football team, but I did ride broncos for a hobby. Got a lot of blue ribbons."

Rufus piped up. "Just call me Bax, if you will. I got lots of blue ribbons also."

"Bax, did you ride broncos at Georgia?" Frank asked innocently.

"No, I was president of the debate team," he said with a snicker, as we all cracked up.

"Let's hit the 'O' Club for happy hour and then dinner at the BOQ mess. The poor cadets are probably all marching while we're having a wind down at the club."

After a big steak dinner, Frank asked, "Have you boys been to Trader Jon's yet?"

"What's that?" Joe asked. "Some kind of shopping area?"

"You'll see," Frank said with a sly grin.

TRADER JON'S

During dinner at the Mustin Beach "O" Club, Cal could not contain his suspense. "Dammit, Frank, tell us about Trader Jon's!"

"Okay, but I'll only tell you about the background and origin. You'll have to judge the place when you see it. I can't adequately describe it. Trader Jon was a yankee from New York City who arrived in Pensacola around 1953. Pensacola was known as the snapper capital of the world, and it was one of the finest fishing ports in the country. Pensacola was evolving as a Naval training center, and Trader established his business as a stopover for sailors and naval cadets. As a marketing tool, Trader offered to trade artifacts for wall decoration for drinks. The gimmick worked and people began bringing all types of memorabilia to decorate the place. Hundreds of aviator photographs, airplane and sailing ship pictures, toilet seats, a stuffed dog, a picture mural by a student of Frank Lloyd Wright worth $100,000, and many other things.

"Trader himself is a very unimposing little fellow. He is short, New York accent, proudly wears two different colored socks, has a big bulbous nose, and an infectious smile. Everyone agrees he is one of the nicest men you'll ever meet. He doesn't give drinks away, but he is known to be a very generous person and absolutely loves Blue Angels and dignitaries.

The list of 'Who's Who' attending Trader Jon's is unbelievable. It's the number one tourist attraction of Pensacola. It is said every single Naval aviator who has traversed the Naval Air Station has visited Trader Jon's. At least three astronauts have pictures on the wall."

"What about the non-matching socks?" I asked.

"Well, the sock colors are always red and green. Rules of the road are for red to indicate port, and green to be starboard. So, he calls them port and starboard socks. Makes perfect sense, doesn't it? He advertises a thousand-dollar reward if someone catches him wearing a match. He married a girl from South

Alabama who is an artist. She has her paintings all over the place. They adopted two daughters who are usually helping out around the place.

"He was the first to have a stripper show that nobody watches. It was hard to get strippers when he first opened, so he didn't necessarily hire on beauty. They were required to wear G-strings and pasties which was a good thing. The girls loved to circulate and push drinks and treated everybody as friends. They never seemed to have trouble with the clients. Since every Naval aviator (including admirals) had attended Trader's at one time or another, it was the perfect excuse for anyone who got in trouble with the shore patrol to blame a night at Trader Jon's. It might help with leniency.

"John Wayne made a movie in Pensacola called 'Wings of Eagles.' He walked into Trader's one day and Trader said to him. 'You sure look familiar.'

"He said, 'I should, I'm John Wayne.' They became good friends while he was there. He even took a ship's wheel from the bar and put it on his yacht, 'The Wild Goose.'

"Astronauts who have left pictures are Alan Shepherd, John Glenn, and Deke Slayton. Senator John McCain was known to terrorize the place after graduating from the Naval Academy. Tennessee Williams was another regular visitor. A ship's bell was left by oceanographer Jacques Cousteau. Twenty-year-old Prince Andrew of England visited while he was a crewmember on Her Majesty's ship 'Hermes.'

"The news rags back home in England gave him hell for getting off the 'royal path' and being around American strippers."

"Frank, you sure know a lot about this place. Have you been hanging out there a lot?" Cal asked as he gulped down his dessert.

"Naw, I actually took a Greyline Tour when I first arrived. This place is high up on the list of tourist attractions."

Frank kept us in more suspense as we drove through the gates and returned salutes to the Marine guard as we left the base. We drove toward downtown and eventually turned onto Palafox Street and parked in a lot across from a somewhat run-down old building which could pass for a warehouse of some sort. There was a dimly-lit streetlight which added to the desolate atmosphere of lower Palafox near Trader Jon's.

Frank continued to give us a background as we exited his blue convertible and walked toward the building. The front door was a simple wooden frame about eighteen feet high with patches of naval aviation squadrons attached. A sign beside the door simply read "Trader Jon's," and below the sign was a picture of two red and green socks. Two huge columns supported the roof and the wooden siding was unpainted.

An attractive hostess greeted us as we entered. She quickly surmised we were of age and probably from the air station. We later found out she was one of Trader's adopted daughters. The lighting inside was adequate but not dim. Our first view encompassed walls which were completely filled with artifacts. There was no room for anything new. Trader told us later it was permissible to keep adding pictures and cards on top of others as long as you didn't obscure Blue Angels and other celebrities. Music played familiar music of the times from a disco. The ceilings had all manner of gadgets and model airplanes and you name it hanging down. There was a two-foot-high stage which was empty at present.

We were seated and within fifteen minutes Trader himself came by.

"Hello, boys, welcome to Trader Jon's. Have you gone to survival school yet?"

We were caught off guard by the question. Then we realized Trader probably knew more about flight school than we did. Frank's description of Trader was right on target. He was a very small man with big dimples and a huge smile. He definitely had on mismatched socks. His voice had a certain warmth despite his New York accent. "Tell me your first names, boys. I'll try to remember. None of you are going to DOR (drop on request) on me, are you?"

"Heavens, no," Cal blurted out. "We have a new celebrity here for you, Trader."

"Is one of you a new Blue Angel?"

"No, not exactly. One of us was in the news recently."

"Knock it off, Cal. This is inappropriate," I protested.

Trader perked up on this unexpected news.

"Well, you're welcome here. What's it all about?"

"Ensign Pinson, here, was the officer who survived the plane crash in the Bahamas and was stranded at sea with the stewardess for two weeks. He was lucky to survive the ordeal."

"It really wasn't that bad, vastly exaggerated," I said.

"I recognize you, now." Trader said. "You were in all the papers. Come on up to the bar with me. I want you to meet my wife and some of the girls."

Trader dragged me away from the table and ordered me a bar drink.

I was really embarrassed. Everybody in the place was staring at me.

"Trader, please keep this down home. I don't need to be recognized. I'm only a student pilot now."

"Okay. We'll keep it quiet. I want to introduce you to all the dancers who are also waitresses. They'll give you special treatment when you come in. Can you get me a picture to put on the wall?"

"Sure, I'll bring it when I come back again."

"You and your buddies get the first round on the house."

I slowly slipped back to the table with my buddies.

"Dammit it, Cal, why did you bring that up?"

"It was good for a free drink, wasn't it?"

"I would have preferred to pay for it myself."

The show started at 2100 and each of the dancers came over and performed in front of our table. We had a good laugh and wondered if this was to be a regular bailout out place for R and R. We were now alumni of the famous Trader Jon's—soon to have an artifact on the wall.

TORTURE SWIMMING

Lt. Cassidy informed our class there was a back up in training and we would have a one-month pool awaiting flying status after the ground school was completed. Washington issued a command to deliver more foreign-trained pilots to assist in the Vietnam war. The idea was to have them fight their own war and for the U.S. to simply advise. There were a half dozen Vietnamese student pilots in our current class accompanied by their own interpreter. These student pilots were immersed in a six-month program to learn English and the results were less than desired. You must be English proficient while flying. English is the universal language of aviation around the world. No matter what country you fly into, there will be a controller versed in English (Russia, China, France, etc.).

The unexpected backlog resulted in the affected Navy and Marine student pilots being required to check in at 0800, and then remaining secure for the rest of the day. Each had to check in each morning in person—no substitutions. This left us free to have the latitude to travel around in the Pensacola area. We would be required to finish with our ground training before the backlog kicked in.

At lunch in the BOQ mess, we met Cal's roommate, Ensign David Anderson. "Andy, where are you from and what's your claim to fame?" I asked.

"I'm a Hoosier from Indiana and went to IU. I was the head manager of the football team my last two years during our streak."

"What were the numbers of the streak?" Bax asked.

"I managed the football team through twenty-one straight Big Ten losses. The referees never gave us any breaks."

"Right," Bax chuckled.

Cal, Andy, Bax, and I pondered over the implications of the upcoming pool. We decided the proper option would be to rent a house on Pensacola Beach so we would have a daily crash pad. The next afternoon after torture swimming, we decided to run the idea by some of our classmates. There was immediate interest.

After lunch, we went to our second session of survival swimming. Lt. Williams was waiting with a scowl on his face. After roll call, he asked me to step forward. "Ensign Pinson, how's Commander Pinson doing today?"

"I don't know, sir. I haven't talked with him."

"So, you do know him."

"No, I didn't mean that I know him."

"Well, I'm going to find out. You can lead off the drownproofing demonstration today."

"Yes, sir." I dove into the pool and commenced the procedure. I had vastly improved from the first day.

The remainder of the class jumped in and Williams focused his attention on another ensign named Jack Haines who was completely inept in the water. After finishing the session like drowned rats, we were informed the test for proficiency would be required on the third session. Any failures would become remedials with a chance to wash out.

The Fleet Post Office is the US mail service for the Navy. This service has the ability to track down sailors all over the world and deliver the mail very efficiently, even at sea. I picked up my mail from the desk of the BOQ and received a big surprise.

Dear Peter,

Lisl and I hope you get this letter. We are stuck up here in Hamburg in this cold winter weather and need a good beach vacation. We thought of you in the States somewhere and hoped you might meet us in Florida. We don't know where your ship is but maybe you can work it out to meet us. We have some flexibility on dates because of my job as a Lufthansa flight attendant and Lisl as a travel agent. We hated that the Navy took you away from us just as we were getting you trained to drive on the autobahns. We missed you at Oktoberfest this year but maybe you can slip away from your ship again for the festival next year. Ha, ha! We hope to tour Las Vegas as well.

If you get this, please write back and let us know if this is possible. We are doing great, but Lisl has lost her driving license, and I am having to drive her around in the Mercedes convertible. My driving is much better!

Love,

Brigitte and Lisl.

Dear Brigitte and Lisl,

I was just thinking about you two. A lot has happened since I saw you last. I am no longer on the USS Neptune. Of all things, I am in Navy flight school in Pensacola, Florida. I had quite an experience on the ship when I finally got to it after the diversion to Germany. I'm sorry the Navy found me. I was having a good time over there. At any rate, I somehow got accepted to flight school which got me off the ship. I have no idea if I can fly or not, but we'll see. I may not be able to pass the survival swimming tests. They are not so easy.

I just received word today that we will have a thirty-day pool of waiting to start flying which will begin about a month from now. That will coincide with prime beach weather here. We have some of the most beautiful beaches in the world, so you two will really love it. I hope to rent a house near the beach where you could stay while here. I will send the exact dates shortly. You will absolutely love Florida. Send some pictures when you can.

Love,
Peter

P.S. Has the Mercedes been wrecked yet?

Day three of survival swimming loomed large to all of us. It would be a huge embarrassment to wash out this early in the program. Lt. Williams was waiting for us with his usual frown. I led the group into the pool again and after everyone was in, Williams blew his whistle. I thought the thirty minutes would never end. The biggest problem was to stay calm and keep the air in your lungs. I was able to touch bottom when Williams wasn't looking which helped. I wondered if any of the other guys were able to figure that out. When the whistle blew, we all crawled out and lay on the poolside. Ensign Haines and the Saudi Prince were called aside.

"You two will be coming back tomorrow for remedial training. The rest of you are dismissed. Tomorrow we'll go through parachute training."

Cal, Bax, Tiki and I rode back to the BOQ in Tiki's car.

Ensign Ricky Williamson got the name "Tiki" from his love of the Tiki bar and restaurant on Pensacola Beach. He attended Purdue University and was the head cheerleader. He was commissioned an ensign through the ROTC program.

"Man, it's good to get that one behind us. I hope the rest of survival swimming isn't so tough," Tiki said as we pulled up to the BOQ.

"I've heard the parachute training is no piece of cake either," Cal added. "Maybe we'll have a different instructor for your sake, Peter."

"Second that, man!" I echoed.

The next day's morning class of power plants was pretty boring. We learned about the engine of the T-34 Mentor. This power plant is a six cylinder in-line motor with about 400 horsepower. It will be our initial single engine trainer. Those of us who have never been pilots were more attentive than those who had previous flight time. I felt sorry for the Vietnamese student pilots because they had to work in groups to try to understand the lessons.

At 1300, we reported to the survival school area for the parachute landing training. The first part was jumping off a tower and learning to roll properly on impact with the ground. It was fairly easy, and everyone passed even though Ensign Haines was required to do a second jump. He had passed the remedial drownproofing yesterday. From there we donned swimsuits and reported to a long, narrow pool about fifty yards long.

An apparatus with a motor was located at the far end. A cable was attached and extended to the end of the pool where we were standing. Our instructor appeared, the one and only Lt. Williams.

"Good afternoon, gentlemen—you, too, Pinson. You will enjoy this maneuver. What we'll be doing is attaching a parachute harness to you and attaching you to the cable you see by the pool. This device will simulate a parachute ditching at sea with the wind dragging you through the water and drowning you. We prevent this by teaching you how to loosen your parachute harness before water impact. Once you have done that, you are ready to roll out of your harness at entry. You with me, Pinson?"

"Yes, sir, I believe so."

"Okay, as you hit the water, you'll throw up your arms, push your head forward, and let the cable, which is acting as the wind, pull the harness over your head and off your body. The wind is quite strong at sea and has drowned many pilots who did not perform the maneuver properly. If you do this properly, the harness just slides right off and you are free to do your drownproofing, or whatever."

At the mention of drownproofing, everyone groaned.

"Pinson, let's see you do a dry run."

After the walk-through dry run, Williams hooked me up to the cable. The motor started running and before I realized it, I was jerked toward the pool. I didn't have time to unlock the harness and I hit the water and was quickly pulled under. The cable began dragging me through the water. The motor stopped and I came up coughing. I swam out of the pool and Williams unlocked the cable.

"Troops, Mr. Pinson just demonstrated what happens when you don't get out of the harness." Williams was grinning and enjoying the scene.

"All right, we'll try it again the correct way. Are you ready, Pinson?"

I couldn't believe he did that to me on purpose. I can see I may have to call on the "Phantom" for revenge some day soon!

I hooked up to the cable and was unlatched when the motor started running and it took me toward the pool. I released it and did the maneuver perfectly and rolled out of the harness as I hit the water.

I knew I had passed successfully as Williams then called on Ensign Haines. Jack stepped forward and nervously put on the harness. The cable was attached, and the motor pulled him to the pool. I don't know what happened, but Jack didn't get the harness released, and into the pool he went, being dragged along. He was upside down and his foot was sticking up out of the water. He looked like a submarine periscope moving through the water. Williams mercifully stopped the motor and Haines came up looking like a drowned rat. You could tell Williams enjoyed his job. He must have great stories to pass on to his buddies at happy hour.

"Haines," Williams said, "you'll have a repeat after everyone else has completed."

Cal, Bax, and Tiki completed the maneuver successfully on the first try. The Prince also failed and would need a retry. Jack's repeat was done successfully, and the class was dismissed.

On the way to the "O" Club, Tiki muttered, "That Williams is a real SOB, isn't he?"

"Yeah. He blindsided me on purpose to demonstrate what happens if you don't get unbuckled. Haines would have provided that demo anyway." We all laughed.

"Yeah, Jack has really been struggling," Cal observed. "The Prince hasn't been doing so hot either. Jack has been tearing up the academics, however. I think I saw on the syllabus we'll be doing the Dilbert Dunker tomorrow."

"Oh, crap!" Bax said. "I may just opt for sick bay. I've heard it's really tortuous."

"Aw, it can't be that bad unless Williams runs it. He would be happy if a couple of us drowned." Cal laughed.

"Guess who will do the demo tomorrow?" I smiled. "I learned about revenge when I was on the ship. The 'Phantom' will bide his time. We're going to set him up."

"How?" Tiki asked.

"I'll think of something. There are ways. The 'Phantom' never sleeps. I'll let you know."

THE DREADED DILBERT DUNKER

Every aviator who goes through Navy flight school must successfully pass the Dilbert Dunker. The mystique of this trainer is so well known that it has caused many a pilot to DOR.

It doesn't help that a student pilot was drowned at the Dunker long ago. He apparently got so tangled up in his parachute harness that the frogmen could not get it undone. In trying to cut him out, the pilot expired! It was a black eye for the Navy and terrible public relations. It took all the admirals in Washington to convince the Secretary of the Navy it was safe to use again. The benefits of the training proved to be worth its risk.

The Dunker is located on its own swimming pool. The simulated cockpit looks kind of like a roller coaster on a set of rails. The Dunker is a generic looking airplane cockpit and there is no canopy. The cockpit is open—simulating the canopy having been previously discharged. It is a typical Navy airplane seat and contains a seat belt and shoulder harness as well as a parachute pack to strap on. The pilot climbs in and straps on the seat belts and chute packs then signals the instructor when ready. Once he is cut loose, the cockpit slides down the rails and flips upside down when it hits the water, as a real airplane might do at sea. Now the pilot is upside down, and he must get his bearings with an airplane pressing down on him. He must get his breath as he hits the water, hopefully, a deep breath.

Now, he must feel for his seat belt buckle and figure out how to get away from the sinking airplane, remembering he is upside down. He probably can't see well with all the bubbles from the wreckage. He knows he has limited air in his lungs so he can't make mistakes. The Navy has added an extra frogman as a result of the previous loss of life. Unsatisfactory performances must be repeated until proficient. Three "downs" (unsats) will be disqualifying and lead to discharge from the program. This might lead to duty at the Great Lakes Training Center in Upper Michigan in the winter!

After power plants and lunch, we slowly made our way over to the survival school building and there to our chagrin was Lt.

Williams. "My Lord," Bax whispered as Williams stood there with crossed arms and a twisted smirk on his face. "We can't seem to shake the bastard."

"Okay, you turkeys, get your flight suits and hard hats on and keep your boots on. Hard hats are required and furnished for the maneuver. I'm going to explain how the operation works so pay attention. If you flunk the maneuver three times, you get a 'down' and will have to go to the SPDI board (Student Pilots Disposition Board). There's no reason to flunk, but there are two frogmen in the water to save you if you can't get out of your harness. You'll all become Navy, Marine and Coast Guard pilots so there's always a chance you'll go down at sea and need to get out. We lost way too many men in WWII because they weren't proficient. Once you're strapped in and comfortable, give me a thumbs up and I will cut you loose. When the Dunker hits the water, get a good breath because you may be under for a minute or two. Remember the airplane is pushing down on you so you've got to get away from it after you get unbuckled. Does anyone want to DOR now?"

All of us wanted to DOR now but no hands went up. I guess we are all committed.

"Where's Ensign Pinson? You're going first."

I felt my blood run cold, but I totally expected it. "Here, sir."

"Okay, climb in and let me know when you're ready."

I slowly climbed up the ladder and into the cockpit. It seemed much higher than it actually was. I guess it had to be high enough to get a good start to flip over. I took my time before Williams hollered at me to hurry up. I wanted to be damn sure the harness was buckled properly for me to get loose. I finally gave the thumbs up and away we went. We hit the water with a terrific impact and the cockpit began to flip. I had been in water slides at Disney World but nothing like this.

Before I knew it, we were upside down and water was rushing in. I took a breath, hopefully deep enough. My head was suddenly surrounded with water and I could hardly see for all the bubbles. I knew I had to settle down and get the harness off. I decided to shut my eyes for a few seconds to see if the bubbles would clear up. I reached down and found the buckle and thankfully got it to release. The Dunker was pushing down fast, and I wasn't sure how long I could hold my breath. The adrenalin was flowing which didn't help matters. I got out of the harness and opened my eyes. I grabbed the cockpit windshield and pushed sideways with all my might. I used my legs and then kicked. I broke free and went as fast as I could to the surface. My lungs seemed about to burst. I came up feeling like a drowned rat but I had survived! Williams will really be pissed.

I climbed out of the pool as Williams bellowed out. "Well, somehow Pinson made it. If he can, anybody can."

Everybody sheepishly laughed. Nobody was very cocky. Most of the guys going through this program start out with a lot of self-confidence but after these swimming drills a lot of humility sets in.

"Ensign Haines, you're next." Williams picks on him as bad as me, maybe because he is struggling. Heck, everybody is struggling.

Jack climbs up the ladder slowly and tentatively slips into the cockpit. You can see the perspiration rings on his bright orange flight suit. At sea, you would most likely be wearing the hard hat and heavy boots which would make the water landing even more difficult. No frogmen there to pull you out. Jack reluctantly gives the thumbs up and the cockpit picks up speed. It flips and all we see is bubbles. We can make out the frogmen underwater, and after thirty seconds or so, they move toward the sinking Dunker. Seconds later, they have Jack out and bring him to the surface, coughing and sputtering.

"Okay, Haines, go sit over there by yourself."

It's bad enough to have the frogmen bring you up, but Williams shouldn't be allowed to humiliate him. More fodder for the "Phantom's" revenge. While on the USS Neptune being punished for finding an exit from the cable laying ship, the "Phantom" intervened and leveled the playing field on the senior officers who thought they were so clever. Being relegated to engine room watches on the mid-watch, the "Phantom" gained control of the air conditioning system and alternately burned the seniors up one night and froze them the next. It's time now, for the "Phantom" to re-emerge. But how?

About half the class failed the first time.

"What's wrong with you wimps?" Williams bellowed. "I've never seen such a bunch of basket cases. Do I need to brief it all over? You've got to get a deep breath before you hit, not after. Don't try to unbuckle too fast. Wait till you get upside down. Count to five or something. I don't have all day to try to get you lillies qualified. This whole class will come back tomorrow and do it again, including those who passed today."

We all trudged out, despondent over what had happened. "Boy, what a jerk," Tiki said dejectedly. "That wasn't exactly a great briefing he gave before our first tries. He is trying his best to get under your skin, Peter. Poor Jack, he doesn't deserve that treatment."

On the way out, an officer in khakis came over to us. "Hey, guys, I'm Major Spencer, one of the frogmen. I saw what happened today. How would you like to get even with him tomorrow? I'm senior to him so we can jerk his chain."

"Sir, you're an answer from heaven! What can we do to that jerk?" I asked enthusiastically as I visualized a re-emergence of the "Phantom."

"We have another frogman on our team who hasn't been working over here. We will give him a flight suit and have him take the place of one of you. When Williams calls his name, our guy will enter the Dunker and strap in. When he hits the water, we will have an extra O2 tank for him, and while underwater he will put on the tank and mask and hide behind the dunker away from sight of Williams. We'll pretend to try to help the pilot out, and when the dunker retracts, our guy will hang onto it out of sight as it is pulled back up into position. All of you need to make noise and keep Williams distracted. Say things like 'Look, the frogmen are struggling with Anderson.' We'll pretend while underwater that we are struggling with Anderson. After our guy has hidden out of sight, we will come up and innocently ask, 'We had to struggle with Anderson to get him out. He was taking on water. Did he get out okay?' You guys will all be in 'shock' and say, 'No, we didn't see him come out.' We'll say, 'We'd better take another look underwater.'"

Spencer continued, "We'll leave his empty flight suit, hard hat and boots lying on the bottom of the pool. Williams will go nuts. Y'all enjoy the show."

The next day I went first as usual and managed to get out okay. Haines was next, followed by Anderson, who was first alphabetically, after he had singled out Jack and me.

Haines hit the water and finally got out after help from a frogman. He was escorted to the surface, coughing and sputtering.

"Haines, you're a pitiful excuse for a naval aviator. Go sit by yourself again."

Williams was completely distracted while the new frogman hung back wearing Anderson's flight suit and hard hat with the sunshade pulled down over his face. "Okay, Anderson, you're next. Get a move on."

The fake Anderson climbed up into the cockpit and strapped in. After the thumbs up, he hurtled down the tracks. After flipping upside down, he quickly slipped out and donned the extra oxygen mask the other two had slipped into the pool. Hiding on the side away from our line of sight, he hung on to the Dunker as it slowly retracted into position. The frogmen waited until the Dunker was clearing and swam to the surface.

"Williams, did the last student get to the surface okay? He was struggling a bit when we last saw him," Major Spencer asked innocently.

"What are you saying? We haven't seen him come up yet. Take another look," Williams said with a puzzled look.

"I don't think he's down here. Surely, he came up."

Williams looked all around. "Anybody see Anderson?"

"No!" We all shouted frantically. "He never came up."

Williams now was getting worried. "Where the hell is he? We all saw him go down. He's got to be in the water."

Spencer had taken his mask off and said, "He's not down here. He must have come to the surface."

Williams's face now was as red as a beet. "Dammit, what's going on here? This is crazy!"

He looked around again with no Anderson in sight. He looked hard into the water and saw the orange flight suit on the bottom. I was seriously afraid he was going to have a heart attack. The two frogmen had climbed out of the pool and were casually taking off their tanks and gear. Williams dove into the pool and went straight down to the bottom. We all peered into the pool.

When Williams emerged with the empty flight suit, the look on his face was priceless.

The real Anderson emerged from the locker room wearing a wet flight suit and a big grin on his face. After seeing the grins on the frogmen's faces, he knew he'd been had.

"Anderson, I'm going to have your ass!"

"No, you're not. I'm senior to you and I ordered Anderson to participate." Major Spencer laughed.

The fake Anderson walked out of the locker room in his khaki uniform with his gold Lieutenant Commander bars shining brightly. He walked over to Williams and introduced himself.

"I'm Commander Guin. I've always wanted to do that trick. I hope you weren't offended."

Williams reluctantly had to smile. "I guess you got me. I'll have to buy drinks at happy hour."

Humble pie is never easy to digest, particularly for someone like Lt. Williams. Hopefully, this was my last encounter with him.

Never say never.

ESCAPE AND EVASION

The gang of eight met at happy hour to celebrate the end of ocean survival and swimming. We were joined by Jack Haines who came in with a smile on his face.

"Why so happy, Jack?" Joe asked.

"I knew I was on the way to a SPDI board, so I DOR'd instead. You won't believe what happened. Commander Ringer looked at my academics and found me a billet at NAS Barber's Point, Hawaii. I will be in charge of the Officers' Club. He says they have a magnificent golf course there. I'm an avid golfer, so I think destiny awaits."

"That's great Jack," I said with envy.

"Jack, how can you do that to us? We're about to go on Escape and Evasion and you're going to the beaches of Hawaii. Don't you feel bad about it?" Andy said with a scornful look.

"Sorry, boys, I can't help it. Y'all come by to see me at the club when you come through on the way to 'Nam."

"Frank, what do you know about Escape and Evasion training?" I asked after breakfast in the BOQ.

"Not a whole lot, since the Coast Guard doesn't have to do it. There's little chance we would be exposed to Vietnam, so they don't make us go through it."

"The admin officer informed us yesterday that Vietnam was a possibility for most Naval and Marine Officers, so all of us will get a week over in Eglin, as well as a beach survival course one day. There's still a back-log of slots in basic airplane training over at Saufley Field right now, so the Navy wants to utilize our time. We're being bused over to Perdido Bay in the morning for the beach survival first, and then over to Eglin Air Force Base in Fort Walton the next day."

"Sorry I'm not getting to go with you," Frank laughed.

"Yeah, I'll bet."

About sixty of us were picked up the next morning at 0900 and taken to a pristine beach area which was owned by the Navy. One rock jetty and a long dock extended out into the bay with a few small vessels tied up to the dock. On the beach was a huge black pot with white cloths of some type and what looked like sticks surrounding the pot. Firewood was neatly stacked beside the big pot. Another big box nearby contained some awful smelling objects of some kind.

Our group consisted of ten commissioned officers, thirty cadets and twenty non-commissioned officers. We mustered around the big iron pot and were greeted by none other than Lt. Williams.

"Morning, gents," he uttered with his usual sardonic smile. "Here's what we're going to do today. COMNAVAIRLANT has determined that a majority of you will end up in the South Pacific somewhere so we want you to be prepared if you wash up on some shore. Many sailors in WWII would have survived with some basic knowledge of beach survival.

"We'll demonstrate to you how to capture and prepare crabs here on this beach. They aren't very big but fairly abundant. It takes some time and skill to cook and crack these small crabs, but they may save your life. We'll give you two matches to start the fire, so make them count. Two of you will be responsible for the fire. The pot is two-thirds full of fresh water.

"The remainder of you will take these forked sticks we have prepared for you and assemble these torn cloths on the sticks to make a home-made net. You will use these stinking fish heads in the box to use as bait. Dip them in the water near the jetty and you will get results after about five minutes or so. Be patient. After catching a few, assign a runner to transport them to the cooks. The cooks will boil the crabs for about fifteen minutes and you all are in for a crab fest."

Tiki rolled his eyes at me and whispered, "Yeah, right."

Williams continued. "I'll demonstrate how to crack the crab for maximum results."

After working on the formerly cooked little crab, he produced a spoonful of meat. He seemed proud of the little bite. "You may not think much of the results, but it could save your lives."

"I'd rather die," Cal whispered to me.

"I see we have Ensign Pinson here today. Mr. Pinson, I haven't forgotten the incident at the Dilbert Dunker recently. I presume you had something to do with that deception."

"No sir, I had nothing to do with it. It was strictly the frogmen's idea. It was an awful thing to do to you," I said with a straight face.

"Well, you'll be in charge of lighting the fire. If you fail, plan to give me some pushups."

"Aye, sir."

I carefully got a five-man shield to protect from the wind. Next, I acquired all the loose paper we could drum up. I lit the paper on the second try and threw in a couple of the cloths and we had a good fire going. The kindling caught and soon we had a roaring fire.

"Okay, Pinson, lead your men down to the jetty to start crabbing."

We all scattered and began putting our nets together. I buddied up with a chief petty officer named Barringer and we decided to work the dock instead of the jetty. About halfway down the dock, the chief looked over at a line in the water.

"Wonder what this line goes to?"

"Dunno. Pull it up and let's see."

The chief pulled on the line and soon a trap surfaced. It had two nice sized langostino lobsters in it.

"Damn, this is a lobster pot!" the chief cried out. "These are Florida lobsters. Somebody must be poaching these things at night. Think we should let them alone?"

"Hell, no. You get one and I get one. Chief, we're feasting tonight. Get 'em out and put your fish head back in. We'll get some more lobsters for the rest. Let's don't let Williams know where we got 'em."

We quietly passed the word about the lobster trap on the jetty. Slowly others came over and were able to find three more pots. They had the same success as we did. We slipped the lobsters into the boiling water and soon had a nice dinner. Meanwhile, Williams was sitting down beside a tree drinking a beer, which he obviously wanted us to see. Before the period was over, we had cooked sixty langostinos which provided some to every person. Williams came striding down to the beach after finishing off a few beers in the shade.

"How'd you like the crabs?" he smirked.

Soon he realized there was more than crabs in the trash.

"Where in hell did you get those lobsters?" he bellowed. "Pinson, what's going on here?"

"Sir, the fishing was good. I guess lobsters like fish heads as well."

There was nothing Williams could do. We utilized all our assets as they taught us in the briefing.

"Okay, everyone, get on the buses. You'll be going to Eglin now for Escape and Evasion. You won't be seeing me again."

I hoped that would be true, but he always seemed to be turning up when we least expected him.

We boarded two buses and began our trip to Eglin, about forty miles away. We would spend the night in tents near a tributary of the Choctawhatchee River. Eglin Air Force Base is southwest of Valparaiso, Florida, and encompasses 640 acres. The Navy and Air Force combine to train personnel from both services in escape and evasion techniques. We would be in the wilderness area designated for this training for six days and nights.

Arriving at nightfall, we exited the buses and were directed to our camp. Approximately fifteen tents were pitched to easily accommodate our sixty-man group plus instructors. Five men were assigned to each tent. The local instructors had built a huge campfire which we all gathered around.

A camouflage covered individual with his face painted emerged from the darkness and established himself in a strategic position around the fire.

"Evening, gents. I'm Sergeant Ortiz, US Army Special Forces, Fort Benning, Ga. Here's what we're going to do the next few days. You'll be able to sleep on cots tonight, but that will be your last taste of civilization. Tomorrow, we will give you a training and geographical briefing of the area you're in. We'll expect you to survive in the environment and make your way safely to a place away from foreign forces. You won't have your weapons with you, so you must be very stealthy and smart. Use all your resources and techniques which we will teach you. Do not lose patience in case you are captured. These aren't actual foreign forces who may capture you, but they are so well trained you may think so. They are not trained to kill you, only to train you in foreign techniques. Always bear this in mind. Any questions to this point?"

Everyone was silent.

Ortiz went on. "Tonight, we're going to spoil you. We've prepared some stew from local snakes, fresh caught today. I just sampled it, and it was delicious. We also have some turtle soup which is very good. This may be your last square meal for a few days so eat up to give your body some reserve strength."

"Thank god, I had a lobster at the beach survival," I told Cal.

"This is going to be a tough week if we're going to look for snakes and turtles."

We went through the line with our canteens and cups and served ourselves. I decided to take a minimum helping of each. The snake was oily, and I could only down one small bite. It badly needed a healthy shake of Tabasco. The soup was a little better but needed some water to wash away the taste. So much for a square meal.

We all turned in early knowing it would be an early reveille. Being tired, we easily fell asleep. Naturally, having five men in a tent would produce snoring, which made for a restless night. Unfortunately, this would be the last night on a cot.

We were awakened around 0500 by loud yelling from the instructors. Part of the harassment I assumed. Latrines had been dug and were available to everyone.

At 0600 the sun was rising, and we mustered by a small stream. Sgt. Ortiz showed up again and briefed us on the landscape of our first phase, the escape and evasion. "Men, we'll hand you all simple maps of the area you will be traversing to arrive at a safe zone in the hands of friendly forces. North is indicated on the maps so you will be able to check the sun to get your orientation. The first day of travel is free from enemy, so you must all agree on the direction of travel. Use all of your newfound skills to use the environment to forage for any food you might find. At nightfall pick any shelter you might find and realize you will be on your own at daybreak on day 2. On day 2, you will be traversing territory inhabited by enemy forces, and will need to be evasive on your trek to the safe zone. After daybreak, you all must split up as individuals in your quest to escape. Those of you who are successful will be rewarded with ham and cheese sandwiches. Those of you who are captured will be subjected to some form of limited torture—so be very, very evasive and stealthy. Do not lose your temper or get physical with the captors or you will be dropped from the program.

"You must not get in the open or you will be easily captured. The captors will be in fatigues and will speak little English. Do not resist or they will shoot you with paint balls. If you are captured, they will demand that you raise your hands and follow them. You may be led to a prison camp. The distance is about eight miles to the safe zone which is identified by a small pond being fed by a stream flowing east west. You will find the terrain leads you toward the goal, which is in a northerly direction. Good luck on getting to your goal safely. Any questions?"

There were no questions and we all enthusiastically dreamed of getting to the safe zone and had thoughts of a ham sandwich.

I gathered with my friends Andy, Cal, Joe, and Tiki. We plotted our direction of travel. The sun was in an obvious easterly direction, so everyone started out going the same way. Since we were safe from enemy today, we were loud and raucous as we began our journey. In the middle of the day, one of our group shouted out, "We have surrounded game for food!"

Everyone got excited, and we all arrived at a circle of men who had an animal surrounded. It was a jack rabbit. "Tighten the circle so we can keep him trapped!" someone shouted.

The rabbit just sat in the open, trying to decide his course of escape from these frightening men in his territory.

An officer, whom I didn't know yet, suggested we get rocks for everyone, and take him out with rocks thrown in waves, much like musket battles in the civil or revolutionary wars. This seemed like a good plan, so those outside the circle brought rocks for those guarding the circle. On the officer's command to fire, every other member hurled a rock at the jack rabbit who dodged all the rocks effortlessly. On the next command the next group fired with terrible results. The rabbit dodged and broke for freedom. He easily breached the circle and away went our lunch. Unfortunately, we had several members with slight injuries from the barrage of rocks. The worst injury was a head wound from an errant rock. Fortunately, we had a medic among us who took care of all the wounded.

We made a mile or two on day 2, the terrain suggesting the northward route. At nightfall, everyone fanned out looking for some semblance of shelter in the event of rain. Being late into spring, rain could come at any time. We had no ground cloths of any kind, since we were evading capture in unfriendly territory. I found a pine grove and bundled up some pine straw to make a bed under a big birch tree. Most everybody was dead tired and seemed to get some restless sleep.

At sunrise, we all shoved off on our own. I said goodbye to my buddies and ducked into the forest in cautious strides. I tried to get as far away from the group as possible to avoid the noises from the less cautious. Going was slow and I only progressed about a half mile before noon. I could hear yelling and screaming from some of the group who must have been caught. It was impossible to know what was happening to them as they surrendered. It was every man for himself at this point, so I had to just push on. I made it to nightfall without seeing anybody, but I could hear my comrades occasionally not far away. I was really getting tired and hungry.

I was so tired I went to sleep immediately. After several hours of sleep, I felt something scratching my leg. I suddenly sat up. It was a snake cuddling my leg. I almost shouted but managed to keep my voice down. I jumped up and slung off the snake. It was obviously not poisonous, or it would have had me. It was just looking for a little warmth.

Sunrise the next morning found me looking for water. A stream was mentioned in the briefing as being on course for the safe zone. I listened for sounds of running water and slipped cautiously toward the sound. Something told me danger lurked. I decided to stay in hiding for awhile before chancing a drink. My intuition paid off. After watching for an opening for a few minutes, two men in camouflage appeared speaking quietly in English.

"We've caught all but three. An officer, a chief, and a first-class gunners-mate. It shouldn't be long. They are hemmed in with no place to go."

I figured this stream was the key to finishing their captures. I decided to wait it out till dark to get a drink if I could stand it. The temptation to slip over for a drink was compelling. I observed the enemy on three more occasions patrolling around the stream. I wondered where the other two evaders were located. I climbed a big birch tree and waited till dark.

After sunset, I crawled slowly over to the stream. Suddenly, a bright light shone on me and a man in camouflage came running and screaming toward me. "Hands up, you capitalist dog," he yelled in very broken English. "Get on your knees."

He thrust a rifle in my ribs as two more came running from the woods. They all spoke in broken English, obviously emulating our enemy.

"This is the officer!" a short, stocky man with his face painted beyond recognition shouted. "What is your name?"

"Peter Pinson."

"What are you doing here?" he asked.

"I can't tell you," I said.

"We shall see," he said in a condescending manner. "Put your hands behind your back."

One of them tied my hands together. I knew there was no need to resist. I thought I was so cautious and careful. I wondered how they captured me in the dark. Too late to worry about it now.

"March behind my comrade!" the first soldier commanded.

We marched in the dark on a trail my captors obviously knew well.

"Where are we going?" I demanded.

"Shut up!" Commie #1 said firmly. "No talking at all."

We marched all night. I guessed about five miles. I was given water periodically which I desperately needed. I didn't hear any sounds of my shipmates and wondered if they were all captured.

About daybreak, I heard Commie #2 whispering on a walkie talkie in a terrible English imitation. "Yes, comrade, we have the officer now. We're only missing the chief petty officer."

We marched on for another mile or so and came over a hill. Ahead was a compound of some kind. As we approached, it was obviously a prison camp for us. I could see my shipmates milling around and being harassed by some of the camouflaged captors. The compound was enclosed by a fence with barbed wire at the top. Several dogs were tied to stakes with hungry looks on their faces.

As we approached the compound, Commie #1 suddenly turned to me and said, "What is your hometown, Pinson?"

"I am Ensign Peter Pinson," I said cautiously.

"Not what I asked you, dog."

"Ensign Peter Pinson, serial number 670015, DOB April 1,1956."

"Get on your knees, pig, and lean backwards."

I did so and he began to tap me on the chest bone. It was all I could do to keep from fighting back. I knew I would wash out of the program if I resisted.

"Now, pig, where are you from? We want to notify your family you're okay and being treated nicely."

"I'm only required by the Geneva Convention to tell you name, rank, serial number and date of birth."

"Have it your way for now, dog. We'll see what happens later."

I entered the compound and received a small cheer from my shipmates. Andy, Tiki, Joe, and Cal hurried over.

"We thought you might have escaped!" Tiki exclaimed. "You must have given them fits. The guards were talking about how you would pay."

"I usually do," I said sarcastically. "I'm usually the one who gets picked on."

Within minutes a guard came over to me. "Pinson, come with me. You will give us information."

I knew what was coming. Private interrogation.

I went with a new Commie I hadn't seen before. He was awful big for a Commie but dressed like one for sure.

We entered a dark room with a single chair. "Wanna smoke, Pinson?"

"Sure," I answered.

"Just answer a few basic questions and we will grant you food. What unit are you with?"

"Sorry, I can't tell you that."

I received a quick back hand I wasn't expecting. "Get in position!" he suddenly shouted. He pushed me to the floor and bent my legs under me. He then proceeded to do the chest thumping ordeal again. It was painful but I could stand it, at least for awhile.

"Pinson, I don't know why you are so stubborn. All your comrades have given us what we need to know. You could make it so easy on yourself."

He then walked out of the room leaving me all alone. I wondered what my chances of escape were. It was getting very dark outside, and maybe I could slip away. I peeked out the door and couldn't see any of the guards close by. I quietly slipped over to the fence close to the gate entrance. Then the big Commie interrogator came running out shouting. "Where is he? Where is Pinson?"

Then it erupted. An automatic rifle started firing in my direction. I wasn't hit, but almost had a heart attack. I quickly surrendered and Commie #1 commanded me to get in position. I knew what that was by now. So, I got on my knees. The chest tapping went on for way too long.

The interrogation continued. I knew they wouldn't kill me, so I held out again—name, rank, serial number and date of birth. Soon they sent me into an isolation area away from my troops. The idea was to make my men think I had broken and given in. I had no way of communicating, so I just had to wait in isolation. The next day I was in isolation again. Everyone must be wondering what is going on with me.

Later that day, I was blindfolded and led to another area. My blindfold came off and I saw about ten black boxes lined up. Each was approximately four feet square. "Get in the first box," a new Commie commanded.

I folded myself up and did as he said. The door closed and was locked on the outside.

It was a devastating feeling. Another box was quickly filled beside me. After everything quieted down, I whispered to see if the new occupant could hear me. I recognized the return voice immediately. It was my friend Andy.

"Peter, how's it going?"

"Not bad, so far. Remember that round of golf we played last weekend?"

"Yeah, what about it?"

"Let's replay it, stroke by stroke."

"Great idea."

We replayed each other's shots which golfers would never do, ordinarily. It helped pass the time and eventually we were let out. Everyone in the boxes came out at the same time and no one was physically able to walk. We were made to crawl with guns punching in our sides. After a period of recuperation, I joined up with my troops. Everyone wanted to know my fate the last couple of days.

"I went through interrogation and isolation to make you all wonder if I had caved."

"Yeah, they were putting out the word you had spilled the beans. You didn't, did you?" Joe asked with a smile.

"Of course not. I could stand on my head till we get out of here. I'm a little hungry though."

"Everybody got fed except the officers," Andy injected.

"Figures," I said.

The next event was for all of our troops to muster together in formation. We lined up according to seniority, the officers in front.

"You capitalist pigs are all wrong!" Commie #1 hollered out.

"Officers move to back row, now! You are so stupid. Everyone give ten pushups."

"Don't anyone move. Stay in formation!" I shouted.

No one moved. The lead Commie then got on a platform with the PA microphone. He began to chastise us and started a dialog about how bad capitalism is and how great communism is. He droned on for awhile and suddenly said, "Aw hell, let's quit."

We were all stunned. What did he mean?

"Gentlemen, we are finished. How did we do?"

A chorus of boos came from our ranks. We had learned to hate the captors in less than a week. The captors took off all their camouflage and disguises and roamed among us. They were now trying to make friends, but after our treatment all week, we had a hard time getting in a forgiving mode. We slowly began to realize what a good job they had done as part of the necessary training.

Tiki got the attention of everyone and said loudly, "Men, let's give the Commies a round of applause. They are true professionals."

Slowly everyone joined in. Our guards acknowledged the token of respect and gave us a round of applause as well. Commie #1 introduced himself as Marine Colonel Robert Whitton of MCRD based in San Diego.

"Men, we're sorry for the discomfort of the week. You have witnessed a few of the enemy techniques used on us, so we want you to be prepared. You must stick together and keep your chain of command at all times. You have done well but remember this is only a taste of what may come.

Buses will meet you at the gate and drive you back to Pensacola. There is a hamburger joint down the road in case any of you want hamburgers after the good food we've given you all week. Uncle Sam is footing the bill. Have a good day."

Needless to say, the hamburger joint was swamped but they were ready for us. They had already prepared for three per person.

MONTH OF NOTHING

Upon finishing ground school and sea survival at Mainside, we were all called in for orders by the training admin officer, Ltjg. Cassidy.

"Gentlemen, you have passed the first major test of your naval aviation challenge. Now you will be sent to Saufley Field for your basic flying experience. All of you will be reporting for training in the T-34 Mentor. Saufley is eighteen miles north of Pensacola. The Saufley experience will be a true test of your aviation aptitude. We expect you to report for every flight thoroughly prepared. This means studying as well as being properly equipped with flight suits, hardhats, boots, gloves, kneeboards, checklists, etc. The Navy philosophy is to put maximum pressure on you from the start. If you can't handle pressure, we want to find out early. There is a lot of pressure in combat, so we don't have time to just teach you how to fly an airplane. Your instructors will have different techniques, but all will test your ability to handle pressure. Our washout experience is quite high, so be prepared. It is no disgrace to DOR. We don't want to waste your time or ours.

"Having said all that, I have some updated information. You will report immediately to Saufley and procure your flight equipment as well as berthing slots at the field. However, there is still a backlog of flying for students currently due to the addition of Vietnamese student pilots who have been given a rush to qualify. So, you'll have a one-month pool of waiting your turns to fly as we previously reported. You will report to schedules every morning at 0800, and then secure for the rest of the day if there is nothing for you to do. As long as you check in every morning, you are free to do what you want. You are dismissed."

This news shocked us all to the core. We'd been busting it for two months, and now they force us to take a month's vacation. This aviation life is great. I should have done it sooner.

"Andy, can you believe this? I've got to write my buddies on the Neptune. They'll be so jealous. What're we gonna do for a month?" I said excitedly.

"Let's get the beach house we talked about. We'll have a crash pad for a month after we check in each morning," Andy said.

"I'm in," Cal added. "This is beach weather. I'll go check it out today. Anybody wanna go with me?"

"Yeah, I'll go," Andy said.

"Okay. Y'all go see what you can find. Got to be close to the beach. We'll meet at the 'O' Club at six for happy hour." I could see the enthusiasm rising.

The four of us in the class who were most interested met at the Mustin Beach "O" Club at 1800. Two Marines, Paul Nick and Everett Haymore, asked to join the discussion. Andy, Cal, Frank, and I nodded approval, and they pulled up chairs to the table.

Everett is from Oklahoma and attended OSU. He is a newly-commissioned second lieutenant, who was a MarCad and graduated here in Pensacola. We found out after some prodding that he was a champion calf roper in several rodeos, including the "Calgary Stampede," while at Oklahoma State.

Paul is a "Cajun" from New Orleans. He was commissioned as a second lieutenant through the Marine PLC program, a program that runs through summers. He says his claim to fame is being the base ping-pong champion at Parris Island, South Carolina.

Andy announced the findings. "We met with a realtor at the beach who showed us a house on Ariola Avenue, which is practically on the beach. We have to cross the road to get on the beach, but the price is right if we split it up six ways. It's a three-bedroom concrete block wall house built to withstand hurricanes and Marine parties."

Everett gave Andy a cold stare.

"They'll give us a six-month lease, but we must give a damage deposit. I don't believe even you marines can damage this place," Cal said, glancing at Paul and Everett.

"What about furniture?" I asked.

"Durable stuff from Walmart. Quite beautiful. Nice velvet paintings of bullfights and cock fights." Cal smiled. "We'll all have to be on lease. Everybody in?"

Everyone nodded.

"Here's to our good fortune and new crash pad," Everett toasted.

"'Crash pad' is terrible terminology for potential aviators," Paul said sarcastically.

"Right," Everett added. "Let's just call it our Ranch."

All six of us took the trip out to Pensacola Beach to check out the Ranch.

"Good job, Andy. This will do nicely while we're in Pensacola. If all goes well for each of us, we'll be in the area for at least six months."

Since we were in three different branches of service, we decided to split the bedrooms into Navy, Marine, and Coast guard: Cal and Andy the Navy, Everett and Paul the Marines, Frank and me (honorary), Coast Guard. Andy agreed to get a locksmith out to protect the integrity of the three bedrooms. We set up strict regulations on cleanliness and order to prevent any parties from getting out of control (primarily for the Marines). We agreed this was designed to be a gentleman's beach retreat.

We all co-signed the lease and gave the deposit, which was a little heavy. "We don't normally rent to Marines," the leasing lady said.

I checked my mail at the fleet post office and found an interesting letter which was postmarked from several different countries. It was from Brigitte.

Brigitte Ludwig
1 April 1968
10 Alderhorst Court
Hamburg, Germany 12321

Dear Peter,

Lisl and I are planning to come to the States for a visit from 1 May to 20 May. We want to see you if you are available in that time frame. We're hoping to see some good beaches after this cold winter in Germany. I have a good airline pass policy with Lufthansa which will include Lisl. We can go just about anywhere we want to. Where are you currently located? Not at sea, I hope. Send a telegram to Lisl's office if you can and we can make some plans.

Love, Brigitte

What a timely letter, I thought. *We have a month off and they are looking for some warm weather beaches. I have the perfect place for them.*

15 April 1968
Ensign Peter Pinson, 670013
Fleet Post Office
NAS Pensacola, Florida
31111

Brigitte Ludwig
10 Alderhorst Court
Hamburg, Germany 12321

Dear Brigitte,
    Perfect timing. I am in Navy flight School in Pensacola, Florida. I left the USS Neptune in Barbados in January and reported for flight training. I don't have a clue how to be a Navy pilot, but they are supposed to teach me because I passed the entrance tests. We'll see. I haven't been in an airplane yet, because I'm going through ground training first. We also do some survival training because the Navy flies a lot at sea. I'll tell you all about it if you can come to Pensacola. I also have rented a beach house so you can stay there on the beach. You will love it because the weather is getting warm, and the water temperature is nice for snorkeling and swimming. I am in a holding status for beginning training in the T-34 airplane, which is the initial trainer we learn on. All I have to do is check in every morning at 0800, and then head

out to the beach or wherever I want. Weekends are free as well, so maybe I can take you both to Disney World.

Every tourist must go there. I have a Chevy Corvette which you can use when I'm on base. My roommate has a Buick convertible we can use when all of us go somewhere. Of course, my roommate will want to come along at times.

Let me know if you can make it. It will be better than Oktoberfest. You will be the envy of Hamburg when you go back with suntans.

Love, Peter

I quickly told Frank of the news. His eyes lit up when I told him about Brigitte and Lisl. One of the problems single guys have in Pensacola is there are way too many sailor boys and pilots for the single girls around. The guys are in intense competition with each other. To have two gorgeous German girls coming over to see the USA seemed too much for Frank to digest.

"Peter, you do want me to hang around with y'all, don't you?"

"Well, I'll give you a tryout. If the girls can stand you, maybe I can let you tag along occasionally. Just don't think it's your right, okay? If I sense they don't like you, I'll give you the cut sign. Fair enough?"

"Okay, just give me a chance."

"Don't let anybody else know about this. We don't want to be fighting off the Marines. They'll cut in at the drop of a hat."

"Mum's the word."

Brigitte Ludwig
22 April 1968
10 Alderhorst Court
Hamburg, Germany 1232

Dear Peter,
Lisl and I are planning to arrive in Pensacola on 3 May. We are flying standby on a Delta Air Lines flight coming in

from New York, arriving at 1500. Can you please meet our flight? We don't know our way around but can catch a cab if necessary.

Brigitte

28 April 1968
Peter Pinson
18 Ariola Drive
Pensacola, Florida 25766

Dear Brigitte,
Certainly, I will be there to pick you up. My roommate has a convertible which should accommodate all your bags. I will not be in uniform but hopefully you will recognize me. Can't wait to see you both. The beaches are beautiful right now.

Peter

The big Delta jet rolled in right on time. Lisl and Brigitte were the first ones off the plane. They were giggling as they came down the ramp stairs. We saw each other immediately and exchanged big hugs.

"How was the flight, girls?"

"Wonderful," Lisl laughed. "Maybe the best flight I've ever been on. The pilots got us moved up to first class. They were so nice. The stewardesses may have over served us."

"Did the pilots try to get your address here in Pensacola?"

"Yes, how did you know?" Brigitte asked with a smile.

"Just a guess on my part," I answered smugly.

We picked up the bags and piled into Frank's car.

"Top up or down?" Frank asked as we strapped in.

"Definitely down," said Brigitte. "We're ready to soak up this Florida sunshine."

I hadn't seen Lisl and Brigitte in over a year when I was in

Hamburg, Germany, looking for my ship, the USS Neptune. The Bureau of Naval Personnel had inadvertently sent me to the wrong ship, the German SS Neptune, located in Port Travemunde, Germany. My tickets were all one way, and I had no way of getting back to the States with the small amount of money I had with me. Luckily, I met the two of them in the Volksbath of Hamburg, and they were good enough to give me shelter for a few weeks. The Navy finally found me and helped to get me back to my real ship, the USS Neptune. I had promised to sponsor them for awhile if they would come to the States.

Lisl is a tall, blue-eyed blonde with a mischievous smile. She owned a Mercedes convertible and had a lead foot. I will never forget the drives on the autobahn at 200 kilometers per hour and being passed by faster cars.

Brigitte is shorter and has dark brown eyes and dark hair. They both have dynamite figures, and I fear they may turn too many heads in this pilot-loaded environment. I will need to be on my toes to protect them like a father from unwanted advances. Brigitte has been a stewardess with Lufthansa for over a year now. Lisl worked for a travel agency named Mediterranean Adventures.

"Brigitte, how are you liking Lufthansa?"

"I love it. I've been to so many great places. I take Lisl with me and we go skiing in the Alps, and beaching all over the Mediterranean. I've been to the US a few times since you and I came over together on my first flight. My supervisor counseled me on giving you too much service on the flight to New York."

"I thought the service was just fine." I grinned.

"Lisl, are you still the leading sales rep for the travel agency?"

"I was for awhile, but now I'm the store manager."

"I'm not surprised—you'll probably own the place before long.

"Okay, we're going out to the beach first to show you our beach house. It's not too fancy but it's right across the street from the Gulf. You'll have your own bedroom and bath. We share the kitchen with some other pilot trainees, two Marines and two Navy friends."

We drove out through downtown and crossed a long bridge to Gulf Breeze, located on a strip of land which separates Pensacola from the beaches.

"Gulf Breeze is just a connector town on Santa Rosa Island. We'll cross another bridge which will get us to Pensacola Beach, home to the most beautiful sand in the world. We try to keep it secret so all the snowbirds don't come down from Canada. You probably hear all about Miami's beaches, but these are much nicer."

Our Ariola Avenue address provided easy access to the beach. The girls were ready for a dip. I anticipated this and produced some modest bikinis for them. "Do we have to wear these?" Lisl asked.

"Of course, this is not the French Riviera. However, I'm not a policeman."

They reluctantly donned them and headed for the beach.

"Can you both swim proficiently?"

"You bet! We have many indoor pools in Germany."

The tide was out, and the beaches were sparkling. "Maybe we can stay a little longer," Brigitte shouted as she romped into the surf kicking up the water.

The beach was love at first sight for them. "These beaches are more beautiful than the French Riviera!" Lisl yelled.

"I know. That's why we don't advertise them to the rest of the world. We're keeping them a secret. You need to be careful about the undertow. When I'm not here, stay within sight of the lifeguards." (I immediately wished I had not said that. It might distract the lifeguards too much.)

After the swim, we dressed, and I took them on a tour of the area. We went east to the giant water tower. "Pensacola Beach" is emblazoned on the shoreward side.

"If you can keep the tower in sight, you can always find your way back to the house. This is the eastward edge of the city limits. Everything east of the tower is federally owned property. It is a pristine natural area, only beaches and no homes or buildings for about forty kilometers. We'll take a spin down there tomorrow. It ends at Fort Walton Beach."

We had dinner and I showed them the Tiki Club, a famous

stop for all naval aviators and student pilots. School teachers like to go there as well. I dropped them off at the beach house.

"You'll stay here tonight by yourselves. Are you comfortable with that? I've got to go into the base so I can make muster tomorrow morning at 0800. After that, I'll be back. I'll have a car for you tomorrow."

"Sure, we'll be fine. Lisl has a black belt in karate."

"Keep the front door and bedroom doors locked. There may be Marines in the area."

THE GERMAN GIRLS

Frank and I mustered out the next day at 0800. Frank wanted to go to the beach, but I held him off.

"Let me get the girls tucked in and I'll let you meet them. They aren't ready for some dirty old Coast Guard officer. I'll give you a good word, however. Just be patient."

"Okay, but don't let anybody else meet them."

I switched cars with Frank and arrived at the beach house about noon. There seemed to be more cars parked along Ariola than normal. I jumped into some shorts and wandered down to the beach. I spotted the girls quickly and realized they were attracting a crowd.

"Morning, girls. How's the beach? Have you been in the water yet?"

Lisl answered, "The water's great, but Brigittes's top got knocked off by the waves. They're pretty high. It took a few minutes to find the top."

"That explains the crowded beach. We may have to get her a one piece."

"Oh, no. We'll be more careful. We've got to take a good tan back to Germany."

"Let's take a break and I'll show you a beautiful drive. We're going to take a scenic drive over to Fort Walton Beach."

We hopped into Frank's convertible and turned east. We passed the huge Pensacola Beach water tower and were quickly removed from civilization and speeding down Highway 399. The only thing to be seen were beautiful sand dunes and sea oats and sparkling Gulf coast waters.

"Have you ever seen a more beautiful and natural beach in your life?"

"No, Lisl said. "Maybe in some of the brochures in the office on some remote islands, but nothing like this."

Highway 399 is amazing in that the National Park Service has been able to prevent any development though I know it will not last forever. The drive is almost boring because of its natural beauty.

"Why are you poking along, Peter?" Lisl called out.

"I'm not poking, Lisl. I'm doing 70."

"Something wrong with the car?"

"Of course not. This isn't an autobahn."

"I was just curious. I'm not used to going so slow."

"You may not know it, but we have speed limits in the States. I'm going to let you drive back to familiarize yourself with driving here. You drive halfway and Brigitte drives the second half. I may let y'all have my Corvette while I'm away if you prove yourselves."

The drive back was uneventful except Brigitte kept tapping the brakes too hard to slow down. They were trying to manage the speed limits better than I expected. I can still remember the harrowing drives with Lisl in Germany.

We spent the rest of the day driving all over the Pensacola area to get them familiarized with the geography. We toured Santa Rosa Island before coming back to downtown Pensacola. The girls wanted to go to Trader Jon's, but I wasn't sure they were ready for that step. Trader might try to hire them as dancers. I wasn't sure but that they might take him up on the offer. But then, it would certainly up the quality there. We went west to Fort Pickens and around Perdido Bay. They were amazed at the bountiful white sandy beaches everywhere.

We ended up at the Naval Air Station where I was training in the initial phases. We drove up to the main east gate where the Marine guards stood watch—crisp uniforms, polished white helmet liners with yellow and red stripes on the side and the large golden Globe and anchor on the front. Even to the uninitiated, you knew you were entering a special place.

"Girls, I will be the tour guide and you can ask questions or comment anytime."

We took the left fork onto Murray Road and passed the beautiful A. C. Read golf course and a static displayed Blue Angel F-11 fighter jet, painted in the famous blue and yellow paint scheme.

"Almost everything on the base is named for some famous old pilots, mostly World War I pilots, who were the first Naval aviators. This base was opened in 1914. Off to the right is the Bachelor Officer Quarters where I'm staying. Many of the pilot trainees aren't officers yet. They will live in the barracks you see on the left. You'll see them marching in a minute. You can recognize them by their shaved heads."

"Do they have to become officers to fly?" Brigitte asked.

"Yeah, they become officers and learn to fly at the same time."

As we crested the top of the hill, I pointed out Captain's row—antebellum homes overlooking the parade field, football stadium and the base chapel.

"The area off to the left is Chevalier Field. It became too small for today's airplanes so you can see it has buildings there now. This is where most of the ground school training is done."

We continued down Murray Road and turning left, the aircraft carrier USS Lexington appeared, tied to its dock, dominating its surroundings.

"You're not going to have to land on that thing, are you?" Lisl inquired.

"Probably so if I learn how to fly, which I haven't done yet. I'll get about six months' training before I get to that stage."

"Why didn't you just stay on your other ship?"

"Long story. Look at my surroundings. Not bad, huh?"

"Yeah, I love your beaches," Lisl exclaimed.

"You can have a full day of sun tomorrow."

"Can we get an all over tan?"

"I'll see if I can find you a place. The beach is closed east of the Pensacola Beach water tower."

Just past the carrier, the road made a right turn and brought us along a seawall and a bunch of old hangars on our left.

"This base was the real birthplace of Naval aviation where long forgotten seaplanes and float planes were launched and trained the first of those to go before us. It shared the bay with old sailing ships in service at the time."

We continued west on Radford Boulevard past some brick buildings.

"This is the altitude chamber and Navy Exchange. Just past the old hangars on the left is the aquatic center housing the indoor swimming pools. This place is called the torture chamber, officially the Dilbert Dunker. The Navy tries to drown you by crashing you upside down into a big pool, then see if you can get out. I passed it somehow. Not everybody does!"

Next up was the survival school.

"This building has a collection of wild animals you might encounter if your plane goes down on land. I encountered a snake while asleep on my survival week near here. Scared the hell out of me but I was able to identify it from the one I saw on display here.

"Next is the water tower and obstacle course and base hospital. Here we had to sweat out our indoctrination physical. The medics stuck a bunch of needles in us to see if we would pass out. Frank, my roommate, passed out."

We passed the Mustin Beach Officers Club on the left.

"We'll come back here later and have dinner at the club. That's the advantage of being commissioned before you get here. The cadets don't have 'O' Club privileges yet. I've invited my roommate, Frank, to join us. You don't mind, do you?"

"Of course not," Lisl said. "Why are you driving so slow?"

"We're not in Germany, Lisl."

Driving up the hill we passed the lighthouse.

"Let's go in the lighthouse," Brigitte urged.

"Sure, it's a great view," I said.

We clamored to the top and were treated to a great view of the area—Forrest Sherman field to the north, Pensacola Bay to the south, Perdido Key to the west and Santa Rosa Island to the east.

"Hey, I can see the Pensacola Beach water tower, close to the beach house, right?" Brigitte excitedly informed us.

"Right on," I said. "I think we're about to see the Blue Angels take off."

"Who are they?" Lisl asked.

"They are the most prestigious pilots in the Navy. They periodically perform acrobatic maneuvers in airshows all over the world. They are home based here at Sherman Field. They are practicing today. Want to watch them?"

"Oh, yes," Brigitte said. "Maybe I can teach my Lufthansa guys some new tricks. Might spice up some of our long ten-hour flights."

"Don't think your company would go for tricks on a 747."

We could see the six bright blue F-14 Tomcats taxiing slowly down the taxiway toward the runway. They taxied onto the runway in pairs and applied power together with a deafening roar—smoke blowing from the exhausts. The takeoffs were breathtaking, and the planes very quickly joined up in perfect formation.

"Will you be doing this one day?" Lisl asked slyly.

"I can only dream," I laughed. "I haven't made my first takeoff yet."

We watched the practice for about half an hour.

"Let's head on out and go to the 'O' Club. Frank should be waiting for us. He probably wants to get his car back."

We descended the lighthouse and drove back to the Club.

Frank was waiting for us in the parking lot. I could tell he was anxious to meet the infamous German girls. I had briefed the girls a little about his background without propping him up too much.

Frank tried to be matter of fact through the introductions. The girls were peppy about everything as usual. We took a table overlooking Pensacola Bay and the USS Lexington standing guard over the base.

"Thanks for the use of your car, Frank," Lisl said. "Peter's Corvette just wasn't big enough for the three of us."

"You're welcome to use it anytime while you're here. I was quite happy using the Corvette, anyway. I had no idea it would do 160."

"Better not have, roomie. I don't want to give any ideas to Lisl. She is having a hard time adjusting to our speed limits."

Lisl replied, "I just have trouble converting to your miles per hour speedometer readings compared to our kilometers. I go by feel anyway. We don't have your ridiculous speed limits in Hamburg."

"We're having our indoctrination physicals all day tomorrow, so I'm going to give you the Corvette to take out to the beach tonight. Lisl, you'll drive. Brigitte doesn't get to drive until I give her a better checkout."

"Aw, Peter," Brigitte protested. "I'm not that bad. I have a certified German license now."

"You just make sure Lisl doesn't get lost."

"Okay, if you insist."

A well-heeled man in a coat and tie approached our table. "I don't want to interrupt you all. Are you Ensign Peter Pinson?" he said as he looked directly at me.

"Yes, sir," I said as I stood to face him.

"I'm Lieutenant Commander Buck Stonewall, leader of the Blue Angels. One of the staff recognized you and I thought I would like to meet you. That was quite a survival story you had in the Caribbean."

"Oh, it wasn't as bad as you might think. The Caribbean is certainly a much better place to land in than the North Atlantic. Besides I had good company. Would you like to join us?"

None of us could believe a Blue Angel would come over to us. Much less the leader. I could see Frank was not anxious for the addition.

"Sure, just for a quick drink. I don't want to intrude. Tell me a little about the experience."

I introduced Frank, Lisl, and Brigitte. Frank stood up. Buck grabbed a chair and pulled it over.

"I didn't know anything about your survival," Brigitte asked inquisitively.

I could see I was trapped into telling the story which I really didn't want to talk about at this time.

"I'm going to give the short version or else we'll be here all night."

I proceeded to fast forward the story and took the anticipated questions.

"Amazing story!" Buck said.

"We saw a little of your practice this afternoon. When is your next performance?" I asked.

"We're off to NAS Jax next week for a show. We're a little rusty. Hard to keep the three-foot wing separation on positions #2 and #3."

My lord, I thought. *Only three foot separation between*

wingtips at three hundred miles per hour.

Buck was obviously impressed with himself. He quickly changed the conversation to the girls. He wanted to know all about them.

"How long will you ladies be in town?" came the obvious first question.

"Just a few more days. We're over here to see some sights and visit Frank and Peter." Lisl smiled.

Buck, undeterred, continued, "We're having a private party over at Trader Jon's tomorrow night. You're all invited. It's for Blue Angels and friends. Starts at 1900. Love for you all to attend."

"We'll check our schedules. Do we need to RSVP?"

"Yes, if you don't mind. Trader is a big friend of ours. Should be a fun party. Hope to see you."

Buck politely excused himself and joined another group in the bar.

"Wow!" Frank sneered. "These guys are good. They know how to get a party going. Trader Jon is the perfect foil."

Lobsters were on special at the Club and we all feasted. I wanted to leave the girls with the Corvette for the next day while Frank and I were in physicals, so we took both cars back to the beach. Lisl rode in the Corvette with me, and Frank drove Brigitte in the convertible. Frank seemed to hit it off pretty well with Brigitte. After a moonlight swim, we left the girls at the beach.

"Remember girls, keep your door locked and don't let anybody in. Drive within the American speed limits."

"Okay, Dad, we'll be careful."

BLUE ANGEL PARTY

Frank and I showed up at 0830 at the base hospital for our indoctrination physicals. This was the most thorough physical I had ever received. We were given ECG's, EEG's, gave tons of blood, peed in multiple jars, were stuck with needles big enough for horses, ran on treadmills, jumped up and down on one leg, did pushups for five minutes, checked blood pressure, performed hearing and eye tests, and topped it off with an interview with a shrink. Also receiving physicals were twenty-five or so other pilot candidates and one of the Blue Angels, Rocky Stonebridge, who flies position #5. It was refreshing to know he took the same physical as I did.

We finished up at 1500 and headed out to the beach. The girls were not in so we figured they went for a ride somewhere.

We were out on the beach when we observed the yellow Corvette returning from the east, from the barren national park direction.

"Did you drive over to Navarre Beach?" I asked.

"No, we didn't get that far," Brigitte grinned.

"Let me see your tan lines," I demanded with a stern face.

As I suspected there were none.

"So, you found a nice secluded beach, huh?" I tried to keep a straight face.

"You won't turn us in, will you, Peter?"

"No, I want you to look good when you get back home. Besides, if I turned you in, the sheriff would probably make you go back to the scene and demonstrate what you did in order to determine if a crime was perpetuated."

"Now, do we go to the Blue Angels party tonight or not? We know they will hit on you girls big time," I cautiously asked, unsure of their response.

"Listen, Peter. We have handled French and Italian men on the Riviera. These guys won't be a problem." Lisl laughed. "Wait till I throw some German words at them. They won't know if they're on foot or horseback!"

"I trust you. Let's go have a good time on Trader's dime. I'm sure they'll have good music and food. Just know that the Blue

Angels will be coming after you."

"We'll be up for the challenge," Brigitte grinned. "I take care of aggressive passengers on Lufthansa all the time. Part of our training."

"Pilots also?"

"They're probably the worst, but easiest to handle. I always check out their watches, to see who has the biggest."

The four of us climbed into Frank's car for the drive to Trader Jon's. Frank and I figured we would be the only student pilots attending. The parking lot was guarded by an attendant to make sure of the invitations. We mentioned Buck's name and he waved us through.

The music had started when we entered the huge brown wooden door and Trader was at the door to greet everyone. We signed in and Trader took an immediate interest in Lisl and Brigitte. I had advised them to speak to Trader in German to throw him off. It worked, and he stuttered a bit and waved us in.

Shortly after seven the music stopped, and Buck took the mike. "Good evening, everybody. Welcome to Trader Jon's. We have lots to celebrate tonight and thank you all for participating. We're especially appreciative for the Pensacola Teachers Union to send so many charming ladies over tonight. Trader was good enough to let us use this special place for the celebration. It's the Blue Angels' last get-together at home before we start our road tour in Jacksonville in two weeks. We have just been given a 20 x 25 watercolor painting of the six of us to be placed on the wall here at Trader's, in addition to all the other pictures and paintings we have here. Trader has placed it in the center of the stage, right behind the shows."

I whispered to Frank, "I think we're the only non-Blue Angels guys here. We're the only ones who need name tags."

Actually, there were four more who were not Blue Angels pilots. They were staff members who were on the traveling team. Just guessing, there appeared to be three ladies to every man. The party organizers knew what they were doing.

Buck continued, "Everyone will have a name tag with first names only. Some of us will have nicknames but you can ID us by the pictures on the walls if you need to. Ten of us are attached to the Blue Angels, and we have two special guests who are just beginning flight school, Ensigns Peter Pinson and Frank Hammer, and their guests from Germany. Please make them welcome."

Frank and I rolled our eyes. Lisl and Brigitte just smiled.

The band started up and everyone began mixing and getting acquainted. Trader's dancers doubled as waitresses. Trader came over to find out what the heck was going on with the German girls.

"Do you girls speak English?" Trader asked curiously as if he had never seen a German.

"Guten tag, Trader. Of course, we were just pulling your leg," Lisl said. "We're just visiting our friend Peter, whom we've known awhile."

Trader looked over curiously at me. "Peter, you sure get around. I remember you got pulled out of the Bahamas recently. You still owe me a picture."

"These girls took me in when I was wrongfully sent to Germany. I'm reciprocating as their host in the States."

"Do you girls need a job? I need some dancers and you both qualify."

"I told you about him," I said looking over at Lisl. "How do you know they can dance, Trader?"

"I can teach them." Trader smiled. "You boys are on to me. I can try, can't I? Have a good time. By the way, have you started flying yet?"

"Naw, we're just about ready for T-1s. We're not real pilots yet."

"Doesn't matter, you're welcome here."

Trader had the reputation of being the friendliest man in town.

The Blues all looked alike. Similar military haircuts, Izod shirts, pleated trousers, Weejun shoes. They must have the same tailors. They could probably be a dance line or barber shop quartet. Probably get their haircuts at the same time. It's not by accident they are the most famous flight demonstration team in the world.

It didn't take long before the guys dropped by to say hello. They wore nicknames like "Rocky," "Buzz," "Slick" and "Burner." Under each name was the number of their position in the flight formation, (3-6). There was no #1 or #2 under Buck or the Executive Officer who flew #2.

Buck simply had "Skipper" under his name and Lt. Chuck Veale, the Executive Officer, had "XO" under his name.

Brigitte asked why there were no numbers under their names.

"No one is allowed to call the leader and Exec #1 or #2 without consequences," Chuck said with a straight face.

It went right over the girls' heads.

Buck came over and thanked us for coming. "My boys were excited about you all coming, especially you girls. I told them you were versed in martial arts so be on your best behavior. We have to fly out at 0700 tomorrow, so I may have to put a curfew on them."

One of the crew not in the pilot rotation, came over and introduced himself. Under his name, "Jocky," were the letters FA-1.

"What's "FA-1?" Brigitte asked.

"Fat Albert One Captain. I'm the pilot of the C-130, which is a support plane for our team," Jocky proudly proclaimed. "We perform some maneuvers with our souped-up, jet-assisted plane. After the Blues are put out to pasture, they might want to come back and fly Fat Albert.

Another person by the name of "Skunk" came by to introduce himself. "I'm the announcer for the shows," he explained. "I narrate the show along with all the introductions and explain the individual upcoming stunts."

Under his name were the letters "DT."

"I give up," Lisl said. "What's that stand for?"

"Deep Throat. Makes sense, huh?"

"Of course." She laughed.

The only one left to come by went by the name of "Foxy." His initials under his name were LL. "You'll never guess what the LL stands for, so I'll tell you. I head up the camera crew, so they call me "Lima, Lima" for long lens. Pretty corny, I know."

The band started up, and I wondered about the condition of the Blues for takeoff the next morning. I knew they were pros, so they should be fine. We left about 2300 despite the pleas to stay longer. As we walked out the door, Lisl handed me a stack of calling cards. "What's this?" I asked.

"Calling cards from each of the Blues. I got one from everyone except Buck. Peter, you can use them better than me."

"I'll bet the schoolteachers got cards, too." Frank grinned.

"I'll bet you're right. Well, girls, how many offers did you get?"

Brigitte laughed. "Rocky offered a trip to New Orleans when they get back next week. Buzz offered a dinner cruise around the bay. Slick offered a beach date with lunch. Burner offered a trip to Disney World."

"Lisl, did you get any hits?"

"Yes, I did. Buck knew we drive fast in Germany and offered a ride in Blue Angel #1 during a training session. I politely declined. I like to drive fast but get sick on roller coasters. I believe a ride with him would do me in. Probably missed a chance of a lifetime. He laughed and said not many girls take him up on the offer."

A harvest moon shone brightly as we sped back to the beach in Frank's convertible. The top was down, and the cool air flowed through the girls' long hair but did not disturb the flat tops on Frank and me. We arrived at the beach house, and it was no surprise the girls were ready for a moonlight swim.

"Suits required, girls. We might encounter a beach Nazi. Besides, Frank just met you."

"Killjoy." Brigitte scowled.

Frank gave me a look of disbelief. I winked back at him.

The tide was going out and the waters were calm with gentle waves breaking quietly on the beautiful white sands. We raced down to the beach which was completely empty. Lisl noticed the emptiness and was the first to pretend to lose her suit. Brigitte was right behind.

"You two are so subtle," I yelled out sarcastically.

The next morning, we woke up to Brigitte making a

breakfast of German potato pancakes. "My grandmother in Hamburg taught me the recipe. What do you think?"

Pretty fantastic. When do we get wiener schnitzel?" Frank laughed.

"Maybe later if you're a good boy." She smiled.

Frank and I left early for Mainside to make our 0800 muster. I left the Corvette for the girls.

"Frank, do you think that is a good idea? Can they possibly get in any trouble?"

"Those sweet, innocent things? Of course not. Somebody will take care of them."

As we crossed the bridge from Gulf Breeze to Pensacola we looked over to the west and observed the Blues taking off. The sounds became deafening as they flew right over the top of us. Numbers 5 and 6 were just catching up and magically they were in perfect formation as they roared upward. They turned eastward toward Jacksonville and were soon out of sight.

Minutes later, another roar came from the west. Fat Albert was taking off using the jet-assisted rockets. "Jocky" pitched her up to an impressive angle of attack until she finally leveled off about 3,000 feet.

"Frank, do we really get paid for all this?"

We laughed heartily as we hit the morning traffic into Mainside.

We picked up the results of our physicals which were all positive. I received another message after lunch to report to security at the main gate.

"Do you mind dropping me over there, Frank?"

"Course not, wonder what they want?"

I entered the building and introduced myself to the Marine at the desk.

"Mr. Pinson, do you own a yellow Corvette?"

"Yes. What about it?"

The sheriff in Walton County, Fort Walton Beach has it in custody. Two foreign girls have apparently stolen it and were stopped at the Bridge from Navarre Beach. They were travelling over 120 miles per hour on Highway 399, the beach road through the national park. They speak very little English."

"Thanks, I'll get right over to resolve it."

I rushed out to Frank, who was waiting in the car.

"How about running me over to Fort Walton? The girls have been arrested over there for stealing the Corvette. Apparently, they were going a little fast."

"How fast?"

"Something over 120, on Highway 399, the beach road to Navarre."

We arrived at the Sheriff's department and were ushered into his office.

"I'm Sheriff Machen." A tall, burly man introduced himself.

"Are you Peter Pinson, the owner of a yellow Corvette, license plate Florida 670013?"

"Yes, sir."

"We have in custody two girls from Germany who speak very little English and have no ownership or rental papers from the car. We checked the license and traced the car to you in the air station in Pensacola. You don't know these girls, do you?"

"Actually, I do. What are the charges?"

"They were driving down highway 399, the Navarre Beach road, at something over 140 mph. A Coast Guard helicopter, which patrols the National Park as well as the coastline, noticed the car because it was going faster than the helicopter. The helicopter had a ground speed of 120 knots. The pilot notified our office, and we were waiting when they slowed for a turn at the bridge. The driver, a Lisl Beck, had a German passport and European driver's license. I don't know if that license is recognized here. The other lady, also German, is being held as an accessory to theft. They don't appear to speak much English."

"I will accept responsibility for them and pay any fees if you will release them to my custody. I assure you it won't happen again. I suspect they were using the speedometer in kilometers instead of mph. 140 kph is about 80 mph on our speedometers.

They drive pretty fast on the autobahns. I'm sure it was an honest mistake. They're such nice girls and good representatives of Germany. They're trying to learn our language."

"Okay, I'm going to let it go since they are from Germany

and didn't harm anyone. I suggest in the future you orient them better to our customs and laws. A Corvette is way too much car for young ladies to be driving. They should probably rent a Volkswagen or Jeep. Sign these custody papers and you're free to go."

Lisl and Brigitte appeared with downcast faces, like children caught in a prank. I gave them my dirtiest look. They looked away.

Frank brought the car around, and we made them both sit in the back seat of Frank's car. I would drive back alone.

"So, you girls don't speak much English, do you?"

Lisl countered. "It didn't seem to be in our best interest. We thought the sheriff might have some sympathy if we played dumb."

"Played dumb, huh. How'd that work out?"

"Pretty good, I'd say. We're out, aren't we?"

I burst out laughing. "If it had been me, they'd have thrown me under the jail. The sheriff certainly wouldn't want to offend two sweet young German girls, would he?" I asked sarcastically. "I almost told him you were both fluent in five languages, but he might have locked you up and thrown away the key."

We both drove back over the scenic Highway 399 and arrived at the beach house.

"It's all Brigitte's fault," Lisl said. "If she could have converted kilometers to miles per hour, we might not have been going so fast. I can't drive and do the math at the same time."

"Oh, come on Lisl. You always drive by feel. You've never looked at a speedometer in your life."

Lisl grinned. "You're probably right. But this Corvette was designed to run fast. It's the car's fault, not mine."

"Okay, okay, we'll leave it at that. It's the car's fault. I can't believe you outran a helicopter. That may be a world record. The Coast Guard should be embarrassed."

"What do y'all want to do tonight? We don't have to check in until 0800 tomorrow. This is your last night here."

"Doesn't matter too much. We're kind of tired." Brigitte responded with a big yawn. "We've got a Delta flight out at noon tomorrow for Las Vegas. Maybe we'll get lucky again and get moved to first class."

"You probably will, but luck won't have anything to do with it." I chuckled.

"Girls, if you have any money left after Vegas, maybe you can swing back by here on the way home. We might take you to Mardi Gras," Frank suggested.

"What's Mardi Gras?" Lisl asked.

"Something like Oktoberfest, but different."

SAUFLEY FIELD

We regretfully drove Lisl and Brigitte to the Pensacola Municipal airport. They were decked out in their finest and fit to kill.

"How long will it take to get to Las Vegas?" Lisl asked.

"About five hours," I said. "You'll have to stop over in Atlanta. Everybody stops there to go anywhere."

"We've only got five days in Vegas. Got to get back home with our new sun tans."

"You'll be a big hit in the Volksbaths," I understated.

"You boys are welcome to come see us in Oktoberfest this year." Brigitte smiled. "I can get you buddy passes on Lufthansa."

"I'll sure try, if this backlog continues."

We hugged the girls and watched them board the big Delta jet. I'll bet Lisl and Brigitte will be having cocktails in first class as soon as the door closes.

"Frank, with the girls gone, we've got to get serious about this flight school."

"Yeah, they could've become a huge distraction."

We mustered in at 0800 the next day to find our backlog was over and we were to report to Saufley Field, about seventeen miles north of Mainside. Ground school orientation will begin at 0830 in Building 3. Flight gear will be issued in Building 4 at 1300.

"Wow, Frank, the moment of truth has finally arrived. Are you ready?"

"I don't know, man. I'm getting butterflies."

"You've got some flight time already. I've never held a yoke or stick."

"Theoretically, we're all starting even. I admit it is helpful to have flown some. I've heard the instructors start yelling on your first day. I'm not used to that."

"Let's hit the beach one last time. It won't be the same without Lisl and Brigitte."

"You can say that again."

Saufley Field was named for Lieutenant junior grade Richard

G. Saufley. He was born in 1884, graduated from the Naval academy in June of 1908, and was commissioned as an ensign in June 1910. He trained as an aviator in Annapolis, Maryland, in 1913, was promoted to Ltjg., and designated Naval Aviator #14. He was involved in the Veracruz campaign in Mexico in 1914. Saufley returned to Pensacola to concentrate on seaplane development. He set altitude and endurance records and was attempting to better his own record when he died in a plane crash on Santa Rosa Island on a flight out of Naval Aeronautical Station at Pensacola on 9 June 1916. His seaplane went down at the 8-hour-51-minute mark of the flight in which he was attempting to set an endurance record. In addition to Saufley Field, destroyer DD-465 is named for him.

We dropped our gear off at the BOQ the next morning and learned we would be roommates again.

"Think you can stand me a little longer, Peter?"

"Of course, Frank, we're a team now. You fit in very well with the girls. I noticed you were invited to Oktoberfest. Just don't go without me."

"Wouldn't think of it." Frank winked.

Lt. Van Eaton moderated our orientation class at 0800, which consisted of explaining the syllabus, describing Saufley Field procedures, outlying fields in the training area, limits and recognition features to help stay in protected airspace, relationship with instructors, how to "DOR" (drop on request), and how to manage the Saufley Field traffic pattern. I spotted several other faces in the class which Frank and I had met over at Mainside going through preflight. The Saudi Prince was here along with his interpreter and two aides. In the back of the class were five Vietnamese student pilots along with their interpreter. I was quite surprised by the number of foreign pilots being trained. The Vietnamese had undergone six months of English training in preparation for the flight training. I can't explain why the Prince needs Navy flight training.

"Saufley Field is unique in that it has eight runway options," Lt. Van Eaton continued. "The idea is to always have a runway into the wind, much like a carrier. The carriers are usually able to turn into the wind so that the relative wind comes down the deck to make the already difficult landings easier. As pilots, it is imperative you learn how to navigate properly and land on the correct runway. You must not land on the wrong runway! The same goes for takeoff. Here at Saufley, we take off on different runways from the one we land on!

"Now, let's talk about radio procedures. Your four divisions will all have call signs. For example, 'Fairdale' is the call sign for squadron one. 102 would be the side number of the airplane you're in. Some of you have previous flight time and will catch on quickly. If you are a solo, your call sign is 'Fairdale 102 Sierra.' Your instructors will help you on the first flight. Your radios are pre-set for Saufley ground control, Saufley tower, NAS Pensacola, and emergency. Your instructor will explain how to get other frequencies. Please don't use the emergency frequency unless you need it. If you get lost, don't automatically use emergency. Try to find out where you are. Fly south till you hit the Gulf and turn east.

"Your transponders are pre-set for VFR flying. It also has an emergency function which will alert air traffic control as to your position. Again, don't use that emergency function unless you're in extremis.

"Now, for the traffic pattern. This is unlike any other you men have ever seen.

"We're prepping you for carrier approaches so you will use a similar pattern here. After you return from your outlying training area, you will have two initial checkpoints to arrive at. 'Bravo,' is the bridge at Highway 90 for all runways landing south and east. 'Charlie' is the checkpoint over the bridge at Highway 98 over Perdido Bay and is for all runways landing north and west. You will call these checkpoints on channel 7. Approach control will give you a sequence number so you can keep up with the flight in front of you. The controller will give you the side number of the flight you follow, so keep an eye for him and descend to 1500 feet as you look for the field. You will overfly the field on the same heading as your landing runway.

You will stay in the holding pattern at 1500 feet. You should spot the plane directly in sequence in front of you. If not, call 'not in sight' to the controller. The controller clears you to 800 feet whereby you can switch to tower, channel 6, and fly upwind over the runway and make your left-hand break. After the break, descend to 600 feet on your downwind leg. Abeam at the 90, turn inbound and fully configure with gear and flaps down. Lined up at 325 feet, commence inbound and call three green when cleared to land. Always use your full training call sign. Any questions?" Lt. Van Eaton asked with a smile on his face. He knew full well nobody knew enough to ask a question.

It was clear as mud to me and probably everyone else. I looked at Frank and he gave me a shrug and rolled his eyes. We'd have an instructor on the first few flights, thank goodness.

This course took all morning. I noticed many familiar faces I had seen at Mainside in various courses of training. I was beginning to put names with faces.

Training Wing One (TraWingOne) consists of four flight divisions. I am in flight division 1 and Frank is in flight division 3. By being split up, we would have a different set of training instructors and check pilots. We both were scheduled on the next day, for our PS-1 flights (Pre-solo).

On a brilliant sunlit day, I nervously strode into the division one ready room in my new orange flight suit to meet my instructor for briefing. A tall, red haired, stern-faced, pilot in a tan flight suit was seated behind a desk. I could see that he was a full Lieutenant.

"Mr. Pinson?" he posed without looking up. I would later find out that each instructor had reputations which passed down the line, so student pilots had an idea what to expect of each instructor regarding their dispositions.

"Yes, sir, that's me," I answered cautiously.

"Are you prepared?" he asked without looking up.

"I believe so, sir," I said.

"I hope so," he growled as he looked up at me with no emotion. His eyes seemed to penetrate right through me.

"I'm Jerry Davidson. We have a long way to go and the pressure will increase as you go along. We don't waste time with our student pilots, and we expect you to stay up or be dismissed. Only about half of our initials make it through and it's no disgrace to DOR if you can't hack the program. Most pilots who get their wings have a 'down' along the way—but don't get discouraged. You will have a chance to repeat the flight or check ride to get it right. Three 'downs' and you'll get a speedy board (SPDI) and probably wash out. You must be highly motivated to finish and get your 'Wings of Gold.' The normal time for Naval and Marine aviators is eighteen months. Coast Guard pilots usually take a year because they aren't required to carrier qualify. Are you ready to make the commitment?"

"Yes, sir."

"Okay, let's get on with it. Here's what we're doing today. Today's pretty much a freebie. I'll talk you through and demonstrate everything today. Let's talk about the pattern first. It mirrors what you'll see when and if you get to the carrier phase."

His explanation helped but still my mind was clouded with all the complicated procedures. Hopefully, doing it today will clear it up.

"We're going to do an exploration and identification of the training area today. It's important you don't get lost and end up in Mobile or New Orleans, as one of our foreign students on solo did recently. He landed safely but we had to send crews down to get him and the airplane. Quite embarrassing.

"We'll go out together and do a pre-flight of the airplane. Maintenance generally gives you a perfect airplane, but some things can happen after they have delivered the plane: oil leaks, tires leaking air, etc. So, it's the pilot's responsibility to be the last check for an airworthy airplane. Never hesitate to call maintenance.

"After pre-flighting, I'll get you strapped in and buckle your parachute and seat belt. Have you been given a briefing on use of the parachute?"

"Yes, sir, we checked out in ground school."

"Think you could jump out?"

"I believe so."

"We've had guys DOR after being asked that question. I'll

do all radio transmissions today, so pay attention because you'll be doing them on your PS-2."

We found our airplane on ramp one, side number 210. It was bigger than I expected. My heart began to flutter. The moment of truth had arrived. It's time to determine if I can cut this program or not. My doubts surfaced as to my capabilities. I have no flying background. What is it going to feel like?

After a thorough walk around with Lt. Davidson, he stopped and said, "You can call me Jerry. We're both officers who have been around awhile. I don't need any more formality."

That helped to ease my apprehension. I certainly didn't need any more pressure.

"Climb in and get comfortable. Let me know if you have questions."

I started to climb in the back seat. "No, dummy, you're in the front. Do you think I'm going to do all the work? I'll be demonstrating some things, but mainly I'll be talking you through everything and following you on the stick. When I demonstrate the loop, you won't be on the controls."

The loop! I don't remember the syllabus calling for that on the first hop—and I ate chili dogs for lunch.

I strapped in and clicked the canopy closed. Jerry got in and closed his canopy. When I took the orientation T-28 ride in Norfolk to try to qualify for flight school, I didn't do anything but enjoy the ride. I still remember how the pilot got me sick. Now I'm in the front trying to be a real pilot. The feeling is so different.

"Radio check, Peter?"

"Radio is checked on, Jerry."

"No, say 'loud and clear, how me?'"

"Oh, okay. 'Loud and clear, how me?'"

"That's better. Now I want you to read the before start checklist and then give the answer after you have performed the function."

I was very slow and deliberate in reading and executing the checklist.

"Peter, this is way too slow. Tomorrow, I expect you to breeze through the checklist about ten times faster. Practice with your buddies in the BOQ tonight. We don't have time to waste on the ramp."

Jerry talked me through the engine start and the Lycoming engine began to purr. Jerry read the after-start checklist, so I could grasp the situation. Jerry did all the radio work while teaching me how to taxi the airplane. I felt a surge of emotion as I felt the airplane begin to move at my command.

We reached the end of the runway and Jerry got the clearance to takeoff. "Peter, just add the throttle slowly until you hit the stops. Release the brakes and keep both heels on the deck. Steer with your legs and keep her on the centerline. After you hit takeoff speed, ease the nose back and let her fly off. Remember torqueing causes her to roll slightly to the left. Put in a slight right rudder. Keep her flying straight ahead. Once she's flying at about 300 feet, raise the gear. At 500 feet, raise the flaps. Call for the after-takeoff checklist. Once you start soloing, you'll have to do your own checklist and fly the airplane at the same time. Okay, the checklist is complete, and you're cleared onto runway 6. Always check the markings for the correct runway. Are you ready?"

I wasn't really ready, but I couldn't think of a reason to delay. All of those instructions were causing my mind to freeze up. I was overloaded.

As I added the power, the T-34 started to slide toward the left.

"Ease in the right rudder, Peter."

I overreacted and the plane swerved right.

"Ease it in, I said, dammit!" Jerry yelled. "This ain't a Mack truck."

We hit the rotation speed quickly.

"Ease the stick back, Peter, and she'll fly off on her own."

I pulled back on the stick and the plane lurched upward.

"Peter, do I have to explain the word 'ease' to you?"

"Sorry, sir," I said sheepishly.

My first takeoff was an exhilarating experience. The airplane rose smoothly above the treetops. At last I felt like a real pilot.

AIRBORNE AT LAST

"Get your gear up. Don't forget the flaps. Finish the checklist. Keep the wings level. Climb to 3,000 feet. Turn to a west heading."

After getting the airplane on course and altitude, Jerry took the controls.

"Not bad, Peter. Don't take the yelling personally. That's the way we do it in the Navy. I'm going to let you look around to see the neighborhood. Off to the left is Perdido Bay—very important in helping you find your way back to Saufley. On our return, we'll go down to the coastline and work our way back coming up Perdido Bay to find our way to Saufley. I can't tell you how many solos get lost out here. Dead ahead you can see Mobile Bay. That is outside our training area, so turn around if you find yourself getting close. We don't want locals shooting at you.

"Okay, we're in the operating area now, so I'm going to introduce you to a loop. Are you strapped in good?"

"Yes, sir."

"We will make some 'S' turns first to clear the area. Try not to throw up at the top because it might get on me. I don't want that to ever happen to me again. Actually, the term should be called 'throw down' when in a loop. Notice the wings being level to the horizon throughout the maneuver. Here we go."

The loop was so smooth I didn't need to throw down at the top. I'm glad I don't have to do it myself until later in the syllabus. We continued the flight doing basic air work, steep turns, climbs and descents, things I had never done before. We then turned to the south and Jerry continued the area orientation.

"Peter, can you see the beach extending westward toward Mobile Bay?"

"Sure, looks like a fort at the end."

"Good, that's Fort Morgan. Please turn around and head east toward Perdido Bay if you see yourself at the fort. See this pristine beach leading to the fort?"

"Yes."

"That's called Gulf Shores. Do not, do not, do not, fly down low on the beach. That's called 'flat hatting' and might get you kicked out. I know it's tempting, but don't do it."

As we headed back toward Perdido, we passed a large inlet of water.

"This inlet is Orange Beach and the bodies of water are Wolf Bay and Bayou Saint John which are much smaller than Perdido Bay. I want you to notice the difference in size, so you don't land at the wrong airport on your solos. You can see Perdido up ahead. See the difference?"

"Sure do. Do many students land at the wrong airports?"

"You wouldn't believe it. There are about ten airports in this op area. Most all airports look alike from the air. Please don't do that while I'm your instructor. Come back after you get your wings and I'll give you some stories."

"I'll do my best."

We proceeded over Perdido Bay toward Saufley Field. Jerry called initial over "Bravo," and we were cleared to the 2,000 feet pattern altitude and would be landing east on runway 9.

"Now the fun begins." Jerry laughed. "Everyone is on a visual flight plan so we must be vigilant to watch out for other traffic. Instructors know the pattern, but not so much the solos. You sound off if we start getting too close to another plane. I'll talk you through everything I'm doing on the approach and you follow me lightly on the control stick on the final."

"Roger." I replied even though I was basically lost on what was happening.

Jerry deftly configured the airplane and maneuvered us down to the final approach and confirmed "Three green and cleared to land" with the RDO (Runway Duty Officer). We touched down and Jerry immediately gave me control to taxi back in. Ground control gave us clearance to taxi to ramp 1 where our division parked. My head was still swimming as I navigated the various taxiways back to the ramp.

"Shut her down, Peter, run the checklists, do a thorough post flight, and meet me in the ready room. I will record the flight time today, but you will do it on the next flight. Weather looks good for tomorrow. You get an 'up' for the flight."

"Roger, see you in a few minutes." Jerry could have stated that no one ever gets a "down" on the first flight.

On debrief, Jerry went over the takeoff, landing and pattern procedures. "Tomorrow is a new day, Peter. It gets fast and furious. Study hard and we'll take a big cut at the apple. You'll be doing most of the flying."

I stumbled out of the ready room. I couldn't wait for the fast and furious tomorrow.

Back at the BOQ before dinner, I gathered together with Frank and a few hallmates in the lounge. We all had PS-1s today and were eager to compare notes. Frank Hammer, Callahan, Tiki, Joe, Andy, Bax, Everett and I met in the tail-hook lounge. We compared our first flights. We agreed it was an eye opener.

Everett observed. "I couldn't believe how much we've got to pick up in a short time. We're supposed to solo in ten hops."

"Yeah," Andy said. "I'm not sure I can find my way back to Saufley. I got Mobile Bay mixed up with Perdido Bay. What if we get caught out in weather? We're not going to be checked out in instrument approaches."

I chimed in. "My guy said to just fly south till you hit water and then go east until you see an airport—even if it's not the right one."

"That'll look good in your flight jacket—landing at the wrong airport on first solo." Andy laughed.

"Did anyone have a loop demoed today? It's not in the syllabus," I asked.

Joe Francis, an ROTC grad from Wyoming added, "I did, and I've got to admit I lost my cookies at the top."

We all laughed. It seems he and I were the only ones to get the loop. Apparently, the loop is designed to get rid of some student pilots early on.

"Did anyone get to make the landing today?" Joe inquired.

"I did," Bax said. "I told my instructor I had over 200 hours in a Cessna 182. This was very different, however. I flared too quickly and floated and then hit hard. My instructor let out a stream of cuss words that made me blush in my hard hat. He made me look hard at the tires which he said were probably flat. They weren't."

We all laughed but we knew any one of us might be the next source of mirth. So, we agreed before breaking for dinner to debrief together every night with the understanding that what is said in Vegas stays in Vegas—no loose lips at happy hour with anyone outside our new "Gang of Eight."

UNINVITED PASSENGER

I met Lt. Davidson in the briefing room at 1000 for my second flight. It will consist of takeoffs and landings and some stalls and basic air work. I stayed up late studying the night before because I wanted to make a good impression and to help conquer my nerves. I asked some pretty dumb questions, but Jerry was very patient. I heard he was a plough back, which meant he had come back from the fleet to be an instructor for a couple of years. He may have requested this duty, but quite often the instructors might be short timers (those who have limited contracts to stay in the Navy and don't have enough time left to make a deployment with an operational squadron). He was reputedly a screamer like all of them, but he seemed approachable as an instructor.

"Peter, I'm going to let you take over the preflight duties and radio calls today. You'll make mistakes, but I will correct you on the spot or in the debriefing after we land back here. I'm getting you ready for your solo flight, which hopefully will occur on PS-10. On the checklist usage, you'll read it aloud, and then answer it yourself after accomplishing the item. After takeoff, turn due west and climb to 3,000. Perform the after-takeoff checklist and set cruise power. Switch frequencies to channel 3 and report your position and altitude. He will clear you to the training area for training maneuvers. I'll take over the radios at that point so you will only monitor ICS (intercommunications). You can start the air work by doing steep turns left and right, holding altitude and airspeed at 180 knots. Start on due west heading and end up heading west."

I was taking notes as fast as I could. I hadn't counted on doing this much on just the second flight. I know I've got to rely on the checklists. It's nice to have the instructor aboard to bail you out. I wonder if I can get a "down" (unsat) on my second flight.

"You will have plenty of questions which I will answer as we go. Just do the best you can. You can go on out now and do the preflight. Our plane today is 202 so your call sign will be 'Fairdale 202' in all your outside transmissions. You should be pretty good on radios because of your previous experience at sea on the USS Neptune. After you get your solo hop in, I want to meet you at happy hour and tell me about your adventures on that ship. It sounds interesting. Go on out. I'll be about twenty minutes behind you."

I nervously picked up my hard hat and flight gear and walked out onto the ramp. There were eight shiny, orange and white T-34 Mentors lined up in a row. A plane captain was standing in the "at ease" position in front of each plane. As I approached ship 202, the plane captain came to attention and gave me a Navy salute, not to be mistaken for a Marine salute.

"Good morning, sir. I'm at your service, Airman Lewis. Your ship is fueled and oiled and ready to go. I'm new to this division. I've been working in division 3."

"Thank you, Lewis, I'm Ensign Pinson on my second flight."

"Good luck, sir. I don't know Lt. Davidson. Is he a screamer?"

I gave him a sideways glance. Was he serious? He had a sly smile on his face.

I performed the walk around inspection and climbed into the front seat. I strapped in and Lewis handed me my hard hat. I turned on the battery switch and the cockpit came to life. This is such a shock after coming from a cable laying ship. After going through all the checklists, I saw Jerry's figure in my peripheral climbing in the back seat. Airman Lewis handed him his hard hat. In a few moments, I asked. "Are you ready, sir?"

"All set, sir."

I wonder why Jerry called me sir. I thought we were going informal.

"I've run the checklist and we're ready to start the engine."

"Great," he replied.

I over-riched the engine the first time and she choked down. Jerry didn't say anything, and I tried again, and she cranked right up. I adjusted the power to idle. It was a thrill to feel the awesome engine idling along. My confidence rose and I gave Lewis the thumbs up that we were ready to taxi. He saluted and stepped away. I called ground control for taxi.

"Ground, Fairdale 202, ready for taxi."

"Fairdale 202, Ground, you're cleared to runway 36 via taxiway Foxtrot. You're number one this morning. Contact tower after your run up."

I stopped in the run-up area and went through the procedures as best I could remember from the previous day. I know I screwed up the mag (magneto) check and power check but Jerry didn't say a word. I expected him to start screaming—maybe he has turned into a Santa Claus. He's probably treating me differently because I've been out in the fleet for a year, and now I'm a senior ensign.

I struggled through the rest of the checklist and hoped I hadn't missed anything. I double checked the flaps set for takeoff. My heart was racing—my first real takeoff without the instructor following me on the controls. After full power was set, I released the brakes and we immediately swerved off center line toward the left. I jammed in the rudder and we swerved back to the right. Across the centerline again to the left. I waited for the screaming to start but nothing was said. I couldn't believe the lateral porpoising that was happening. As we approached 80 knots, I was getting a little straighter. At rotate speed I pulled too hard on the stick and we jumped into the air. There was a slight flutter in the plane, so I shoved the nose over.

Tower: "Fairdale 202, switch over to channel 3 reaching three thousand feet. Nice takeoff, boys, but don't forget to raise your gear and flaps."

"Roger, Tower. Switching to channel 3, Fairdale 202."

Despite all these mistakes, Jerry never said a word. He must be seething. He's probably never seen a worse takeoff. I switched to channel 3, which is the area control frequency.

"Area control, Fairdale 202, level 3,000 feet, heading 270."

"Roger, Fairdale 202, you are cleared to the ops area. Call 'Charlie' when back inbound for sequencing into the landing pattern."

I switched off the UHF frequency and called on the ICS (intercom system) to Jerry. "Jerry, I know I screwed up the run ups and takeoff, but I know what I did wrong."

"The voice on the intercom came back. "Sir, why do you

keep calling me Jerry?"

"What? Aren't you my instructor?"

"No, sir. I'm cadet Terry Triplett from the Naval Academy. I'm down here to observe the flight operations. Aren't you a qualified pilot?"

"Hell no. You must've got in the wrong airplane. My instructor, Lt. Jerry Davidson is supposed to be with me. We're up shit creek now. Tune into channel 3 now and monitor with me but don't say a word. Understand?"

"Yes, sir."

About the same time that I changed over to channel 3, I spotted a T-34 approaching from my port side. "Fairdale 202, this is Fairdale 101, do you read?"

"Roger, I read you and have you in sight."

"Peter, this is Jerry Davidson. I presume you know what has happened."

"Yes, this cadet has jumped into the wrong airplane and I couldn't tell it was not you until we were airborne. I guess we need to get this airplane on the ground."

"That's an understatement. I'm going to fly formation on you back to Saufley. I'll be above and behind you and talk you through everything. We'll do a flyover to start and let you get down to 500 feet to get the feel for an approach. Then we'll do as many flyovers as it takes to get you comfortable for a landing. How do you feel?"

"Scared shitless."

"Good. I wouldn't want you to be anything else."

"Okay. Turn to an east heading and maintain 3000 feet. Let's slow to 100 knots and lower your flaps to 1. We'll get configured and stay that way to get that feel and then go flaps 2. Are you caught up on all your checklists? Does your passenger have any flight time that might help you?"

"He says no. This is his first time in an airplane."

"That's great. Tell him not to touch anything."

"Okay. I'm ready for the descent checklist."

"Good, start your descent and I'll handle all the radios. You just answer to me for all instructions." I wondered how Jerry could be so calm.

"Got it. I can see Perdido Bay straight ahead."

"Descend to 1500 feet and we will do a long straight-in to runway 36. I have declared an emergency and all airplanes have been cleared out of the way. Make your heading 120. We're going to come in over highway 98 and turn north for a straight-in to runway 36."

"Okay, I have Saufley in sight."

"Turn north now and descend to 500 feet with landing flaps. Run your landing checklist and let me know when you're finished and comfortable. I'm mirroring you from behind and above so I will give you approximate power settings.

"We're just going to drag it in to get a good look at the runway and landing attitude. I'll shut up for a minute and look you over." Jerry's voice was completely calm and reassuring. I wondered what the unexpected passenger in the back seat was thinking. He probably won't pick flight school as his graduate assignment.

My altitude control wasn't exactly what you'd call precision, but I wasn't going below 500 feet. Jerry's constant power suggestions and confident voice helped a lot. It felt like he was actually in the airplane with me.

I called back to my passenger in the back seat. "Hey, what's your name again?"

"Midshipman Terry Triplett, fourth year at the Naval Academy."

"Well, you picked a dandy orientation. I'm Ensign Peter Pinson and this is my second flight. My first one was just a demo. Sorry I can't give you a handshake."

"Nice to meet you, sir."

We all switched over to channel 2, the tower control frequency. I glanced down at the airport. There were fire trucks and flashing lights everywhere.

As we approached the airport, the Tower and Jerry concurred on a plan to make a couple of low approaches until I was ready to land.

We passed over the airport and I turned downwind for another approach. I was sweating profusely, and my arms were as tight as piano wires. Holding altitude and airspeed was something I had not yet been exposed to. Jerry taught me how to trim on my first flight and I was constantly fighting the pressure after each power setting change Jerry gave.

The second pass was much smoother, and I informed Jerry I was ready. We turned final and the Tower confirmed we were cleared to land.

"You strapped in back there, Terry?"

"Yes, sir. You'll do great."

Jerry began to bark out instructions all the way to landing. "Ease the power back, hold your airspeed, raise your nose slightly, power up a little, looking good."

As we got closer to the runway, Jerry suddenly screamed. "You're getting slow! Put on some power quick!"

I jammed on some power and we leveled out and climbed a little. "No, too much power. Back off a little. Flare a little. Too much. Ease the nose back. Cut your power." We finally banged onto the runway about halfway down it. We bounced once and became slightly airborne. "Push the nose over and make sure your power is idle. Get on the brakes!" he shouted as we approached the end of the runway.

We came to a stop and waited for instructions from the Tower.

Tower: "Fairdale 202, You're cleared to the ramp. The fire trucks will follow you to check for overheating brakes. Nice job, I think this bird may be able to fly again someday."

I detected a note of sarcasm in his voice. *Oh well*, I thought. *We're going to walk away from it.*

"Terry, you okay back there?"

"Yes, sir, but I think I may need to change my flight suit."

"You and me both." I laughed.

Jerry Davidson met me in the debriefing room with a stern look on his face. He couldn't decide whether to chew me out or compliment me.

"Peter, this is by far the most unusual PS-2 I've ever observed. I don't normally get to train my student pilots from another airplane. I've got to give you a 'sat' because you saved the airplane and two Navy men. For headwork, it would normally be a 'down' for loss of situational awareness. I confess to giving you a briefing that could have been misinterpreted so that you thought you would be totally doing everything without my input. We will do the PS-2 over again tomorrow to insure you get the complete instruction. That being said, you are ahead of your peers on PS-2."

I saw a hint of a smile.

Jerry added, "Airman Lewis apologized to me. He thought the midshipman in the back seat was an instructor replacing me from another squadron."

The gang of eight met in mine and Frank's room for the daily debrief. We had the only television, and everyone wanted to watch the latest episode of "The Fugitive."

Andy started it off first. "Peter, how in hell did you do it? Are you trying to make the rest of us look bad?"

"Well, once you get all strapped in, you really can't see who's behind you and I thought my instructor wanted me to take the lead. It got my attention when I found out a midshipman was behind me. Once Lt. Davidson caught up with me, it was a matter of talking me down. I made a terrible landing. Maintenance was checking the 'g' meter for stress on the airplane. I hope I don't have to buy it. Anybody else have an interesting flight today?"

"No, but why didn't your plane captain identify the midshipman?" Andy posed.

"Good question. He said he thought the middie was a substitute instructor."

Nobody wanted to follow my story, so we shared a few tips on landings and instructor's idiosyncrasies. Everyone agreed the message from all instructors was that "We don't waste time on anybody who can't take the pressure. If you can't take the pressure, you should DOR now."

We watched the next episode of "The Fugitive" and everyone split.

THE STUD

Our gang of eight usually ate together every night in the BOQ mess hall. There was one ensign that physically stood out from all of us. We were all very physically fit, but this one guy looked like an All-American linebacker. His shirts looked tailor-made, and he appeared to be lifting weights every day. He even had perfect teeth.

"Wonder who that guy is?" Everett asked as we were finishing up dinner. Everett is a Marine second lieutenant and is the epitome of fitness himself. Everett is from Oklahoma and has a rodeo background. Marines only have two choices for future assignments, helicopters or fighters. Navy pilots have choices of helicopters, jet fighters, and fixed wing airplanes. None of us has expressed interest in helicopters.

"I heard he is from Connecticut—went to the Naval Academy. Played hockey, I think. His name's John McCune, III."

"His father and grandfather were both admirals," Joe added.

"He's driving the red Ferrari you see parked by the BOQ," Andy said. "Someone said he's keeping a Playboy Bunny out in town."

"He's got too much going for him," I laughed. "Just look at those perfect teeth. I'll bet he's aceing all the tests as well. I heard he solos in a couple of days. Guys like him are making all the rest of us look bad. He's a chick magnet for sure. He'll be gone to Meridian for jet training in a couple of days. We won't miss him."

Frank and I met in the BOQ mess the next day between flights. We were doing two-a-day training flights now. Just as we were ordering lunch from the steward mate, the stud came in, looking for a place to sit. I motioned for him to sit with us at the empty table.

"I'm Peter Pinson." I offered and extended my hand. He must not have seen the extended hand.

"The chow here really stinks," he said. "We had much better food at the Academy. Maybe it'll be better when I get to jets in

Meridian."

"Oh, you've already got your jet assignment in Meridian?" Frank asked with a surprised look.

"Well, not officially. My father is a two star admiral, and he told me that's where I would be going if that's the assignment I want. He flew jets himself—the first jets the Navy had. He had over a hundred carrier traps. I don't believe I've seen you guys. Were you at the Academy?"

"No, not me," Frank volunteered. "I was an aerospace engineer at Oregon State University with a master's degree in physics."

"I was only a civil engineer from Georgia Tech," I said as I began eating my lunch. "I probably couldn't get in the Academy."

"Don't feel bad about it. Only the top candidates from each state get in. Some people thought it was a hard school. I found it to be very easy. I hardly ever had to study. Good genes, I guess."

"Yeah, you must be a natural. Did you have prior flight time?"

"Yeah, my dad had a T-28 flown up to Annapolis every weekend with a pilot to give me some training. I was amazed how easy it is to be a pilot. Carrier quals should be a snap."

"I'm just the opposite. I have zero flight time and just came from the fleet on a cable layer ship."

"Boy, you're in for trouble. You know where you go if you wash out, don't you?"

"Yeah, back to the cable layer." I laughed. "I don't have your confidence. Everyone here has such solid backgrounds. I was Officer of the Deck on the cable layer. Hardly a background for flying high performance Navy aircraft."

"You probably won't make it. The washout rate is very high here."

"Well, I'll keep on trying, anyway. They've told me you don't actually need prior time if you study hard and pay attention to the instructors. If I can't hack it, I will DOR before carrier quals."

"I probably won't see you boys much longer since I'll be soloing in a couple of days and heading on out to Meridian, Mississippi. Don't be disappointed if you get helicopters or fixed wing props next. Whiting Field is in the sticks. I'm glad

I'm not going there next after I get my solo Friday."

"Good luck to you," Frank offered sincerely.

"I don't rely on luck," the stud shot back. "I'll leave luck with you fellows."

He grabbed his flight gear and sauntered out toward the flight line.

"Sounds like he's got his act together." Frank said sarcastically.

"Maybe so. Hope he doesn't swallow his silver spoon." I laughed.

I was on my 7th training flight and gaining confidence. Jerry was patient with me but still put on the pressure. Today we were going out to Silver Hill, an outlying field with triangular runways and no tower. Today we were using runway 6 and our call sign was Fairdale 103. There was one other T-34 operating at the field. The two instructors were constantly talking to each other giving our respective positions around the field so as not to collide. Without a tower, we were always flying VFR, or see and be seen.

Today, the other instructor was showing some tension in his transmissions. The student pilot must have been having trouble with his landings.

"Dammit, watch your airspeed. You trying to kill us?" The other T-34 instructor was on UHF instead of intercom and didn't realize he was broadcasting out. "You ain't going to solo tomorrow if you can't land better than this. Where is your head today, John?"

He realized his error and we didn't hear any more transmissions except position relays from Fairdale 111. "Do you know the other instructor?" I asked over our intercom.

"Yeah, it's Jack Krebs, a good friend of mine. He hates his student but can't get rid of him. He has his check-ride this afternoon for his safe for solo. He's scheduled to take the solo tomorrow if he's ready. I don't think he's ready, but Jack's putting him up for the safe for solo check. If he gets a 'down,' he'll have to get another instructor. At any rate, Jack is finished with him. Boy, he's arrogant."

I didn't ask his name, but I was pretty sure it was the stud. What a shock! Not that it was the stud but the fact that he was struggling to qualify. I couldn't wait to tell my buddies.

We finished our landing work and then climbed to work on the stall and spin series. I was not looking forward to the spins. We climbed to 8,000 feet and Jerry explained the maneuver.

"I want you to pull the manifold pressure back to fifteen inches and raise the nose up till you get a slight shudder. Continue holding the stick pressure until she falls off into the spin. I want you to just relax the stick and lightly put in right rudder and she'll roll off to the right. Then take your feet off the rudders. This airplane is so stable that she'll come out of the spin on her own. Just don't do anything to screw it up, okay?"

Everything worked as he advertised, and the T-34 suddenly stabilized from the spinning action.

"Wow," I exclaimed. "That was breathtaking, but not as bad as I thought."

"Yeah, this is pretty gentle. Wait till you get in jets or T-28s. The T-28 is a killer if you do it wrong. You've got to use proper rudder to get out. Impossible to get out of an inverted spin. Pay close attention if you go to T-28's in Whiting Field. That's where I went after Saufley before going to the fleet."

As we turned to go back to Saufley, the throttle slowly came back. "Assume an engine failure, Peter, and try to find a place you can safely land in. Try to stay out of the trees."

I had not done this maneuver yet and he caught me by surprise. I surveyed the countryside. There was the Gulf and its sandy beaches, and there were a few farmers' fields, a few highways, plenty of forested tracts, a few small towns, and one of our Navy outlying fields. As I pointed the nose toward the field, Jerry said, "Sorry pal, the airport is closed. Pick somewhere else."

As we descended through 2,000 feet, I spotted a freshly plowed farmer's field that was relatively flat. I couldn't decide if it was best to land gear up or down. I decided to drop the gear to take advantage of the wheels. At 500 feet, Jerry took over the controls and we climbed back out.

"Not bad," Jerry said. "You dirtied up a little too soon but might have made it. We'll talk about it in debrief. I'll fly for awhile to give you a break."

I took over on arrival at Saufley. The landing pattern was always a circus with solos and duals jockeying for position to land. Cars are parked daily outside the gates to watch the air show, wondering why there are no collisions, knowing student pilots are up there learning the ropes.

I started the descent into Saufley Field, and Jerry informed me we were landing east on runway 9. We leveled at 1500 feet and just as I was about to turn left and descend to 800 feet for the downwind leg, a T-34 went shooting by our starboard side. He must have been doing 20 knots faster than us when the RDO (Runway Duty Officer) screamed out.

"What the hell is going on up there? Identify yourselves."

"Fairdale 103, we're turning downwind to 800 feet," Jerry responded. "Not sure who was in the rocket that passed us to starboard."

A sheepish voice responded. "It's Fairdale 111. We were a little hot. My student forgot to extend the boards. We'll re-enter the pattern and turn downwind at 800 feet."

The sarcastic voice of the RDO bellowed out, "Should I clear the whole pattern for you and your student."

"Not necessary. I hope we've got it under control," Jack replied.

Jerry was cracked up when he said to me on the intercom, "Jack's having fun today. Can't wait for him to debrief me at happy hour."

"Scared hell out of me when he came screaming by us."

"Well, I've seen it all as an instructor. The washout rate is pretty high around here. Beats me why we don't have more midairs in this pattern. It's designed to emulate the carrier landing pattern so there is a reason for this madness."

We finished the pattern and rolled out on final just as Fairdale 111 called downwind.

"Peter, you're cleared to land. I think we're safe from 111. You're a little too fast, so get off some power. Think about a glideslope from here in."

I floated down the runway and the T-34 finally settled onto the runway with a hard thump.

"That's about how hard a real carrier landing is. We don't get graded on smoothness on the boat—just be able to walk away from the trap (landing) and hope the bird is still flyable." Jerry laughed heartily at his own joke.

As we taxied in, we heard Fairdale 111 cleared for landing.

"Slow down, Peter, I want to observe this landing."

Fairdale 111 came in a little high and fast and was late getting his landing gear down. The instructor called the tower and stated he would like to demo a missed approach to his student.

"Bullshit!" hollered Jerry over the intercom. "His student could never have made it. He would have landed in the Gulf with that speed. I can't wait to give Jack hell about that supposed demo go-around."

As we pulled into the ramp to park, we saw 111 coming back in to land. This time he was low and looked terribly close to the tops of the trees. As he got closer to the runway he leveled off and became high over the end of the runway. Then he suddenly started a fast sink. The T-34 hit and bounced about three feet back into the air before settling down onto the runway.

"They just don't pay us instructors enough," Jerry laughed. "Instructors are 'dropping on request' as fast as the students. I'm just kidding. The T-34 does have extra strength landing gear, much like the carrier planes. Shut her down, do the post flight, and meet me back in ops."

I took my time finishing up the post flight inspection and waited around to see who the student pilot was in 111. They parked two planes down from us, and I peered over in time to see the stud climbing out of the cockpit. I quickly darted inside to start the debrief.

"What are you laughing about, Peter?" Jerry asked.

"I'd rather not say, sir. It's a private joke."

"Okay. How'd you like the acrobatics today?"

"Not bad. I think I'll watch my food intake better from now on. The top of the loop felt funny."

"Your status is about average so far. Actually, pretty good considering you haven't had previous flight time. A couple more flights and you should be ready for solo. Legitimate solo, I should say. You are probably the only student pilot in history to go up without an instructor before being checked out. That'll be a story for Trader Jon's."

I couldn't wait to get back to the BOQ to tell the guys what had happened at Silver Hill and the pattern back at Saufley. They were not going to believe it.

LEARNING THE ROPES

Lt. Davidson was an excellent instructor and I progressed along with the other members of the gang of eight. I was lucky to get an instructor who was a supporter rather than a screamer. Pensacola had plenty of both. Some of the guys had previous flight time and were helpful to the rest of us. We were all impressed with one of the Vietnamese student pilots, NavCad Dung. He had only six months of English training but was getting rave feedback on his piloting skills. He was on track to solo with all of us. The great master plan was for Vietnamese pilots to be trained to do their own fighting.

Most of the next few days were spent at outlying fields between Saufley field westward toward Mobile, with the Gulf of Mexico being the southern boundary. This was our exclusive operating area. Silver Hill was the favorite field of Lt. Davidson. He liked this airport because it set up to exclude most crosswind landings like carriers. Every American Naval aviator is required to land solo on a carrier, including helicopter pilots. The thought of it caused many student pilots to DOR. Pilots who complete training, including carrier landings, are rumored to be about 40%. But first, we must solo in the T-34, the basic trainer for everyone.

After three weeks of flight training, all we talked about was our first solo. The requirement was to go to an outlying field with our instructors, make a couple of successful touch and gos, do a full stop, and let the instructor get out. He will go sit by a tree and you will make a couple of landings at the outlying field, stop, and let the instructor back in. If he is satisfied, you are safe for solo. You will fly back to Saufley Field, the instructor clears you, and you will go into the wild blue yonder all by yourself. Of course, I accidentally soloed on my second flight when the midshipman mistakenly climbed in my backseat, and I took off with a non-pilot in the back seat. Next time, I will be a little more careful. It's rather embarrassing to have the whole field shut down and fire trucks all over the place, not to mention the controlled crash landing. As if my reputation around Pensacola wasn't bad enough from the fiasco in the Caribbean. I won't be able to face Trader Jon.

The gang of eight continued to debrief every night as we got closer to the solos. Frank, my roommate, has previous flight time and is ready. Cal, Tiki, Bax and I were a day behind the others. My PS-2 didn't count as a finished flight. Cal was having a hard time with landings and had to repeat a flight. Tiki couldn't get his acrobatics exactly right. Bax tried to land at the wrong airport which resulted in an "unsat."

PS-12 is my safe for solo with a Marine instructor, Captain Frank Smith. He is a veteran of Vietnam and is instructing temporarily before trying out for the Blue Angels demonstration team. He is an intimidating character and I was nervous as a cat.

We met in the ready room and he wanted to know if I had prior flying experience or ever soloed. I told him about my inadvertent solo and he cracked up. That helped a lot because he is a naturally gruff individual. After asking me to explain the emergency procedures, we went out to the airplane.

The start-up, clearance, taxi out, and take off went fine and we turned west toward the operating area. Frank unexpectedly pulled the power back at 3,000 feet and said, "Your engine is simulated failed. What are you going to do?"

I wasn't expecting it after takeoff, and I felt a lump in my throat. I could see a highway and a big body of water, Perdido Bay, ahead. I knew these were my only choices. I chose the Bay. I had already cleaned up my gear and flaps, so I needed to figure out my landing configuration. I decided to use flaps with the landing gear retracted. The winds were pretty high today, but I was too busy to make a good judgement on the direction to make the water landing. I got the wings fairly level and at 500 feet Frank took control and we flew on our way.

"Not too bad, Peter. We'll talk it over in debrief. Take us up to 8000 feet and we'll do our high work."

The high work consisted of stalls, slow flight, and spins. We didn't do any loops on this flight because they were optional on your solo. You get to choose on your solo what you want to do, but most guys told me they just fly straight and level on their first solo. Just go smell the roses and fly down over the beaches.

Everything went pretty well on the high work, but I knew I'd get gigged on the stall series. I could never get them exactly right, but I knew they didn't warrant a "down." We descended to do our landing work today at Summerdale Field. Summerdale is on the western edge of the operating area and uses the traditional triangle direction of the three runways so that you always have no worse than a 30-degree crosswind for landing. Of course, on carrier landings, the ship usually gives you a heading directly into the wind.

Based on Frank's background, I knew he would have a lot of write ups for debrief. I could only hope I wouldn't get a "down." He advised the winds were from the southwest, and we would be using runway 24. There were two other planes in the pattern, and I knew they were two of my friends getting their safe for solos. Frank had me do four landings with him before he decided to get out.

After my fiasco on my PS-2 flight without an instructor, this solo around the pattern was a piece of cake. I couldn't vouch for a textbook landing, but I taxied over to where Frank was sitting with another instructor.

It was my regular instructor, Jerry Davidson, sitting under a tree observing his student in the pattern. I knew from the posted schedule he was checking someone safe for solo.

"Hi, Jerry. What are you doing today?"

"I've got a safe for solo, also."

"Is it Ensign Williamson (Tiki), by chance?"

"Yes, is he a friend of yours?"

"Yeah, he's a great guy. One of the best yankees I know. Do me a favor, please. Tell him to get together with me to let me help him with his landings. He's such a perfectionist. I just want to jerk his chain."

"Okay, he's doing fine so far. He's on his third landing now so I'll probably recommend him for solo tomorrow if he doesn't screw up the next one. I see you're with Captain Smith. He's a tough Marine dude. I'll give you a fifty-fifty chance of getting an 'up.'" He winked and smiled.

Captain Smith motioned me to come back to our plane.

"Come on, sailor. Stop the 'brown nosing.' You don't want a 'down,' do you?"

I didn't doubt him. We climbed in and his only words were, "Let's head on back to Saufley."

I couldn't read him as to whether I had done good, bad, or poor. I wished he would give me a clue. Maybe it's all dependent on the landing back at Saufley.

The pattern was chaotic as usual. Two of my gang were on their solos which probably contributed. I turned on final and dropped the gear when Captain Smith casually stated, "You goin' to try it without flaps, podner?"

Dammit! I thought. *No wonder I'm so fast.*

I quickly got out the flaps and hurried through the landing checklist. I was rushed now and salvaged a pretty good Navy landing, nice and hard. At least it didn't bounce. I could feel the back of my neck getting hot as I wondered if I got a "down."

After taxi and shutdown his only words were, "Finish the post flight and meet me inside." He sounded gruff and indifferent.

Cripes. Must be a "down."

I slowly shuffled into the ready room for the debrief. Captain Smith still wasn't showing any emotion.

"Well, Peter. I'm giving you an 'up' for solo. Not the best I've ever seen, but since you've technically soloed on your second fam (familiarization) flight, I know you can do it safely. I want you to tell me your weak areas today and then I'll comment."

I breathed a sigh of relief and recounted all I could remember about the flight. Captain Smith was very thorough, and I could see how he was a seasoned pilot with attention to detail. You don't survive in the fleet without eliminating mistakes. He wished me well and I bounced out and headed to the BOQ.

Tiki was waiting for me and displayed a big smile.

"I can tell you got an 'up' recommendation. I did, too!"

"I can't believe what your regular instructor, Lt. Davidson, recommended for me."

"What's that?" I said straight faced.

"He told me to get up with you to give me some tips on landings. That makes no sense. I think my landings are pretty good. I don't need help from you."

"I'll be glad to help you however I can. Let's go to happy hour and celebrate."

Andy, Tiki and I all survived the safe for solo flights today. Frank had already passed and soloed. Cal and Everett got "downs" and will be required to repeat with different instructors. We had our usual happy hour table when Everett came bouncing in.

"Hey, guys. Did everything go good today? You probably heard I messed up a bit. I hit the wrong rudder on the spin. Flared a little too high on landings. Tried to dead stick on a busy highway. Other than that, Lt. Peavy said I was above average. Ha, ha."

"Bummer, man. You'll do well tomorrow. Who've you got for the recheck?" Andy asked.

"Lieutenant Commander Morris, a mean SOB. Supposed to hate Marines."

"Yeah, I've heard it's been awhile since he's given a safe for solo." I smirked.

"Aw, come on, guys, give me a break," Everett moaned.

"All right, we'll buy you a beer to drown your sorrows," Tiki quipped.

"You all are so generous."

Cal slumped into the bar with a disgusted look on his face.

"I've met the enemy and it is me," Cal said disconsolately. "I got too busy on landing and forgot something."

"What did you forget?" Tiki blurted.

"Just the landing gear," Cal deadpanned.

We all cracked up. "What's the big deal about that?"

"My check instructor, Lt. Wilson, is a screamer and had me uptight the whole flight. Maybe I'll get Santa Claus, your instructor, Peter, for the re-check. If you can get safe for solo, anybody can."

"I resent that remark. I'll have you know he can be a real hard-ass."

"We do get three strikes, don't we?" Cal said hopefully.

Frank jumped in. "Well, it depends. If your headwork is bad, that's one thing. But if headwork is bad and flying ability is bad, you'll probably get one more chance with a different instructor and then a SPDI board. You'll do fine. Don't worry.

Andy made it, so you can, too."

"Oh, so now it's Andy," Andy protested.

"Now, now, guys," Tiki jumped in. "Time for some solidarity. We're all gonna make it. Here's to the gang of eight!"

Glasses clinked.

We broke from happy hour, and as we settled into our room, I asked Frank what he thought our chances were to eventually get our wings.

"I know the statistics suggest only about half make it through, but I think most of our gang will make it. It's easy to make a mistake or two as long as you understand your mistakes, and don't keep making the same ones continuously. SPDI boards usually mean a discharge from the program. On the other hand, Vietnam is getting hot and there is pressure on the Navy to produce more pilots. They'd like to get the Vietnamese to check out and fly their own planes but that's not working out. I hear one of their pilots is soloing tomorrow."

"Yeah, it's NavCad Dung. Apparently, he's their ace and best hope to keep their program going. I wish him luck."

SOLOS

Today is my solo day. I woke up and felt butterflies in my stomach. I blocked out my previous out-of-control solo with the cadet in the back seat. This is the real deal. I will do everything myself—check into operations and sign for my own airplane. Check the maintenance log for previous write ups and insure the airplane has been fueled and deemed safe for flight. I'll check the weather forecast and direction of the winds. I'll go over my intentions to fly out into the operations area. I will decide if I want to do spins and loops or just fly straight and level. I decided to fly down low over the beaches so I won't get lost.

I methodically put on my flight suit and grabbed my flight gloves and hardhat. It seemed so different to know you're preparing to solo rather than repeating the accidental fiasco. I tied my flight boots and headed out to the flight line. My airplane side number is 107 so my call sign would be Fairdale 107 Sierra, indicating solo. My plane captain was already at the plane and he saluted me as I arrived.

"Good morning, sir, I'm Airman Long. Your plane's fueled and ready to go."

"Thanks, Long, I'll give her a look." (All pilots do their own walk-around check to back up the plane captains.)

I climbed into the T-34 cockpit and strapped on my seat belt and shoulder harness. My parachute was secured, and I went through the pre-start checklist twice to make sure I hadn't missed anything. I gave the plane captain a thumbs up and he returned the thumbs up as a sign that I was cleared to start.

I cracked the throttle, hit the starter, and after the propeller started turning introduced the fuel. She belched a little and soon the sweet sound of starting was complete. I turned on the radios and called the ground controller to get clearance to taxi.

My voice was a little creaky and the controller could tell I was solo. I heard Tiki's voice call for taxi a few minutes later so I knew I would have a friend in the operations area. I finished the run up and switched to tower on channel 2. I was so nervous I couldn't remember my call sign.

Tower: "Ship 107, are you by chance Fairdale 107?"

"Aye, Fairdale 107 is ready to go."

Tower: "Are you solo?"

"Affirmative."

Tower: "Remember to add "Sierra" when you are solo. You are planning to put your flaps out, aren't you?" (Tower has binoculars trained on every plane).

Crap! I thought. *Relax Pinson.*

"Yes, sir, just getting them out."

Tower: "Fairdale 107 Sierra, you're cleared for takeoff."

I slowly applied the power and the T-34 came to life. My first real solo. My centerline control wasn't the greatest, but after playing with the rudders a little she straightened out and at 80 knots I gently let her fly off the runway. My heart was racing as I saw the runway disappear under the nose. The trees below became smaller and smaller. I remembered to bring up the gear and flaps and turned westward toward the ops area. I set climb power and listened intently to the sound of the engine as the rpm was reduced. So far, so good. I climbed to 3500 feet and turned southwest toward the Gulf of Mexico which was a popular place for solos. You couldn't get lost there and you could show off for the beach goers. You couldn't legally go below 500 feet, but I was hoping big brother wasn't watching. I had talked to Tiki before takeoff and told him where I was going. On my descent I looked over at 3 o'clock and saw Tiki descending as well. We hadn't pre-arranged it, but we kept getting closer and closer and all of a sudden, we were flying in loose formation. We weren't allowed to talk with each other except in emergency, but everyone knew to click your mike twice to acknowledge another solo in the area. I nodded my head for Tiki to follow me down to the beach.

Tiki had a lot of flight time while in school at Purdue University. He had over 400 flight hours and he was totally comfortable flying formation. I leveled off at 500 feet and Tiki scared me half to death by tucking in off my right wing. I flew right down the beach with Tiki right beside me. I could sense he was laughing at me. I had no idea how to signal him as the leader and so I just gradually turned north away from the beach. I figured it was time to go back to Saufley since we were supposed to get one hour of flight time. Tiki mimicked my every move and followed me back to Saufley. I switched over to approach control on channel 3 and reported IP at 1032 hours. Tiki came right behind me and reported IP at 1032, same time as me. For god's sake, Tiki. You're going to get us both on report, I thought.

Except for over-running the solo ahead of me and needing to extend downwind, I successfully negotiated the pattern and made a successful landing. My first real solo was over. It was the thrill of a lifetime! Maybe I won't DOR quite yet.

After taxiing in and shutting down, I post-flighted the airplane and saluted Plane Captain Long. "Any problems with the bird, sir?"

"Naw, she performed well for me. No write ups. 1.1 hours flight time."

I was giddy as I walked across the ramp to the flight line. I wish the guys on the Neptune could see me now. A letter from Ensign Dollar had mentioned that everyone on the ship was betting whether I would solo or not. I'll be happy to give them the news. Captain Tuna and CDR Scratchy probably bet against me.

Tiki was grinning as I entered the debriefing area.

"Tiki, you scared me half to death. Had you ever done that before?"

"Yeah, we did it all the time at Purdue—best aviation program in the country."

"That's funny. Cal said the same thing about Auburn."

"Well, we'll have to set up a little challenge down the road. Let's head to happy hour to see how our buddies did today."

The next few days were clean-up flights to give confidence to the solo experience with reviews by instructors to make sure we were safe and hadn't been just lucky. The difficulty of the program didn't let anybody slip through the cracks. Jerry told me that anyone at this stage could fly Navy airplanes, but what got pilots in trouble later on was failure to evaluate and lose concentration on the tactical situation. Of course, getting shot down is probably out of your control.

One of our gang of eight didn't make the cut. Everett couldn't get past his safe for solo and went before the SPDI board. Everett confessed he hated the acrobatics and said he would be much happier driving tanks with the Marine Corp. I must admit I'm still not that comfortable flying acrobatics and spins. In addition, carrier quals still loomed ahead as you continued through the syllabus. Rumor was that when you got to carrier qualifications, the DOR's became numerous.

Solo celebrations take place at the Mustin Beach "O" Club every Friday afternoon. There we follow the tradition of cutting off our ties. Our next step would be getting orders for advanced training. The choices were jets in Meridian, Mississippi, props in Milton, Florida at Whiting Field, or helicopters at Ellyson Field in Pensacola. Some of the Marines and Coasties had no choice—they would be assigned to Ellyson Field for choppers. My choice was Whiting Field to fly propeller airplanes because I wasn't sure yet what I was doing here. At some point I had to decide if I wanted to try to land on an aircraft carrier—the idea was daunting.

ORDERS

Everyone in the gang of eight passed the T-34 basic training except for Everett—the Oklahoma boy who always seemed far away. Dick Wall, his roommate, confessed that Everett's heart was just not into flying and he had a girl back home. His instructor gave him a bad report on his safe-for-solo flight and he would have been required to go to a SPDI (Student Pilot Disposition) board. He requested a DOR and was assigned to a tank command for the remainder of his Marine obligation. Dick said that made him happy because that's where his heart really was.

Paul Nick, partner in the Marine bedroom at the beach house, received orders to go to Meridian, Mississippi, to train in jets. That would result in a fast track to get to the action in Vietnam.

Ensign Tiki Williamson, our ace from Purdue aviation, wouldbe at Whiting Field until after carrier quals, and then report to Beeville, Texas, to train on the A-1 Skyraider, the awesome single pilot, single engine propeller plane with a gigantic bomber payload. The Skyraider is considered a perfect plane for the jungles of Vietnam. That will result in a fast lane to Vietnam like Paul.

Frank opted to take helicopters out of Ellyson Field which will extend his time in the Pensacola area. His other option was to go to school on the C-130 Hercules which would be more of a support type billet. He wanted to be more of an operational type.

Ensign Andy Anderson, in our original gang of eight, will go to Whiting Field to train on the T-28 with requests to go to C-130 school down the road. He hopes to be a pilot on Fat Albert, the C-130 support plane for the Blue Angels. This seems to be a long shot, but Andy is very determined.

Ensign Rufus Baxley stated his desire to end up in the Bahamas, in particular on the island of Eleuthera. He heard of my adventures there and decided that is the place for him. I can't say I blame him. He thinks C-130's will get him to Eleuthera.

The remaining three of us, Cal, Joe and I received orders to

Whiting Field to train on T-28s. Our long-range projection was to train in the P-3 Orion, a long-range patrol bomber with multiple missions including anti-submarine warfare. The T-28 is considered to be the backbone of Naval aviation training.

We gathered at happy hour for our celebratory solo tie cuttings with our instructors and delivered them all a present. It was sad to lose Everett, but we all knew there was a lot of attrition in the program.

We checked out of the BOQ the next morning and wished good luck to our new-found buddies going elsewhere. Paul was really happy about going to be a jet jock, until we told him he would be going straight to Vietnam if he finished the program. As for the rest of us, nobody was absolutely sure of a destination. I came to Pensacola to escape the USS Neptune so I still didn't know if I wanted to or could be a Naval aviator. So far, I was doing as well as most everyone. Some of these guys have wanted to do this for years. I was a Johnny-come-lately.

I packed up my Corvette and headed up to Milton which is thirty miles to the northeast of Pensacola. I will be living in the BOQ on the field, for the third time in the Pensacola area. I am beginning to enjoy the beach and surrounding attractions and the nice balmy weather. Quite a pleasant change from the Norfolk weather. You get to know a lot of schoolteachers and other groupies who know their way around better than us.

Whiting Field is named for Kenneth Whiting, Naval aviator #16. He was an icon of Naval aviation and also commanded a submarine. His widow dedicated the field in 1943. Whiting Field actually consists of two airport complexes, North and South. Training Wing Five (TraWing5) is broken down into VT-2, VT-3, and VT-4 squadrons. I will be assigned to VT-2. Advanced training consists of three parts: basic, instruments, and formation on the North complex. After completing that phase, carrier landing comes into play. That separates the men from the boys, because your first carrier landing is solo! That will be VT-4 and a totally different way of landing an airplane.

We will go to ground school again to learn about the T-28 Trojan. This airplane seems like a monster compared to the T-34. The T-34 is an inline engine, 225 horsepower. The T-28 has a huge radial engine with 1500 horsepower—big difference.

I arrived at the BOQ about the same time as Bax. He had Georgia Bulldog stickers all over his red Pontiac. "Who's your roommate, Bax?"

"I don't know yet, but I hope it's not a Bama or LSU grad. All those guys talk about is football. We're much more cultured at Georgia. We can talk about economics and social engineering. Plus, our cheerleaders put theirs to shame."

"I'll bet our cheerleaders at Tech are smarter than yours at Georgia," I proposed.

"I'd be a fool to take that bet." Bax laughed.

"Looks like Frank and I will be together again. We brought our television over from Saufley, so we'll have a place to gather on Tuesday nights to watch 'The Fugitive.'"

Cal and Tiki arrived a few minutes later and got the room next to ours. Tiki went through the ROTC program for his commission at Purdue and Cal went through the AOC program in Pensacola. I was a year senior to all of them since I had come from the fleet on the Neptune, even though we were all Ensigns (O-1s). Andy showed up an hour later and was assigned a room on our floor with Bax as roommate. I hope a yankee and a grits eater can co-exist.

I was initially awed by the size of the operation. Airplanes were taking off and landing on both the North and South fields—all T-28s with identical white fuselages trimmed with international orange covering the entire nose cowling and vertical stabilizer. Additional orange stripes were painted on each wingtip. All of the markings and identifiers were in bold black paint.

Someone described it as the busiest airport in the world.

We checked into our BOQ rooms which had an outstanding view of the North field. The flight line displayed rows and rows of T-28s all perfectly lined up. The north control tower looked out over the field and over the north operating area which spanned all the way to South Alabama.

Our room consisted of two beds, two desks, two chests of drawers and a head. Quite Spartan considering the officer quarters on the USS Neptune. The mess hall was next door with a covered walkway connection. The Navy Exchange and Officers Club were between the North and South runways. The training buildings were closer to the South runways.

The following Monday we started ground school classes. We were initially briefed on the operating area around Whiting. The area consisted of towns and airports to the north, east, and west of the North field. We were instructed to absolutely stay clear of the South field since they were for carrier field practice and cross-country operations. We began our indoctrination on the T-28.

"Lord, this is a monster!" Cal exclaimed on our first break. "If Lt. Ringer was trying to intimidate us, he succeeded. It's hard to comprehend how much bigger the T-28 Trojan is. I had a hop on one while in school at Auburn. The pilot showed me a spin and scared the hell out of me. I think it scared the hell out of him, too. The scuttlebutt was that the spins cause the second most DOR's. Field carrier landing practice (FCLP) is the worst. Many guys decide they don't want to go solo to the carrier."

Lt. Ringer was our instructor for the entire first week of power plants. The next week would be instruments and procedures with Ltjg. Benson, and then emergency procedures with Ltjg. Nichols. Our first flights would be on the fourth week with various instructors. The syllabus was set up that you have a primary instructor for eight flights (T1-T8), followed by a check instructor to monitor your progress. T-9 will be the first solo. Basic flying will consist of takeoff and landings and steep turns, stalls, spins, loops, and other acrobatics. Orientation of the ops area will be on the T-1. Ringer stressed way too many solos get lost and land at the wrong airports. The Brewton, Alabama, airport had been the recipient of most deviant navigational errors and has a hotline to the Whiting Field tower.

On Monday Lt. Ringer strode into the classroom. He was dressed in working khakis, tan shirt and pants, black tie, the khaki piss cutter and brown shoes. He wore the double silver bars of full lieutenant and Navy Wings of Gold with an I.D. badge underneath. Brown shoes were still a novelty to me because shipboard types wear black shoes. Shipboard types generally call aviators airedales, or brown shoes. He had the cocky air of someone who had been to a few rodeos.

"Gentlemen, I came here from the fleet having been through a year operating in the Gulf of Tonkin. I flew the A-1 Sky raider which you may be familiar with. It's a big 3000 horsepower attack bomber carrier based on the USS Forrestal. The max takeoff weight is about 20,000 pounds, about twice the weight of the T-28. It's a tail dragger and a real handful. There is a single pilot. The T-28 is a real easy airplane compared to the Skyraider."

All of our eyes rolled in disbelief.

"I'm teaching this class because the Navy wants me to emphasize the importance of torque on propeller type aircraft. The Skyraider is used in Vietnam to carry heavy bombs and is known for its pinpoint accuracy. It is known as the flying dump truck because of its ability to carry so much ordnance. The wings fold up to save space on the carrier. The four-bladed prop is monstrous. The torque generated by this huge propeller turns in a clockwise direction during takeoff power which generates a torqueing or twisting force on the fuselage of the aircraft which makes it try to turnover to the left. To offset this force, the pilot must apply hard right rudder on liftoff to offset the torque. The Navy has lost way too many planes because of this basic aviation principle. Short pilots in particular have had trouble getting enough rudder in because of their shorter legs, thus we have a height minimum on the Skyraider. We lost a Vietnamese pilot and aircraft because of this torqueing on takeoff.

"Another Skyraider was lost on the ground in Corpus Christi, where we trained Skyraider pilots. A young Vietnamese pilot who had made it to advanced training was on his first solo flight. He was in the runup area and had set the parking brakes to make his pre-takeoff checks. The procedure called for setting the manifold pressure to 50% power to check that all engine instruments were in the normal range. He accidentally set the power to max and the tail wheel came off the ground. The huge propeller blades began striking the concrete ramp and came loose contacting the main landing gear so hard that the gear collapsed. So then the airplane came down to the ramp and caught on fire. The pilot was able to escape but the airplane burned up. I tell you this not to embarrass anyone but only to illustrate things that can happen now that you're on a more advanced airplane than the T-34."

After these two illustrations, two of the Saudi trainee pilots decided to leave the room and DOR.

Lt. Ringer grinned. "I hate this part of my presentation, but it always thins out the unmotivated."

THE TROJAN

My first flight on the mighty T-28 was on a cold, windy day in February. I met my instructor in the ready room in my flight suit and accessories. I was nervous as this was by far the bigger test I had undergone.

Lt. Sanda was sitting calmly in a lounge chair, legs crossed and smoking a pipe.

"So, you're the infamous Ensign Pinson?" he asked with a sneer.

"Guilty as charged, sir. I must defend myself, though. Both good and bad luck seem to follow me around."

"Well, let me get one thing straight here. You can't count on good luck in this business. Preparation is what this is all about. You're going to find out in aviation bad things can happen in a hurry. I pray you're always up to the challenge. Things happen fast. You must react fast and with a good plan. We lose way too many students and instructors in training because of freeze ups and not following our procedures. Our procedures are time tested and proven to be effective. If you'll train and study to absolute proficiency, you'll be okay. As you know, the culmination of your training here will be carrier landings while you're solo. Way too many students lose confidence right before the carrier quals and DOR. The Navy has lost money and time on these guys. Are you committed to land on a carrier by yourself, Ensign Pinson?"

I gulped and showed a flash of fear and indecision. "Yes, sir," I said, a little more meekly than I intended.

"Okay, Pinson, we're going to train fast and furiously. The Navy wants to work with guys who're motivated. Can't waste time on anyone not committed. Let's go over our menu for today."

My head was swimming after the briefing. The T-28 is a whole new level of flying. I had already heard the scuttlebutt about the danger of spinning this bird. An inverted spin is certain death. The T-34 was so stable that you could literally take your hands off the controls and it would stabilize out of a spin. On the T-28 you must use the correct rudder and ailerons to successfully recover.

"Peter, on day one, we'll do a complete walk-around inspection and the next five days you will conduct it under my supervision. On your first checkride with another instructor, you will be expected to do it flawlessly. You can call me Sandy if you wish. Most people do. Any questions?"

"No, sir."

"Now, the engine start is quite different from the T-34. We'll read the checklist for the first couple of days until you're comfortable without it. There are thirty-five items on the before-start checklist. They will soon be second nature to you. I will demonstrate an engine failure today and show you how to glide toward a farmer's field. Have you heard the expression 'Bought the Farm'?"

"Yes, sir."

"You got the picture now?"

"I do. Never thought of it that way."

"We'll do one acrobatic maneuver today just to ensure you're ready for this program. We don't train people who can't stand a few g's. We'll perform a straightforward loop. What did you have for lunch?"

"Ham sandwich."

"You should be okay, then.

"I'll talk you through the first two landings. Then you'll make a few. Hold your hands lightly on the controls to get a feel for the smooth movements throughout the landings. We'll go up to the Brewton airport where I like to work. The locals like to come out and cheer and jeer since they see some beauties every now and then.

"After leaving the pattern at Whiting, take up a 330 heading, and we'll climb to 8,000 feet and do some stalls and slow flight. Then I'll demo the loop, and we'll get in the pattern at Brewton. Any questions?"

"What if I get sick on the loop."

"Grab a barf bag on the way out, one time only. Naval aviators don't get sick, Rookie. Grab your gear and let's go strap it on."

I didn't want to tell Sandy that I had a demo ride in a T-28 at NAS Breezy Point in Norfolk over a year ago when I was secretly applying for flight school while still attached to the USS Neptune. I was taken up by a Navy Lt. to see if I had the proper demeanor to handle pulling g's and the strain of flying in a high-performance airplane. Except for throwing up (down) at the top of the loop, I seemed to handle it okay. I wasn't allowed to touch the control stick which was fine with me. Now here I am about to get into a T-28 and actually fly it (with an instructor looking over my shoulder, of course).

I had forgotten how big and intimidating the T-28 was in Norfolk. Compared to the T-34, this airplane is a monster. We were assigned ship 519 which was the first airplane on the line. Lt. Sanda performed the walkaround showing me all the things to look for. I then climbed into the front seat and he climbed in behind me in the tandem seat configuration. I closed the canopy and tested the intercom to see if we were in communication. I was amazed at how squeaky my voice was.

"Loud and clear," Sandy announced. "You make the start, Peter. State what you're doing."

"DC Battery and generator-on.

"Starter-press.

"Ignition-both.

"Primer-depress."

The engine turned over and caught after five blades. Then the engine belched and blue smoke appeared.

"Starter-released," I said.

"Mixture rich." Then I released the primer.

"Look for oil pressure, Peter. If none, you shut down the engine immediately, understand?"

I pushed in the inverter circuit breakers and the instruments and gauges came to life.

"Okay, Peter, not bad for the first try. We'll go over abnormal starts on the debriefing. There are a lot of tricks you can try when the starts are stubborn. When you get on the carrier, the air boss will eat you alive for any kind of delay."

I thought to myself all these instructors talk about is getting to the "boat" (carrier). I can't even think that far ahead. I'm not even supposed to be this far along, actually. I meant to just get orders off the Neptune, not to become a Navy pilot. Here I am about to go flying in a T-28. Can't look back now. What the hell!

Sandy talked me through the pre-taxi and taxi checklists.

Ground control: "Sioux Falls 519, You're cleared to taxi."

"Peter, ease a little power on. After we move forward, test the brakes."

I may have put too much power on, and we quickly moved out. I sensed we were travelling too fast and slammed on the brakes. The Trojan lurched forward, and I almost hit my head on the canopy. There was silence on the Intercom. I was afraid Sandy got knocked out.

Finally, a sound on the IC. "Damn, Peter, did I forget to say ease on the brakes. I think I've got a cut on my head. It's not bad. I won't need a tourniquet."

Rats, I said to myself. *I'm gonna get a 'down' on my first flight.*

"Okay, let's go. Taxi at about 800 rpm. That'll work on level taxiways. Head over to the runup area."

We entered the runup area and I set the brakes. This airplane is a bear, I said to myself. I don't know if I'll ever get comfortable on this thing.

I ran the takeoff checklist. "Trim-check 0, 0, 5; flaps-up; fuel pressure-checked; supercharger-low; prop-full increase rpm; mixture-rich; harness-locked; cowl and oil cooler flaps-open; carb air-direct." So far, so good.

I thought back to where I was a year ago—floating in the middle of the Atlantic Ocean on a Navy cable layer ship. No weapons except a shotgun in the Welfare and Rec department which was used to shoot seagulls off the fantail. All I had to do was watch the ship's heading and keep the plots updated and call the Captain if something didn't seem right. It seemed so long ago. Now I'm trying to learn how to fly an airplane the Navy way, knowing that one mistake and I'm kicked out, and might have to go back to the Neptune. Captain Tuna will eat me alive if I show up back there after what I did to the ship's air conditioning system.

"Peter, we're number 2 for 36. Remember, on the roll, just

ease the rudder in to keep her straight. Don't chase the rudder. The torque will increase the faster we go."

Tower: "Sioux Falls 519 you're cleared for takeoff, runway 36."

Sandy: "Roger, 519 cleared for takeoff."

"Now, ease her onto the runway and hold the brakes after you get her straight," Sandy said as I slowly taxied out to the threshold of the runway.

I thought I got it straight until Sandy yelled, "Straighter than that, Stud," in a snarky voice.

Tower cleared us for takeoff with a clearance to level at 3,000 feet on a heading of 330.

I ran the throttle to 30 inches MAP and checked the instruments. The noise was way higher than the T-34. I released the brakes and set 48 inches. I felt awed by the thrust and power as we accelerated through 30 knots and felt the rudder become effective. We started fishtailing and I started chasing the heading on the rudder pedals. Sandy didn't say anything. He can't be happy. One hundred knots came quickly, and the airplane lifted off without my input. I realized I should have rotated slightly at 90 knots.

"Are you flying the airplane or is it flying on its own?" came the sarcastic voice on the headset.

I felt my face flush up. I was way behind the airplane.

"Get your after-takeoff checklist, now."

I glanced down at my kneeboard on my right leg at the checklist. By glancing down, my heading drifted and the airspeed dropped.

Brakes apply, gear up. Throttle-36 inches, prop-2400.

Accelerate to climb schedule, 140 knots at sea level reducing.

"Listen, Stud, you gotta memorize that checklist cold. The checklist is to back up your actions. When you get ready for the boat, you must open the canopy to get down to hook speed. What if your checklist blew out into the ocean? What are you gonna do then?"

"Yes, sir, I get your point."

"Climb me up to 8,000 feet and we'll do some stalls and slow flight."

Sandy demonstrated the maneuvers first and then let me do them. It was not a pretty picture, but Sandy stuck with me and tried to hold the insults back. I could see the Navy applying the pressure at this stage. The curve on DORs was reportedly steep.

"We won't do acrobatics yet. Got to get you more familiar with the T-28. Let's drop down to 2,000 feet and we'll go to Brewton for touch-and-go landings. Run the descent checklist."

I checked the supercharger low, mixture rich, cowl flaps closed, speed brake out, power at 16/1400, and started down. Passing through 3500 feet, Sandy took over control, and asked, "If you lost power now, where would you go?"

I was caught by surprise and looked all over for an airport. There was none in sight and I saw a north south highway off to starboard. I pointed toward it.

"Sorry, Stud, that ain't a good choice. Too many power lines. Also, a few cars. There are some beautiful farmers' fields around here in LA (Lower Alabama). We've unfortunately landed in a few of them. Bought a few of them, too. Most of them are pretty level and can be landed on very successfully. The key is to be a little high and fast as you approach about 1500 feet and you can use your drag devices once you know you've got the field made. Okay, you've got it back. Run your landing check."

I adjusted the carb air, supercharger checked low, shoulder harness locked, mixture rich, tail hook up, canopy closed; wheels, props and flaps to go. Rpm set to 2200.

We approached the Brewton airport and Sandy barked, "You got it in sight?"

"Yeah, about eleven o'clock?"

"Right, now let's talk about the break. It's just like the break we do at the boat, except at the boat we'll be in five-plane formation. The break is to separate the planes and establish sequence between each hook landing, get them released, and out of the way for the next landing. The timing must be perfect—the air boss will chew your ass if you're not right on time."

All this talk about the carrier had become very unnerving to me since I'm not sure I'm cut out to land on carriers. I was pretty comfortable being an OOD on the cable layer. Now we're talking about aircraft carriers. I need time to catch my breath.

The "break" checklist consisted of a precise 40 degree bank, 15 inch-manifold pressure, speed brake extend, gear down when below 140 knots, speed brake retract, slow to 120 knots, prop 2400.

Sandy decided to demo it, talking me through the checklist as he performed each item. We'll land on 36 so we'll break left on a north heading and turn to reach the abeam landing position configured and ready to go full flaps. He demoed it perfectly and said, "See the touchdown point off to the left? That's what it will look like when you get to the boat. Remember this for later. We're not going to worry about that for now. That's where you would turn for final on the carrier. We're just going to teach you to land this beast. You've got control now. Extend on out for awhile so I can get you comfortable and stabilized for your first landing."

I got turned for final with the throttle at 20 inches, prop full increase, and flaps down. The gear was already extended from the break.

"Work your airspeed to 100 knots. I want you at the landing line at 150 to 200 feet. 1200 feet to touch down from the end. You'll transition to 90 knots before flare. Flare at five to ten feet. On rollout, lower nose wheel as elevator becomes ineffective."

My approach was awful, but he constantly hammered at me as we closed in. We were a little slow as I flared, and we slammed down pretty hard. "Congratulations! You've just simulated a real carrier landing. We're not quite ready for them this hard yet. We'll get better. We'll try to land at 90 for now. The carrier speed will be exactly 83 knots. We want to try for smooth landings for now."

I looked over at the hangar area, and sure enough, the parking lot was full of the locals out for a look at the air show of newbies like me making initial landings. As we taxied by the line of cars, I looked over and the headlights came on intermittently.

"The blinking lights are the grades you got for the landing." Sandy laughed. "You got a lot of 'ones.' They also honk horns for grades which you probably can't hear. Not a lot of other things going on over here in Brewton. I expect you to get up to a 'three' before we leave today."

Sandy explained to me we would do touch-and-go landings which saves time by not stopping and taking off on every approach. We slowly taxied back to 36 and took off again.

"I won't touch the controls again unless you convince me you're trying to kill us both," Sandy said with a touch of sarcasm in his voice.

We stayed in the landing pattern for six more landings until Sandy called for us to depart the pattern and head back to Whiting Field. Sandy said I got three flashes from one car but I was too busy to look. I was sweating like never before. I had never done something so dangerous in my life. The pre-flight training at NAS Pensacola was intense but this airplane was going to be way more than that. No wonder so many pilot trainees DOR at Whiting. I realize many of them are done right before going out to sea to land on the carrier. For the first time since joining the flight school, I actually thought ahead about carrier landings. The thought scared the hell out of me.

Sandy had my full attention.

We arrived back at Whiting for our landing at the North complex. The South complex of runways was for advanced and carrier training. I had a long way to go to get to the South complex. I did the break at Sandy's prompt and established a sequence downwind. It seemed like T-28s were all over the place. Anyone out of position would certainly cause a midair. The RDO gave us the green light, and I flared and bounced a few times and decelerated to slow speed. "Be sure to check the tires and record the 'g' meter reading before you come to debrief. You gave the left main tire hell out there."

I made the post flight walkaround and noticed the left main was pretty hot but still had air. The "g" meter read a 6 which I knew was not considered a "down." Navy airplanes have special heavy-duty landing gear for obvious reasons.

I went into the debrief room and Sandy was smiling. "Stud, that wasn't too bad for the first flight. We'll go over each landing and maneuver. There are no 'unsats' on this flight, but

I'll look for improvements as we go along. If you stay on schedule, I'll keep you as my student up until your first checkride. If not, I'll turn you over to another instructor and he'll see how you're doing."

I was amazed at the debrief how thorough Sandy was. He didn't miss a thing I did. I think he was reading my mind. I left the briefing room with my head spinning a bit but the big picture began to take shape. Unfortunately, there were a lot of new maneuvers to be introduced. I couldn't wait to see how my buddies did today!

HURRICANE PARTY

The panhandle of Florida is known as a magnet for hurricanes. My remaining buddies and I were just getting comfortable living in the BOQ at Whiting when Cal came down to happy hour in the "O" Club and remarked he had just heard a new weather report. Hurricane Sally Mae was in the Gulf and had suddenly strengthened and was changing direction. The new prognostication was to hit the Pensacola area in a couple of days and strengthen to a category 4. The pressure reading was already down to 29.80 inches. We all looked at each other.

"Reckon what this means for us?" Andy posed.

"Good question," Bax responded. "Maybe we'll fly to New Orleans with our instructors. Mardi Gras is cranking up and that would be sweet. Can you imagine us all down on Bourbon Street while everyone else is riding out a hurricane?"

Dick Wall had replaced Everett in the gang of eight since Everett's departure. "Pipe dream," Dick added. "They'll probably take the mechanics with them. They sure as heck don't need a bunch of nuggets like us. We don't know crap about instruments or navigation yet. Heck, we've just learned to crank this beast up."

"You're probably right," I added. "Does that mean we're going to have to ride it out?"

"We might be able to make the best of the situation." Andy chimed in. "What's to keep us from having a hurricane party in the 'O' Club?"

"Nothing, I guess. Our instructors will all be gone with the airplanes so there won't be anything for us to do. Let's make sure the club will stay open. Maybe we can get happy hour rates. It's worth a try."

"Andy, you're the biggest party animal. See if you can get a handle on the situation. Let us know something tomorrow. We're still scheduled to fly tomorrow as of right now," Cal suggested.

I checked in with Sandy the next day at the briefing room. I didn't want to push the party idea, so I didn't mention our plans. I hoped Sandy would open up.

"Well, Stud, we're going to do our normal T-2 today with a slight change. We'll get into navigation a bit. There is a low pressure in the Gulf that has turned into a cat 3 hurricane. It has turned toward the Panhandle and may have some influence on our operations. The instructors are having a briefing at 1300 to formulate a plan. There is an outside chance you may ride with me to a safe destination. I just want you to be comfortable with the navigation radios and a few ATC communications procedures. Do you have a flying background?"

"No, just radio communications I had on the USS Neptune. Nothing like what you do in aviation."

"Well, today, you'll do all the communications. I'll prompt you what and when to call for each event. You've been paying attention, right?"

"Oh, yes, sir. I remember what I did on the T-34."

"That's good, but this will be a lot more complex. I'll help. Don't worry."

"I've heard New Orleans will be a safe destination."

"In your dreams. Students always start that rumor, but it never works. We'll probably go somewhere that you can't get in trouble."

"Oh, well, I'll just volunteer to stay here and stick it out."

"We'll see."

After the briefing for the T-2, I headed out to the flight line knowing the demo flight was over and I'd be expected to do it all. The plane captain, Airman Rolf, saluted me and reported the aircraft was ready for service. I can't get over how proficient these airdale enlisted guys are. They take great pride in having your airplane ready, fueled, and airworthy.

I knew loops and stalls would be introduced, so I ate a light lunch. A barf bag was slipped into my flight suit. The flight suit is a bright international orange color with plenty of zippered pockets. The Navy wants to make sure students can be seen in all conditions. Our flight helmets are white, but we are allowed to decorate them with reflective tape. Most guys' decorations have a reference to their college attended. Every student pilot must have at least two years of college so there is a lot of back and forth about football rivalries. I did my backup walkaround pre-flight and jumped in and put on my shoulder harness. I still couldn't get over how big the T-28 was.

Sandy jumped in back and said, "Go to it, Stud. Your airplane." I slowly and deliberately went through the before start checklist.

"Way too slow, Stud. You've got to run it by heart and then come back and double check everything's done. I'll be timing you tomorrow."

I had just started cranking when Sandy yelled out. "Simulated fire in the engine. What do you do?"

Fortunately, I had memorized the procedure.

"Mixture-cutoff, no prime, continue cranking, fuel shutoff-off, ignition-off, carb air-direct, throttle-open.

"That's good, Stud. We'll assume the fire went out. We'll take it a step further on another flight where the fire doesn't go out. Okay, get her started and let's go get airborne."

The takeoff today was just as bad as the first day.

"Stud, you've got to quit chasing the rudder. You're over-correcting something awful."

We climbed to 8,000 feet and Sandy showed me a loop. "This is about the only acrobatic maneuver you'll do. I'll show you the spins and let you get out of it. We essentially want you to get proficient in basic instruments, navigation, formation and carrier landings."

Sandy demoed the loop and rolled out on heading and altitude perfectly. I had done it in the T-34 but never mastered it like Sandy. I still wondered where my aviation career was going. I continued to be amazed by the number of guys dropping out. Once the carrier landings are behind you, you will probably become a Naval aviator.

Next up were the spins. "Stud, the spins are much more dangerous than the T-34. On the T-34 you can pretty much neutralize the controls and she is so stable it will come out on its own. This beast is different. If you get into an inverted spin, you can kiss your butt good-bye. Do not do that. I'm gonna get you in a normal spin and you can follow me on the controls for the recovery. In particular, notice how I introduce the opposite rudder very positively. That is the key to recovery."

I didn't like the spin. It was a very violent maneuver. We did a few until Sandy felt comfortable with me and then went through the stall series. I was sweating profusely after these maneuvers were finished. This was definitely not the fun part of flying.

"Okay, Hoss, head over to Brewton and we're gonna get on the landings. I expect you to get some better headlight grades and honks today."

My landings were much better today, but some were still a little scary. Sandy was not giving me advice like he did yesterday. He would make little sounds when I hit a little bit hard or bounced a bit on touchdown. I knew the critique would be substantial later. The flashing headlights by the farmers around the Brewton airport seemed to oscillate between two and three. My plate was full between learning all about the airplane and flying it at the same time,and he wasn't even throwing emergencies at me yet. Flying the T-28-versus the T-34 was like night and day.

Whiting Field was easy to identify as we returned for landing. The dual airfields stood out because of their multiple runways, but we were warned more airfields existed in the Pensacola and Fort Walton area than anyplace in the world. Most were uncontrolled and without a tower. Landing at the wrong airfield was an automatic "down." This added another dimension to learning the layout of the ops area.

As we taxied in, Sandy came up on the intercom. "Stud, I just heard on the radios we might have to evacuate Whiting. Sallie Mae has strengthened and is heading our way. You students may have a few days off. All instructors will be meeting at 1600 to sort it out. We'll have to cut the debrief short."

I was amazed at how much Sandy had to say on the debrief. He had caught every little detail I missed. "Tell all your buddies to stand by for the latest on the evacuations. Nobody should be hitting Trader Jon's for sure."

We all gathered at the "O" Club for winding down. The word had spread that the evacuation was for real. Andy read the PDL (pass down the line) message being posted all over the base.

To: All Hands

From: ComNavAirLant

All training wings based at NAS Pensacola and associated training facilities under this command shall immediately set hurricane condition 5. Sallie Mae is now a cat 4 and might upgrade to a 5. All aircraft will begin preparation for evacuation to westward military fields. All aircraft in maintenance will be hangared and double tied down. All instructors will prepare for departure tomorrow morning at 0800 and later. Your assignments and airplanes will be posted at 0700 hours. Some student pilots who have finished basic instrument B-15 will be flying out with instructors. Other student pilots will be assigned to stay at Whiting to help with tie downs of ground equipment and aircraft in maintenance. All other ground personnel will begin tie down of ground equipment and find your assigned battle stations. Mess halls will prepare for power outages and prepare meals as required. Married personnel will be granted station leaves as necessary. Other personnel will man the barracks as normal. Contact your individual wing commanders for further details.

Admiral Donald J. Gay
Commander, Naval Air Forces, Atlantic Fleet

We all looked around at each other. "Guess we're all gonna ride it out here, boys," Cal beamed. "Nothing to prevent a hurricane party that I hear in the edict. Andy, you're in charge of arranging for ladies to be allowed in for safekeeping from the storm. Bax, you're in charge of making arrangements for the 'O' Club to have enough supplies to weather the storm. Remember, storms sometimes stagnate in one place, so it may last a long time. Also, some guests may be trapped here and shouldn't try to leave to escape the storm."

That night, we all hovered around the only TV in the BOQ in our room. The antenna consisted of a coathanger wire, so the reception was pretty spotty. The weather lady was pointing out the possible destinations of the storm, but one thing was for sure—it was going to influence Pensacola. We knew every airplane in a flyable condition would need to leave. Whiting Field contained mainly T-28s, but there were a few multi-engine airplanes as well.

The storm was forecast to hit Saturday night which made for a perfect party night. Andy would be the perfect PR person to get the word out to the local girls. Bax was chosen to bribe the Marines at the gate to allow only ladies in who would be coming to the hurricane party. I was responsible to secure bartenders who would ride out the storm at the "O" Club. Tiki was responsible for the music. We needed a live band and he responded with a band called "Clarence Brown and the Hot Nuts." He got a good recommendation from one of the Bama boys who said they were a real clean-cut group of guys with good dancing music.

The next morning, the aircraft were all being prepared for evacuation. Student pilots who were in advanced instruments were chosen to go with instructors. Nuggets like us would be left behind because of lack of instrument training. NAS and Air Force stations were receiving most of the airplanes and pilots while Whiting ground personnel started hunkering down. In the meantime, Sallie Mae turned into a cat 4 so we were worried about creating interest in the party. Our lady-friend targets were young school teachers who would naturally be out of school for the storm. Pensacola was a natural landing area for teachers from Troy State, Auburn, Alabama, and Florida State. Why not come to beautiful Pensacola beaches and meet Navy pilots looking for a good time or to get married. They hated to be called "groupies," even though there was no other term to call the girls that loved the Blue Angels without shame.

Soon the base was cleared of all aircraft and the party began around sunset. The winds were picking up and the sky had an eerie shade of grey. Our band made it by the Marine guards and the Marines did their job with the girls. Actually, we found out the Marines were going a little overboard in asking for identities and phone numbers of the party girls and having them step out of cars for inspection. Just part of security, they later explained.

As the night progressed, I met a dazzling red-haired girl who was a teacher from Brewton, Alabama. She was wearing a University of Alabama necklace of some type.

"What's your name?" I asked.

"Nan Herring."

"Did you get to know Bear Bryant?" I asked sarcastically.

"Believe it or not, I did." She grinned. "My little sister and I were majorettes at Bama and he always had an interest in us and asked us to be recruiters for him. It paid pretty good money, so it sounded like fun."

"What did you have to do?"

"Well, he ordered some outfits for us which my parents did not approve of. We told him that wouldn't work so he relinquished, and we were allowed to go pick out some clothes at the Polytechnic downtown and charge them to the athletic department. We would also be given cash to take the prospects out around town. It didn't work out too well."

"Why not?"

"You wouldn't believe some of the animals they were bringing in. One of them was hairier than a gorilla. He couldn't keep his hands off me. I think his diet consisted of bananas. He wanted to go park down by the creek bank as soon as it got dark. I was lucky to escape with my life.

"I turned in my new clothes the next day."

"Did he sign with Bama?"

"Oh, yes. He flunked out after the first quarter. My little sister had a similar experience. She had one from New York who hadn't had a bath in recent days. She had to keep the windows rolled down the whole time she was showing him around. He was smoking cigarettes one right after another. Who would think an athlete would smoke and play football? Apparently, after the coach put him through his famous grueling workouts, he put the smokes down. I don't know how he survived, but he did and became a star for the New York Jets."

"Did your little sister stick with it?"

"No, she quit, too. Coach Bryant wasn't too happy with us."

"What do you do now?"

"I'm a French teacher at Brewton High School."

"Have you ever been to the Brewton airport?"

"Oh, yes. It's a pastime. We go out and park and watch the airplanes crashing. You wouldn't believe how hard some of the landings are. Sometimes they bounce two or three times."

"Now wait. You're hitting home now."

She winked and smiled. "I was just pulling your chain. I'm sure you only made smooth landings, right?"

"I wish. But you must understand, our landings are harder by design since we land differently on carriers."

"That's what you all say. My ex-boyfriend said he would never want to be a Naval aviator. In fact, he joined the Air Force out of high school."

"Did he become an Air Force pilot?"

"No, last I heard from him he was a radio operator in Shemya, Alaska, on the Aleutian chain of Islands near Russia." She laughed.

"If I get to solo the T-28, I'll let you know I'm coming so you can go out and grade me. If I get a good grade, you'll have to cook me a good ole southern dinner in Brewton."

"Deal, as long as long as my dance card's not too full."

After the band got cranked up good, the club started filling up and just about everybody on base, not flying away, showed up.

Nan was visiting with her girlfriends when I spotted her again after one of my favorite slow dance songs began playing. I went over and grabbed her and said, "Let's dance this one, Nan."

As we were dancing, she said, "What's your name, flyboy?"

"Did you forget already?"

"Yeah, I guess so. Remind me."

"Peter Pinson."

"Oh, yeah. Sorry Peter. You pilots all look alike."

"Where'd you get that line?"

"Well, just look at all of you. Everyone's dressed alike. You all have flat tops. You're all in decent shape. Do your mothers dress all of you?"

"Touche. You've got a point there," I admitted.

"Have you flown up to Brewton yet?"

"You're pulling my leg. I just told you awhile ago, I did."

"That's right you did. I probably wasn't paying attention."

"Listen, Nan. How much have you had to drink?"

"Where'd you get my name's Nan? It's Betsy."

I had seen this trick before. Girls will come to these mixers and pretend to be someone else. I decided to play along with her little charade.

"Can I get you a drink, Betsy?"

"Sure, gin and tonic."

I had to stand in line. After getting the drink, I hurried back and approached her.

"Here you are. Sorry about the wait."

"Thanks. How'd you know I wanted one?"

"You just told me."

"Oh, so I did. Let's step outside for a breath of fresh air."

We went out on the patio. The winds were picking up.

"The hurricane is going to be here in a few hours. Is it forecast to miss Brewton?"

"The last I heard it would miss us there."

"An officer is scheduled to come in and make an announcement on the hour, I think."

I had a sudden urge to hit the head. "Would you excuse me for a few minutes, Nan?"

"Sure, I'll stay out here. It's kind of neat and eerie out here, knowing what's coming."

In the head, I ran into Frank. "Having a good time, buddy?"

"Yeah, I met this really hot redheaded girl from Brewton." Frank smiled.

"I met her, too. She's a bit of a loose cannon. Claims to have met Bear Bryant. Probably making it up."

After leaving the head, I hurried back toward the patio, only to find Nan by the bar.

She angrily said to me, "Since you didn't get me the drink, I decided to get my own!"

"But I did. You must have set it down."

"Forget it. Let's dance. I love this song."

My goodness, this redheaded girl is ditzy. She sure is cute, though. I think she must drink too much.

After the dance I said, "Let's go back out on the patio."

"Sure, I haven't been out there, yet."

Damn, she's out of it. She was just out there, couldn't remember me getting her a drink. She keeps changing her name. She must have been drinking before she got here. I may need to call her a taxi. We strolled out on the patio and another couple was out there who I couldn't see well for the darkness.

"You know, you redheads have quite a reputation."

"How's that?" she asked with a look of feigned innocence.

"Hot blooded, feisty, and energetic."

"You forgot to mention intelligent, beautiful, and rich."

"Are you rich?"

"No, just the other two. My dad's a farmer."

"Oh, a farmer's daughter, eh? They have a reputation as well."

"Well, don't believe everything you hear. You flyboys have reputations also."

"What kind do we have?"

"For one thing, you all talk with your hands, as if you're describing how an airplane maneuvers about. You're not as bad as some. Just watch your buddies when you get together. It's so funny."

"Okay, we won't talk airplanes. Let's go dance, Nan."

"Peter, you have the worst memory. My name's Betsy."

This gal's totally nuts. I thought. She's lucky she's so cute.

The party was a huge success. There had to be over a hundred and fifty people crammed in. I hardly ever saw Frank.

Just before midnight, the officer of the day went to the microphone at the bandstand. "Ladies and gentlemen, I have a bit of good news. The hurricane has changed directions somewhat and the eye of the storm is toward South Alabama now which gives us some relief. But we will still get some effects. Base commander has ordered us to shut down the party at 0100 sharp!"

Boos rained down on the OOD, but he had no choice.

Betsy or Nan, or whatever her real name was, suddenly

cried out, "That's about where I live in Brewton."

"Betsy, as an Officer and a gentleman, I will offer you my quarters tonight with no strings attached to ride out the storm." I tried to be as innocuous as possible.

"Let me call my folks up there to see what's going on. Where's the pay phone?"

I showed her and she ran out the entrance door of the dance floor.

She came back a few minutes later, tears in her eyes. "Mom and dad are planning for the worst now. We have a storm cellar, fortunately. They recommended we find a safe place down here to weather the storm."

"My roommate and I will sleep somewhere else and you can have the room to yourself. Find your little sister and she can stay there, too. Why haven't I met her yet?"

"She's shy and kind of stays in the shadows. You'll meet her soon. That's so kind of you to offer."

I saw Frank over near the bar and pushed my way through the crowd as he was ordering a gin and tonic.

"Hey, Roomie, I have a favor to ask. The schoolteacher from Brewton needs a place to stay tonight, and I offered our room to her and her little sister. They shouldn't be driving anywhere. Is that okay with you?"

"Sure, there'll be some extra rooms with the instructors all gone."

Betsy and/or Nan was still in the same place when I returned. "I cleared my room for you and your little sister with my roommate. Here's the room key. You can give it to your little sister. How long do you want to stay here at the club?"

She said, "We might as well stay until closing time. Okay with you?"

"Sure. Your name is still Nan, right?"

"Of course, what else would it be?" she answered angrily.

"I just wanted to be sure. Let's go dance again."

I was a little worried about her. She might be getting snockered. Or maybe it was me.

The lights started blinking around 0055. Nan and I reluctantly began moving for the exit. I slowly opened the door to my room and realized someone had left the light on in the bathroom.

"Someone's in the bathroom," I whispered to Nan.

"Anyone here?" I called out.

"I'll be right out," a girl's voice answered.

"It's my sister," Nan said. "She may be sick."

"Okay, I'll leave for a few minutes to let you two get situated."

I walked down to the lobby of the BOQ as Frank was coming in with a sack full of hamburgers.

"Peter, I took the liberty of getting some food and coffee for our guests. The gedunk has stayed open late, so I ran out and got a bunch of hamburgers for us."

"You're a good Samaritan. We should probably find an open room for ourselves."

"Yeah, a lot of the instructors' rooms should be empty. We can grab a steward who keeps up with all that."

"I can't get over Nan. She was something else."

"She'll probably get over it with a little sleep," Frank said and hurried out looking for a steward mate to get us a room.

FALLOUT FROM THE STORM

Frank and I went back to our second-floor room to deliver the hamburgers and some coffee to the girls. I knocked on the door and Nan yelled out, "Come on in!"

We entered and gave Nan the food. She said her little sister was sick in the bathroom—not used to drinking gin and tonics.

"We're just going to drop off some burgers and coffee and let you two get some rest. Hope y'all had a good time tonight."

"We absolutely did. Sis'll be fine."

We left and found a steward who got us a room for the night. Frank and I were tired and didn't say much except to talk about the ditzy redhead we both had met.

"The redhead we left in our room was something else. I knew she was a groupie because she knew a lot about Naval aviation and airplanes. When she started talking about lift and drag, I knew this wasn't her first rodeo."

"Yeah, she pretended to change her name at times. I've seen her kind just playing games with us aviators. Most of them are looking for husbands. Did you meet her little sister?"

"No, she is apparently a wallflower."

"Looks like the storm isn't so bad. Let's get some shuteye and get the girls up for breakfast in the morning. I hope the sick sister's okay."

The next morning the winds were still howling but the storm had obviously passed through. It was 0930 as we dragged ourselves out. "Let's take some coffee up to the girls."

We knocked and Nan's voice cheerily said, "Come on in, boys."

We entered as I said, "Morning, Nan, how do you feel?"

"I feel fine but my name's not Nan. It's Betsy."

"Oh, my god. Here we go again."

Nan came out of the head grinning. "Didn't you idiots know we were twins?"

Frank and I looked at each other. We were both stunned.

"You played us, didn't you?"

"Of course, not. We're just being ourselves. We were never dishonest, were we?"

"No, but you could have cleared it up for us a little earlier. You called Betsy your little sister."

"She is. She's five minutes younger than me."

"How are we going to tell y'all apart? You're dressed just alike."

"Being older and wiser, you'll be able tell quickly." Nan laughed.

Betsy chirped back, "When she opens her mouth and makes a fool of herself, that'll give you a clue."

"No fighting, girls. You're lucky we're such nice guys and saved you last night."

"We did recognize that about you. Let us buy you breakfast because of your confusion."

"Who wouldn't be confused by you two?" Frank laughed as he poured coffee for everyone.

After calling home and finding Mr. and Mrs. Herring survived the storm, we jumped in Frank's convertible and headed for downtown Milton. Dunk'n'Dine was open and we found a booth in the back.

"Now, how do we tell you apart?" I asked Nan. I knew it was Nan because I had noticed she had one blouse button unbuttoned. Or at least she was the one who said she was Nan.

"Very astute, Peter. Most people can't tell us apart so quickly. You're one of the sharper pilots I've met."

I turned red. I didn't want her to think I was staring at her blouse. "I think it was the way you walked."

"So, you were fixated on the way I walked, is that it?"

"No, no, no." I was getting exasperated. "You just had this gait about you."

"So, I walk with a gait now."

"Come on, Nan. I meant it in a good way."

Betsy piped in. "Nobody can physically tell us apart. Peter was just guessing."

I couldn't tell them about the blouse.

We exchanged stories about our hometowns and colleges and how we got here. They told us all about Brewton and their teaching jobs. They have an older brother who played football at Auburn named Red Herring. He was an All-American and later played for the Redskins.

"Yeah, I know him. I played against him while at Tech. He was an animal. He would bite you in the pileups."

"I don't believe you. That's not like our sweet brother. He's a pussy cat."

Nan was a French teacher and taught PE. Betsy was an English teacher and taught Music. They were twenty-five-years old and knew their way around the Pensacola area.

Nan began to tell us about the beach. "We should have told you about our family beach house, but we don't know you that well. We could have gone there at last resort. Our parents think we are there. We are on strict orders to never let a pilot come in after dark."

"Does that mean a pilot can come in before dark and stay after dark."

"Technically, yes." Nan grinned. "But we would never allow that."

"I'm sure it has never happened," Frank said sarcastically.

"Absolutely." Nan giggled.

"I've heard all these stories about farmers. Does your father own a shotgun?"

"He does, but our big brother was the bigger threat. If Dad didn't particularly like someone who came for us, he would trot Red out and that usually scared boys off. It was hard for us to get a date growing up."

"And now?" I directed toward Betsy.

"We just selectively pick up sailors. You two seemed to be the most harmless of all we met."

"You judge well." Frank laughed. "I really want to get my wings. It's hard enough to pass the flight exams without being kicked out for behavior. Do you know where you go when you get kicked out?"

"No clue."

"The Great Lakes Training Center. You'd better hope it's not in wintertime," Frank said as he pretended to shiver.

"Others get cable repair ships," I added. "I happen to know one who got kicked out for being a smart ass. He is now a good friend and the reason I'm here. But that's a story for a different day." I hadn't thought of Ensign Dollar (who is still on the Neptune) in a long time.

Frank and I didn't know how to take these two. They were so playful and kept us on our toes. We were amazed at their appetites. They both finished a half-dozen pancakes and looked like they were still hungry.

"You farm girls sure have an appetite. How do you stay so small?"

"Dad makes us pitch in on the farm. We have to plow behind the mule and slop the hogs." Betsy chuckled.

Frank and I just rolled our eyes. "You girls are too much. You must have driven Red crazy!" Frank laughed.

The girls paid the bill and we all went out to Frank's convertible.

"Well, since we're all off today, do you boys want to hit the beach? After all, we told the folks we would be at the beach. And you boys were the only thing we could come up with last night." Betsy smiled.

"We normally study a lot but might make an exception," Frank said with a straight face.

"I'll go with both of them if you want to study," I volunteered.

"No, you couldn't handle them without me," Frank said with a solemn look.

Betsy yelled out, "Get the top down Frank, time's wasting!"

"Nan, you get in the back with me," I said while opening the door.

"I will, but how do you know I'm Nan."

I instinctively looked at her blouse. It was now buttoned.

She grinned and said, "Maybe one day you'll get to know."

THE BEACH HOUSE

We made the trip to Pensacola Beach in thirty-five minutes. Betsy was constantly on Frank about driving so slow.

"Frank, you drive like an old maid. You don't fly airplanes this slow, do you?"

"Hell no! I'm just trying to enjoy the scenery."

"Why are you girls still living at home? At twenty-five, isn't it time for you to launch?" I asked innocently.

"We're saving our money. We live on a nice farm with about eighty acres. Pinta and Nina don't want us to leave. Mom is a wonderful cook. Plus, we have this beach house. We live in it all summer when school is out. Most of the pilots are too cheap to buy us dinners. You saw that this morning when we had to pay for all our breakfasts." Nan feigned a disgusted look.

"Wait a minute!" I protested. "You bought because of all the trouble you put us through."

"Were we all that much trouble? I thought you put us up because you liked us. Did you have other motives?" Nan gave me a look of pity.

"I guess we're shamed into buying dinner tonight, Peter."

"By the way, who's Pinta and Nina?" I asked curiously.

"Why, our horses, of course. Don't farms have horses?"

"I wouldn't know. I grew up in Portland, Oregon. I've never seen a real horse," Frank informed us.

"If you buy us enough dinners, maybe we'll let you ride one."

I couldn't decide if that was a good deal or not. These country girls sure knew how to eat. It's hard to get ahead of these redheads. Their brother really did bite in the piles.

We pulled up in front of a Spanish-tiled stucco house with a definite Florida flavor. Two huge palm trees with azaleas and irises in full color lined the cobblestone path which led from the road to an arched front door. A single car garage door opened as we drove in.

"No wonder you both stay here all summer. This is a cut above the beach house we rented while going through pre-flight. Our house was just a concrete block house built to withstand hurricanes and Navy pilot parties.

"This place is totally livable," Frank said as he carefully maneuvered the car into the garage.

"Yeah, Mom and Dad bought this place years ago and we all grew up in it. Wait until you see the beach."

We didn't have swimsuits, so we had to borrow suits Red had left around. Luckily, they fit pretty well. Hope Red doesn't mind.

The girls came out in different bikinis, thank god. Maybe we'll be able to tell them apart.

"I'm Nan," the one in the polka dot volunteered. "This the last time we're going to tell you. It's up to you both to remember from now on."

That meant Betsy was in the flowery bikini.

"You boys bring the cooler and umbrella and we'll bring the towels and tanning oil."

The beach was amazing today. The hurricane left strong winds and a huge breaking surf with whitecaps as far as you could see.

"How'd you boys do in survival school?" Betsy asked as she broke out the tanning oil.

"What do you know about survival school?" Frank asked.

"I know about drownproofing, Dilbert Dunker, parachute dragging, swimming a mile in a flight suit," Betsy rattled out.

"Damn!" Frank uttered. "Where did you get all that information?"

"Well, I've heard y'all talk about it so much, I figure I know a little. We actually got a tour one time from one of the Blue Angels."

"I should have known you would have met one of the Blue Angels."

"Yeah, they throw a party every year and only invite girls."

"We already found out about that. We got a special invite." I couldn't tell them why we got the invite.

"You boys want to try the surf today?"

"Yeah, let's hit it," Frank called out.

We went dashing into the vicious waves and were immediately all knocked down. Betsy was the first to call "uncle." "Enough of this! I've never seen waves this high."

We retreated back for a more relaxing afternoon on the beach and decided on an early dinner.

We headed to the Tiki Room restaurant and were immediately treated to the best table in the place. I commented on the special treatment.

The manager quickly came over and said, "Hey Nan, Betsy. Great to see you. I see you have some pilot friends with you. Separate checks, I presume?"

I quickly retorted, "How dare you! We are paying pilots."

He quickly responded, "Don't take me seriously. I was only kidding."

After he left, Nan said. "He does that all the time—loves to put pilots on the spot."

"How can he be sure we're pilots?" Immediately I knew I had set myself up.

"You must be kidding, Peter." Nan chuckled.

"Okay, okay! I know we all look alike and have big watches."

After a big dinner where the girls again exhibited large appetites, we headed back to Whiting.

Tomorrow would be back to training for us and teaching for the girls.

We dropped Nan and Betsy off at their car at Whiting and bid goodbyes.

"No charges for room rent yesterday," Frank cheerily said.

"Who would charge for such austere accommodations anyway?" Nan shot back.

"Would you girls like to put up with us again next weekend?" Frank cautiously asked.

"Sure, if you're still paying," Betsy said with a smile.

"Okay, if you promise not to embarrass us again."

"Can't promise that. See you later."

Frank smiled as their car disappeared out the front gate. "It's amazing what hurricanes blow in."

POST SALLIE MAE

"Frank, I hope I didn't speak out of turn obligating you to see the redheads next weekend."

"Heck no. They were a breath of fresh air. They kinda keep you on your toes. I get the feeling they know more about the flight program than we do. Maybe we can get them to study with us."

"We've determined they seem to know everybody in town. We'll have to figure out which one is which, somehow. Their personalities are definitely different, but unless they start talking you can't tell 'em apart. They're certainly not making it easy on us."

Frank and I spent all Sunday night cramming for the coming week. The schedule got pushed back because of the hurricane so tomorrow will be full bore. I am scheduled for eighty-five T-28 flights in the syllabus which includes a solo landing on a carrier. I peeked at the schedule and found that if I made it that far, I would be landing on the USS Intrepid, a storied carrier from WWII. I'd probably flunk out or DOR before then.

My next flight would be with Lt. Sanda again. I wonder where he went on the flyaway?

Monday morning came and I hurried through breakfast. I was still nervous about flying this T-28. Butterflies have always been a problem, dating back to sporting events.

Lt. Sanda was waiting for me in the briefing room. "Sorry you had to get stuck here through the hurricane, Peter. Must have been pretty boring, huh?"

"Yes, it was. You wouldn't believe how much I studied."

"Actually, I could believe it. I heard about the hurricane party you guys had. You had more fun than me. I went to NAS New Orleans with another instructor. He had family down in the bayou and they stuffed us with Cajun food for two days. I had no idea you were supposed to suck the juice out of the head of crayfish.

"I'll have you for four more days and then give you another instructor for evals. Then I'll get you back to prep you for your solo on T-9. After that you'll pick up Basic Instruments for 10 flights. Today we'll work on slow flight and stalls and one more spin. I want to warn you about the spins. We only do normal flat spins. We don't do inverted spins. They will kill you. We don't even demo them. They're too dangerous even for instructors. I'll probably throw in an emergency or two. We'll do our landings at Choctaw Field. Been there yet?"

"Nope."

"Choctaw is like all the outliers. Uncontrolled, triangular runways like all of them. Grab your gear and head on out and do the walkaround. I'll be out shortly."

Sandy came out and did a quick look around and hopped in the back seat. "Think of this as a solo flight today, Peter. I'll tell you where and what to do and you perform as if I wasn't here, okay?"

"Okay."

I went through the preflight and before start checklist and got clearance from the plane captain to start. The start went normal until Sandy said. "Your engine's on fire."

I had the checklist memorized cold. Fuel shutoff-off, mixture-idle cutoff, throttle-open, ignition-off, dc power-off. I was feeling pretty good when Sandy blurted out. "What else?"

I froze. What else?

"Let me know when you think about it. Okay, get clearance from the plane captain and start it again."

The start went fine and as I taxied out, I kept wondering what I'd forgot. All part of the subtle pressure in this program. My radio transmissions were getting better each day. I'm still in awe of this airplane.

We took off normally and climbed to 8,000 feet to do stalls and spins. The stall series was okay but a little ragged. Next was the spins which I didn't particularly like. It was a violent maneuver and pulled "g" forces which are uncomfortable. Sandy put me in the spin and I really did a crappy recovery.

"Let's do another one, Stud. That one won't pass your check ride on flight T-9."

Sandy took control and began setting up the spin. He inadvertently overdid the entry and suddenly we were in an inverted spin. We both immediately knew what was happening and Sandy yelled, "I've got it!"

It was a very violent maneuver. The feeling of being upside down and spinning was getting really scary. Round and round we went, and I could feel Sandy on the rudder pedals and control stick moving back and forth trying to get the spin slowed down and under control. The altimeter was spinning wildly as we descended through 6,000 feet. The rudder pedals were going from one stop back to the other. The fuselage itself caused blanking of airflow to the controls. Descending through 5,000 feet, the controls began having some small effect on the rotation of the T-28. The control stick was pulled straight back into my lap as we passed 4,000 feet. Sandy was now holding full right rudder. He then jammed the stick full forward and the airplane finally responded. We then did a roll to the right and then Sandy had full control of the ailerons and elevator. We were upright and the wings were leveling at 2,500 feet.

"Whew, podner, I sure didn't mean to demo the inverted spin. That's only the second one I've been through. You see why we don't do them. We've still got to get you proficient in the normal spin. We'll save that for another flight. That's enough spins for today. Head us over to Choctaw and we'll do some landings."

Sandy pointed out Choctaw from about twenty miles out. I picked it up and dropped to a maneuver altitude of 1,500 feet. I called the common frequency and checked for other traffic. Sioux Falls 124 was already in the pattern using runway 4. I gave our airport position and dropped to fly the upwind leg at 800 feet. I could see the other aircraft downwind, so we had good separation. I recognized the voice of the student as Joe, and I knew he had a screamer for an instructor.

I executed my break five seconds past the airport and turned 180 degrees and dropped to a downwind altitude of 600 feet and heading 220.

"Damn it, Joe, get your speed back! You're 10 knots fast!" I knew Joe's instructor was Second Lieutenant Jenkins, a notorious Marine screamer. Joe told us every night how much he disliked his instructor. He had accidently transmitted on the UHF instead of the intercom.

"Are you gonna get the damn gear down?" he hollered.

"UHF," Sandy reminded Lt. Jenkins.

"Oops!"

"Jerry gets a little carried away, sometimes," Sandy uttered with a laugh.

I laughed to myself after what Joe had told us during our gatherings after flights. We always debriefed each of our instructors to each other. Jenkins was well known to all of us.

My landings were getting better each day. Most of the T-28 "Charlies" we used at Whiting also were used for the actual carrier quals, so the landing gear was designed for hard landings. "Bravos" did not have tail hooks. Instructors did not particularly mind the hard landings. I did my share to keep up the image. I still cannot envision myself landing solo on a carrier. I wondered what might intervene, if anything.

Joe and Lt. Jenkins were departing the pattern and I couldn't resist a transmission. "See ya, Joe." I got no response.

My last landing was a squeaker which was a touch-and-go.

"Forget that kind of landing, Peter. That won't work at the carrier. You would land in the drink."

"Roger," I said. "I will try to forget that image."

Back at Whiting, the pattern was not nearly as chaotic as Saufley. Sandy told me over half the initial student pilots drop out for one reason or another. I wondered why I haven't dropped out yet.

At today's debriefing, Sandy apologized for getting us into the inverted spin. "I've seen one before and thought that was the last. You can see that you want to avoid it at all costs. I would recommend not doing any spins on your solo flights."

"You don't have to worry about that!"

"Peter, you've made it through four months of preflight, ground school, and survival and I believe you can make it through. You don't have any background in flying but have the ability if you will grind it out. I hope you have the motivation to stick it out. The program is about to get more intense so you will need to strap it on. I'm known as a Santa Claus instructor, but your next flight will be with a hardass Marine first lieutenant named Autry, so be prepared, okay? Don't take anything personally he may throw at you. Like all of us, we want the best Naval aviators possible."

"Yes, sir. I've heard he tries to eat Ensigns alive. Got shot down in Vietnam and is still on the warpath."

"One last thing about your landings today. To make a smooth landing means you're floating. We don't float on Navy landings."

"Aye, sir. No more floating. Get her on the deck."

"Just relax tomorrow, and you'll be okay."

On debriefing in the BOQ I asked Joe how his flight went today.

"That SOB was on my case all day. After calling me every name in the book, he ended the debrief by saying, 'Nice job, today, Joe.' Kind of shocked me. I thought I was terrible."

I laughed. "Makes me feel better about my flight tomorrow with Lt. Autry."

"Frank, how'd your flight go today?"

"Well, being a Coastie, we try for smooth landings since we won't land on carriers. I got the word today that I might be going to helicopters at Ellyson after I finish basic instruments here on the T-28. Most instructors go Santa Claus on us because we're mostly going choppers. A few of us go seaplanes and a few go to the Herkies (Hercules). Seaplanes are a horse of a different color altogether."

Tiki informed us there was a need for A-1 pilots in Vietnam and he would be in that pipeline after Whiting. The A-1 is a single engine bomber with a huge radial engine that carries a big payload of rockets and bombs. He said he had requested that duty. I can't say I would have done it. It is a low altitude bomber that will take a lot of hits. On top of that, it is a single pilot, tail dragger (two main gear forward and a wheel on the tail).

"Tiki, you gonna leave us a little something in your will?"

"Oh, boys, you're just jealous. Wait till you hear that three thousand horsepower puppy sing. I saw one come through Mainside and you couldn't believe the sound of that big radial engine. Sexiest airplane I've ever seen."

I studied extra hard that night in anticipation of flying with Lt Autry. If I screwed up, it wouldn't be from lack of preparation.

The morning was overcast and bleak as I hurried down to the flight line. I wanted to get there before Lt. Autry. As I rushed in, I saw Lt. Autry already sitting behind the desk.

"Good morning, sir," I cheerily said.

"Mornin'," he grunted back. He didn't speak for awhile and I didn't offer anything.

"I heard about you," he simply said.

I didn't know what to say.

Finally, he asked, "Why did you get off that cable ship?"

"I had always wanted to fly, and I was lucky to get the opportunity. I got a ride in a T-28 at NAS Breezy Point in Norfolk. I got sick in the loop but otherwise enjoyed it." I hated not telling him the full story.

"Is it true you hid out in Eleuthera for a month before reporting?"

I'd prefer to think of it as being stranded."

"Whatever. This will be no picnic compared to the ship."

"I know, sir."

He started off by asking me to describe the engine-out landing procedure from 3,000 feet to touchdown.

I thankfully had studied it well and guided him through the five checklist items: approach, high key, low key, 90-degree position, and final.

"Okay, but what if you had to land in a farmer's field with no runway available?"

"I would probably land gear up depending on terrain."

"Okay, now give me the electrical fire in flight checklist."

That one was easier than the engine-out procedure because it only had four items.

"This is not a check ride but only to determine if you're on track to solo on T-9.

"You make all the radio calls and I will just listen except to guide you to Silver Hill Airport near Fairhope. Climb out to 8,000 feet and go right into your stall series and recoveries. Then do steep turns at 45 degrees, 360 each way. I'll then vector you to Silver Hill. You announce our name and position and ask if any other airplanes are working there. Got it?"

"Yes, sir."

"Let's go on out to the airplane, ship 911. We'll do the walkaround together and you tell me what you're looking for."

Lt. Autry didn't talk a lot but had an intimidating manner. His gaze seemed to penetrate right through you. Supposedly he had been shot down but was able to escape capture. I certainly wasn't going to ask him about it.

I was nervous but so far hadn't screwed up anything. I knew the walkaround procedure pretty well and climbed into the front seat and strapped in. It wasn't that Autry was so loud, but he was very intimidating, and apparently gives a lot of "downs" to Navy pilots. The takeoff was okay, and we climbed to 8,000 feet. I was about to go into the stall series when he suddenly said, "Stud, you've got smoke and fumes in the cockpit. What would you do?"

I was so surprised my mind just froze up. I couldn't remember step one which was to open the cockpit air control. He said, "Forget it. Start the stall series."

It's hard to get a screw up off your mind because it now affects everything else. I tried to put it behind me and started the stall series which consisted of the clean and dirty configuration stalls. I was grinding on everything and not outstanding in anything.

Steep turns were next, and I liked them best. They came naturally to me. I rolled out on heading and altitude perfectly.

"Turn to 260 and let's go to Silver Hill for landings."

I was much more relaxed now after doing the steep turns. I called field in sight and descended to 2,000 feet. I called to Silver Hill traffic and got no response, so we had the pattern to ourselves. Autry offered no help, so I had to pick which one of the runways to use. I could see the wind tetrahedron on the field and picked runway 3, almost directly into the wind. I set up the pattern entry and dropped to 800 feet upwind. Over the field, I made the break and descended to 600 feet and shot for a heading of 210 degrees. Abeam the 90 position I turned inbound and started dropping to 350 feet. *Flaps dammit!* I quickly started them out and dropped the gear all in one motion. Through some miracle I rolled out on final at the exact altitude and speed. Pure-ass luck. The first landing was touch-and-go and it worked perfectly, and I made a decent landing.

After finishing the landings, we were climbing out to return back to Whiting when after raising the landing gear he blurted out, "What's the procedure for smoke in the cockpit?"

He caught me offguard again but I stammered out. "Cockpit air control-open."

"Okay, that's better, take her to 4,000 feet and head back to Whiting."

After landing at Whiting, I met Lt. Autry in the debrief room. "Listen sailor, your flying isn't too bad. When you forgot your flaps in the pattern, I was about to give you a 'down' but you made the most amazing recovery I've ever seen. I couldn't tell if it was luck or not, but I'll give you the benefit of the doubt. A word about the emergencies. Emergencies aren't textbook. They come in all sizes and shapes. Usually when you least expect them. Try to remember to think outside the box. I'm giving you an 'up' but don't get too cocky. Keep your nose to the grindstone, you've got some tough days ahead."

"Thank you, sir."

"Don't thank me, Sailor. You're dismissed."

SAFE FOR SOLO

I figured out early on, my roommate Frank was a special guy. He was smart as a whip and had an ROTC scholarship at Oregon State University. He was breezing right through this program. He had almost 400 hours flight time in college and got an instrument rating. He interned in the summer on a Coast Guard cutter and in a seaplane squadron. He is also a scratch golfer. Too much talent for one person. His only shortcoming is that he is height challenged, which doesn't seem to bother him.

"Peter, what are we going to do with the redheads this weekend? They'll have Saturday and Sunday off, and I know we're off the flight schedule as well."

"Let's take 'em to New Orleans. Have you ever been?"

"Nope." Frank's eyes lit up.

"Me neither. Should we drive?"

"Heck, no. I can check out a Beech Baron at the flying club. I've got a hundred or so hours in it and I'm still current. It's a twin engine and seats four. The club's over at the municipal airport. Are you game?"

"Why not? Should we surprise them?" I wasn't sure they would go flying with us.

"No, women need to plan. Get the right clothes, you know."

"Okay, I'll call them today."

I called the Brewton operator who rang the Herrings' house. Mrs. Herring answered.

"Mrs. Herring, I'm Peter Pinson. I met your daughters last weekend. I am a student pilot at the Navy flight school down in Pensacola. I apologize if we create noise from landings at the Brewton airport. It is my favorite airport because of all the beautiful scenery around here—such a gorgeous little town. Your daughters were so nice and well mannered. May I speak with either of them?"

"Well, certainly. You're the first to say such nice things about them. Here's Nan."

"Hello. Nan. It's Peter from last weekend."

"Peter who? Do I know you?"

"C'mon, Nan. Surely you do."

"Are you the tall one or the short one?"

"The tall one. How do I know it's Nan?"

"My mom doesn't lie. Just like her daughters."

"I have an offer for you. Are you on a party or private line?"

"Private line. Why do you ask?"

"Because I want privacy. Have you ever been to New Orleans?"

"No."

"Frank and I want to know if you and Betsy would like to go to New Orleans this weekend. We've got a twin-engine airplane we can rent. It won't take but a little over an hour to get there. We can stay in the Navy Officer barracks at the Naval Air Station and rent a Volkswagen bus to ride around in."

"Okay, but you boys stay on the base. Betsy and I will stay down on Bourbon Street. We don't ride in Volkswagen buses either. You've misjudged us. We're not those kinds of girls."

"Unfortunately, we've noticed that. We're actually looking at The Roosevelt Hotel down off Canal street."

"Now you're talking. We do have quite a few other offers for this weekend, but we'll consider it. I'll go ask Betsy."

Nan came back a few minutes later. "She said okay but to tell Frank he will have to use deodorant this time."

"That's quite an order but I'll make sure he complies. Speaking of that, would you mind going a little light on the Jungle Gardenia?"

"I don't know about that. If I didn't wear it, nobody would notice me."

"Well, let's try it and see."

"You're so demanding."

"What time do you get out of school Friday?"

"Three o'clock."

"Can we pick you up at the Brewton airport about 4:30?"

"Okay, we'll be there. Will you be able to recognize us?"

"I don't know. There will be hundreds there waiting for a Baron with two good looking pilots on board. Please wear name tags if you don't mind."

"You can easily recognize me. I'll be the best looking of the two of us. Bye."

Frank and I both had Friday morning flights. His was the (T-9) solo flight and mine was safe for solo (T-8) with Lt. Homan, a check instructor from another squadron. Frank wasn't even nervous. His regular instructor was Lt. Perkins, known for his attention to detail and discipline. Frank said he was a pain in the ass, but he demanded attention to detail, quite often repeating himself to no end. He was a plough back from the fleet who would be going to the airlines after his tour at Whiting was over.

"Frank, how can you be so calm before these check rides? I'm much more nervous than I was playing sports in college."

"Two keys, Peter. One, staying ahead of the airplane, always planning for down the road. Secondly, expect things not to always be normal. Some great thinker once said, 'Flying can be defined as hours and hours of boredom punctuated by moments of stark terror.'"

"Good analogy, Frank, except flight training is many minutes of stark terror punctuated by moments of boredom."

"Come on, Peter, be positive. You don't want to go back to the cable layer, do you?"

"That is a strong motivator, I assure you."

Friday's weather was not so great. Partly cloudy and very windy. I met Lt. Homan in the briefing room. He was a no-nonsense type guy, so I didn't enter in any small talk.

"So, you think you're ready for your solo, Ensign?"

"I've got some butterflies for sure."

"I've never lost a student on his solo when I have approved him. So, expect a thorough checkout today. We'll mainly do safety of flight items. No acrobatics or spins. Nobody ever does them on solos. Do you have a choice of airports for landings today?"

"I'll take Brewton. I've been there the most. I'm still trying to get more car lights flashing."

"That's fine but I want Navy landings."

"Yes, sir. I understand."

After quizzing me on emergencies and checking the maintenance log, I went on out to preflight ship #131, a "Charlie." I could tell because it had a tail hook. The plane captain informed me it had just come out of maintenance and checked out okay. Lt. Homan followed me around on the walkaround inspection but didn't ask any questions. Check airmen seemed to be able to read your mind.

We climbed into the plane and strapped in. The engine start was normal, and I made all the calls correctly taxiing out. So far, so good. The flight went smoothly—the stalls, slow flight, steep turns were the best I had done. He simulated an engine failure and I found a good farmer's field and took it down to 200 feet before Lt. Homan signaled to take it away. We headed over to Brewton and I called ahead to check out the pattern.

"Brewton traffic, this is Sioux Falls 131, twenty miles Southeast for pattern work. Any local traffic now?"

No one answered so I elected to do the traditional carrier approach. The weather report showed the winds out of the Northeast at 11 knots, so I chose runway 6. There was no traffic, so we did the typical carrier pattern approach and began the landings. The first was a touch-and-go which was okay.

"Make a full stop this time and if it's okay, I'll get out and you'll make two landings solo and I'll get back in. I'll be over at the terminal. Any questions?"

"No, sir. Just one touch-and-go and then a full stop, right?"

"Right."

The first solo touch-and go was good, and as I turned downwind for the full stop landing, I felt a slight vibration in the engine. Then the engine began coughing. The rpm was vacillating. I remembered what Frank had said. Stay ahead of the airplane. I determined it was a rough running engine. What do I do? My speed was 160 knots. Gear was retracted. Flaps were 5. What if the engine quits altogether? What checklist do I use? All these things were spinning through my head. Conserve airspeed and altitude as long as possible. I had no time to consult the checklist. It's all memory now. I slammed the mixture to rich. Prop went to 2000 rpm. I opened the cowl flaps to let in more air to the engine. It was still coughing. Abeam the 90 position I turned inbound. At the 45, the engine seized. I held flaps and gear. I knew it was going to be close. I rolled out on final. I was high, thank god. I started dropping everything out to get down. Gear went out, flaps came down, I even dropped the tail hook. I came over the threshold with plenty of speed to dissipate. I started the flare too early and started to float. I touched down way long and jammed on the brakes hard. The right main blew, and we swerved to the right. I hung onto the stick with all my might. We came to a stop with a few feet to spare. I let out a big sigh of relief. My heart was thumping so hard I could feel the vibrations throughout my entire body. Lt. Homan came running over to make sure I was okay. I gave him a thumbs up. He had some chocks in his hand and yelled at me not to set the brakes. The hot brakes could start a fire. He gave me the cut sign to turn everything off. I did and he yelled to get out. I was happy and literally leapt out to the ground.

"Good job. You okay?"

"Yes, sir. A little rattled."

The local fire truck finally showed up but there was no fire. The local sheriff also came by to get a statement.

"We'll have to leave the plane here until maintenance can get equipment up here. We'll need to get this runway closed as well. Runways 30 and 36 are still usable. The FBO should have the 'closed' markings to put out. I'll call base and get them working. Maybe a couple of training flights can come up to take us back to Whiting."

"Do I pass? Am I cleared for solo flight?"

"Of course. We'll debrief a few things, but you handled a real emergency very well. You'll probably be required to go before a safety board next week to give some details and take a psychological evaluation. I'll pass on a positive report."

Two trainer flights were diverted over to pick us up within the hour. A C-130 Hercules with a full maintenance crew also landed shortly later. The Navy doesn't want a Navy airplane sitting around on a public airport any longer than necessary.

Frank was sitting in the BOQ all packed up and ready to go when I finally showed up.

"Hey, dude, you're sure taking your time. Get your butt packed. We've got business in New Orleans."

BOURBON STREET

Frank had reserved the Baron and taken care of all the paperwork so all we had to do was pre-flight and jump in and go.

"We're going VFR up to Brewton to get the girls. We'll fly VFR all the way to New Orleans, so we can sightsee if we want, and the weather's not too bad. I might want to pick up an IFR clearance into Moisant International Airport so as not to interfere with the airliners coming in. This will be good cross-country training for you. I might even let you fly a little."

"If it's all the same to you, I think I'll just relax."

"You didn't have a rough checkflight today, did you?"

"No, but it was interesting."

"Good, you'll enjoy the solo on Monday. Mine was fun today. I just flew down to the beach and looked for whales."

"Did you see any?"

"A couple—pretty badly sunburned I might add."

Brewton quickly came into sight and I called for traffic.

"Brewton traffic, Baron 411 Tango Alpha, twenty miles south for passenger pickup—any traffic in the pattern?"

"Baron 411 Tango Alpha, this is Brewton FBO. There is no reported traffic. We have two passengers in the terminal waiting for you. Be advised runway 6/24 is closed until further notice. 36 is open if you want the straight in."

"That'll work," I said.

Frank smoothed her onto the runway, and we made the turnoff at midfield and taxied into the ramp. Nan and Betsy were outside waving, as if we couldn't see them. They were all decked out in jeans, sweatshirts, baseball caps, and tennis shoes. Fortunately, their sweatshirts didn't match.

"Peter, did you see the T-28 sitting over there off runway six? Wonder what happened to her?"

"I'm sure I wouldn't know," I said with a big grin on my face.

"You rascal. You're holding out on me. What happened?"

"I'll tell you later. Everything is okay. Let's concentrate on New Orleans. Look at those hot chicks waiting for us. Which one do you want?"

"I don't know. They both look alike." We laughed.

Nan and Betsy each had bags which must have weighed forty pounds each.

"We may have to take off fuel to accommodate these bags, Frank."

"We assumed we'd be taken to some upscale places in New Orleans. Don't tell me you're going cheap on us now," Nan grinned. "We saved you money by not renting the VW bus, you know."

"You don't realize how low Junior Officers' pay is in the Navy. Way below schoolteachers," Frank added.

"Maybe we'll buy you a drink along the way." Betsy smiled. "By the way, looks like one of your pilot buddies left his airplane up here. The FBO manager said he had lost an engine, but it still looks like it is there to me."

"Maybe they found it and stuck it back on," I said.

Frank got the girls strapped in and gave a safety brief. "We have parachutes aboard if we have to bail out. Peter and I will jump first to demonstrate how to do it. It may be a little bumpy so if you get sick there are some barf bags in the seat pocket in front of you."

"Maybe we'll just take the bus and catch up with you," Betsy cracked.

"We're flying right over Tuscaloosa on the way over, so we'll drop down and give you a bird's eye view. I'm sure you'll want to see the football stadium or your sorority house."

"No, we'd rather see the creek bank where we used to park with our boyfriends." Betsy chuckled.

"Can you fly over the farm after taking off? It's right by the Conecuh River. Maybe we can see the horses." Nan gestured off to the left.

We took off on runway 36 and Nan hollered, "I see it. I see it! It's almost straight ahead. Fly right over the red brick house. I see Pinta and Nina."

"Did you tell your folks you were flying to New Orleans?"

"No," Betsy answered. "They didn't ask. We're mature adults, you know."

"No comment," Frank said, as he adjusted the heading

toward New Orleans.

Within twenty minutes we were over Tuscaloosa. "I see the football stadium," Nan said excitedly.

"See if you can see Bear Bryant down there walking on water," I said sarcastically.

"Don't laugh," Betsy said. "We were once his recruiting girls. Don't know how he survived without us."

The skies began to cloudy up and the ride continued to get bumpier.

"Peter, you fly it awhile. I'm gonna get us an instrument clearance into New Orleans. This way we'll have separation from the airliners and won't have to worry about staying clear of clouds."

We soon were completely in clouds and the bumps got worse. The girls got very quiet for a change. We only had twenty minutes left in the flight. The girls both had the barf bags in their hands. Frank guided the Baron in masterfully and landed at Moisant International Airport. We turned off the runway and taxied into the Fixed Base Operation.

"Beats driving, doesn't it, girls?"

"Not sure," Betsy replied. "Greyhound's not all bad."

"You didn't use the bags, did you?"

"No, but it was close."

The FBO gave us a ride in their van into town and dropped us off at the Roosevelt Hotel.

"You boys have outdone yourselves," Nan said approvingly.

"We got you the economy room. Frank and I have the penthouse, but you may be allowed to visit."

"We would be honored unless someone gives us a better offer."

"Well, we only have two nights here so let's make the most of it," I suggested. "Thirty minutes and we meet in the lobby."

They were down in fifty minutes as we predicted. They were dazzling, but unfortunately dressed alike."

They're throwing us another curve," I whispered to Frank. We had decided that Nan and I, and Frank and Betsy were best suited for each other. We could tell them apart from their speech and personalities, but the looks were absolutely identical.

"C'mon, Nan. Let's go over to Felix's Oyster Bar and get some raw oysters to start."

Frank wanted to see Bourbon Street, so he got Betsy and they headed off to check out Pete Fountain's bar. "Meet you at Galatoire's for dinner at eight."

I wasn't sure Nan would like raw oysters, but she did. She started off with a dozen. "I actually love them. We get them in Pensacola all the time. Not quite the same ambience as here. I think I'll have another dozen."

"Were you close to using the bag, Nan?"

"Yep, I can handle commercial planes, but these little ones are a challenge. Same for Betsy. We're a lot more different than you think. I've always gotten in more trouble than she did. At least I got caught more. I guess I'm a little more outgoing than she is. We've always been a kind of protection for the other. I admit it's fun being a twin. It gives us a big advantage over men."

"So I've noticed."

She polished off another dozen.

"Where do you put em?"

"I don't know—high metabolism, I suppose."

We headed over to Galatoire's for dinner. Frank and Betsy were already there. "We've got a table already. I learned that when the maitre d' keeps standing in front of you, he wants his tip."

Galatoire's had a notoriously stuffy reputation. "Nan, I want you to order in your best "French" to see how "French" the waiter really is."

Antoine, our drink and wine waiter, came over and in a snooty voice asked for our drink orders. Nan immediately started asking questions in French which took Antoine by complete surprise. He lost his poise altogether. We laughed as he stumbled off.

Our dinner waiter was named Marie. She was a very polished older lady who had been through the wars. Nan stayed French throughout the dinner and we pretended to help her with her broken English. Marie appeared totally confused since her twin was speaking English, and the other only

French. She was too aloof to ask what the heck was going on. I suspect she had a good laugh back in the kitchen.

I was dragging after the dinner. It had been a long day. Frank could tell. He knew I had been involved in the T-28 incident.

"Let's catch Al Hirt for a little trumpet action and then hang it up for the night. It's been a long day for us."

The girls were just getting wound up but graciously agreed. The big horn perked us up a bit. Al was everything we'd heard about him. New Orleans is a special place.

"We've been to Mardi Gras in Mobile a couple of times but it's nothing like this," Betsy exclaimed as we followed Bourbon Street back to the hotel. "And we're just getting started. Nan and I have agreed to spring for 'Breakfast at Brennans' tomorrow if you guys are game."

"Are you sure you can handle it on teacher's pay?" I asked.

"We robbed our piggy banks."

Before turning in, Frank looked at me and asked, "You want to tell me what happened today?"

"Sure. I'll give you the short version. Everything was going fine on the check ride. High work was okay. Emergencies okay. Landings were okay so Lt. Homan got out at the terminal to let me go solo around the pattern for two landings. On the full stop approach, I had a rough runner on the downwind, and she just quit at the 45. I hadn't dropped the gear or gone full flaps, so I just held everything until I turned final. I forgot to go full flaps and floated a bit, but I got her stopped at the end of the runway. Blew the right main tire getting her stopped."

"Sounds like you did a perfect job except the flaps. I don't think you'll get gigged for that. It's not like you had time to review the checklist."

"The airplane had just come out of maintenance. It'll be interesting to see what caused it to quit."

"These airplanes get a lot of wear. It could be a lot of things. You should be fine."

"Lt. Homan said I would go before a safety board next week to give my version."

"You've got good flight grades so I wouldn't sweat it."

"Let's get a good night's sleep. We'll need it tomorrow with the twin terrors raring to go."

OUR KIND OF TOWN

Breakfast at Brennan's is a misnomer. It is a production. You may not eat another meal all day. Nan and Betsy looked gorgeous as usual. They were dressed alike to our disdain. We had heard about this place and luckily got advance reservations.

"Ooh, what a menu!" Nan exclaimed. "Turtle soup, crawfish quiche, eggs hussarde, oysters j'aime, blackened redfish, duck andouille. I'm in hog heaven."

"That's not so lady-like, Nan," I laughed.

"I can't help it. I've never seen a menu like this."

"Look at the dessert menu," Betsy added. "Bananas Foster, Baked Alaska. We're gonna pig out for sure."

We did pig out. We waddled out around one o'clock. We spent an afternoon walking around the French Quarter and ended up at Piano Red's place around six o'clock for some more Bourbon Street music. Food and music are the staple of the French Quarter. After the big breakfast we settled on "Po Boys" for dinner instead of getting stuck in a long dinner.

We ambled into Pat O'Brien's around nine o'clock just as it was beginning to rock. Two giant grand pianos faced each other with two very seasoned ladies pounding away at popular songs of the day. Each had very throaty voices and seemed to know every fight song in existence. One of the ladies was a redhead.

"Is she one of your kinfolks, Nan?"

"Probably one of our more talented relatives."

Requests were coming in from the audience and were heavy from Southeastern schools. "Hold that Tiger" from LSU folks, "Ramblin Wreck" from me, "Okie from Muskogee" from the Sooner bunch in the corner, "Yea Alabama" from Nan, "War Eagle fly down the Field" from Betsy in honor of her brother Red Herring.

"I have a request!" Frank shouted out after a short intermission.

"What's your request, Shorty?" The redhead shouted back.

"Fight song for the Oregon State Beavers."

"Don't know it but I can sure make one up. You say 'Beavers' are the mascot?"

"Yes, Ma'am."

What she made up brought the house down and Frank turned red.

"Should'a kept my mouth shut," Frank muttered as everybody roared.

We had to try the famous "Hurricanes" from Pat O'Brien's. That turned out to be a mistake as it did us all in for the night. We opted to take a cab back to the hotel.

"Let's ease up a little tomorrow, boys. This was a full day," Betsy slurred as they stumbled into their room.

"Good by me," Frank said in a raspy voice.

Sunday morning broke bright and sunny. We took a stroll down to the Mississippi River. We passed the famous Saint Louis Cathedral on Church Street and landed on the wharf at the river. We gorged on the famous beignets and strong New Orleans chicory coffee at Café Du Monde to get us going.

Frank had checked the weather back in Brewton and decided we needed to get on back. The FBO sent us a van and drove us to the airport.

"Betsy and I decided we're definitely coming back to this place. It's our kind of town," Nan purred.

"Do we get to come back with you?" I innocently asked.

"Maybe if you're not broke." Nan winked.

The flight to Brewton was smooth. We landed just as the rain was beginning to fall. The T-28 had already been removed from the field. We unloaded the heavy bags and ran for their car just as it started to pour.

"Seems like we're always cutting it close," Frank yelled.

"The same can be said for us," Nan yelled back as she raised the window and waved goodbye.

We dropped off the Baron and slowly recounted the weekend.

"Certainly a weekend to remember, Frank. Boy, a lot happened. Do you think the girls enjoyed it?"

"They should have. It was their element."

"I'm a little worried about what's ahead."

"Don't. You did everything right. Don't sweat the small

stuff. The board has to do a job. It won't be anything personal."

Arriving at the BOQ, a note was attached to our door.

It read:

To: Ensign Peter Pinson, 670013
From: ComNavAirTraWing 5

Please report to Bldg 211 at 1000 hours Monday for a debriefing of the incident at Brewton airport on 20 May at 1115 hours. Disregard your training flight this day.

LCDR DQ Housel, USN
ComNavAirTraWing 5

I showered and shaved on Monday and suited up in my dress khaki uniform. I hardly ate anything for breakfast. I had been through similar meetings before, but they were never routine.

I knocked on the door at 1000 sharp. The secretary ushered me in. "Ensign Pinson?"

"Yes."

"Come on in. They're expecting you."

Commander Housel introduced himself and Major Matthews.

"I'm Commander Housel, Commander of TraWing 5, and this is Major Jack Matthews, USMC, safety officer of TraWing 5. This isn't a SPDI Board—it's a safety board. We need to get your account of what happened Friday for our records. We expect you to tell the whole truth. We're not here to trap you, just get the details. Please tell us exactly what happened as you remember. We are also here to evaluate your fitness to go back to flying. Something like this can be quite traumatic.

"Yes, sir. I understand." I was very nervous.

I told the whole story as I remembered it. I also told them I forgot to put down landing flaps.

"Mr. Pinson, regarding your mental state. Could you tell us how you felt after the incident? Did you second guess yourself? Were you able to sleep this weekend? Did you have any nightmares? Did you go into isolation? Were you able to talk about it? Do you dread going on your solo now?"

"Well, sirs, I guess it hasn't hit me, yet. It all happened so fast, I just reacted. I feel the Navy has trained me well for something like this. I was able to sleep okay because I had some relaxers. Some friends helped me get through it. Luckily, I wasn't in isolation. I feel ready to fly again."

Major Matthews commented, "That all seems well and good, Mr. Pinson. What exactly did you do to calm yourself through this trauma? Go to church, visit family. Anything like that?"

"No, sir, I went to New Orleans with my girlfriend and her sister."

Major Matthews almost choked on his coffee. Commander Housel looked dumbfounded.

Commander Housel finally let out a belly laugh. "Well, I guess that's not a bad way to relieve the stress. How long was the drive?"

"Actually, we rented a Baron from the flying club." I didn't want Frank's name to be brought up.

"I think I've heard enough, Mr. Pinson. I know more than I need to know." Commander Housel just shook his head and then began to smile.

"Mr. Pinson, I've got news for you. Whether you knew it or not, you were best not to go full flaps. You might not have made the runway with full flaps. Our preliminary findings about the cause of the engine failure was fuel contamination. We think some jet fuel got mixed in with the avgas. We use tremendous amounts of fuel around here and that may have happened. It's under investigation. How do you feel about flying tomorrow on your solo?"

"I'm okay. New Orleans was good therapy."

"I'm sure it was. Did you go to Pat O'Brien's?"

"Yes, sir, I did."

"The redhead at the piano is an old friend of mine. You're dismissed and cleared to fly tomorrow."

MISTAKEN IDENTITY

"Frank, what did you do on your solo?"

"I only did the basics. No acrobatics or spins for sure. I did a few touch-and-go landings at Choctaw. I shouldn't have, but I infringed on Saufley's op area to go look at Perdido Bay. I thought it was so pretty when we were on the T-34's. There is no radar down there and I took a chance no instructor would turn me in. First of all, they couldn't catch me in a T-34. I could outrun them so they couldn't get my number. They're usually too busy trying to keep their students from killing them, anyway."

"I think I'll go to Choctaw as well. It's pretty easy to find. I'll probably just do three touch-and-go landings and enjoy the scenery. I think Cal is soloing today. Maybe we can do some loose formation work."

"It'd better be 'real' loose. Have you seen his flight grades?"

"No."

"He's a bit of a loose cannon. Went to Auburn, your biggest rival. Just kidding."

I met Cal at breakfast in the Officers' mess hall. "Hey Cal, you still soloing today?"

"Yeah. How about you?"

"Yep. Got cleared yesterday. When I told the safety board I went to New Orleans, they were convinced my mental state's okay. Where you gonna go today?"

"Thought I'd go over to Choctaw. Only one runway open today is 18/36, but it's very long. Kind of like an Air Force runway. Nice and long."

"Yeah, me too. What say we join up in a loose formation after landings?"

"Sounds good. I'll be looking for you. Maybe we can fly over the Yellow River and then swing up to the Blackwater River State Park and over to Cobbtown and then south to Whiting."

"We're not allowed to communicate with other solos, but we'll recognize each other. Probably be the only ones at Choctaw."

I like ole Cal, but he has to be the cheapest guy I've ever

met. Once he loaned me twenty cents for a drink and wrote me an IOU. Hard to forget that.

My ship today was 134. Cal was fifteen minutes ahead of me. The duty runway was 36. I took off and immediately headed for Choctaw to do my landings. As I entered the pattern, I saw Cal finishing up his touch-and-go landings and heading north toward Blackwater or Yellow River.

I called in for traffic and had no response, so I had the airport to myself. I made three landings to my satisfaction and departed on a 020 heading toward the Yellow River. I climbed to 2,500 feet to maintain a VFR altitude. It was a beautiful cloudless day with visibility forever. I picked up the Yellow River and thought how last year I was floating out in the Atlantic Ocean on a cable layer standing mid-watches in the engine room. I still had lingering thoughts of our weekend in New Orleans. What's the future with these crazy girls? How will I tell them apart? Are they really different?

Out of my periphery I picked up a T-28 on the horizon. There's Cal. I increased the rpm to 2000 and 35 inches MAP and took off after him. I caught him as he was turning west toward Cobbtown. He didn't see me yet and I crept up as close as I dared. At Cobbtown, he made a left turn south toward Whiting. I matched his turn and ventured even closer. Formation flying was easier than I thought. I was within about thirty feet. He would see me if he looked aside.

As I looked into the cockpit to my dismay there were two people in the airplane! Crap! I had joined up on an instructor and student. I quickly threw out my speedbrakes and pulled the power back. The other airplane quickly distanced himself. I was mortified. *Now it's going to hit the fan.*

The transmission quickly came out. "T-28 who just joined up on Sioux Falls 107 identify yourself immediately." By now I had turned north toward Brewton as fast as I could go. I decided now was a good time to do a full stop for a few minutes. Luckily, the instructor was too busy with his student to take chase.

I came into the pattern and one other trainer was there. I recognized the voice of Cal. I called for the full stop and Cal recognized my voice and also made a full stop. We taxied in and shutdown our engines. I sauntered over to his airplane.

"What's up, mate? Is everything okay?"

"Just a small problem. I accidentally joined up on an instructor, but he didn't identify me I don't think. He'll probably be trying to find out who it was. If you don't mind saying that you were here with me, I would appreciate it. That's not a lie, is it?"

"Of course not. Your secret is safe with me."

"I owe you." Somehow, I knew he would collect.

The instructor spread the word for the student who joined up on him to identify himself. There were five solos in the area at the time, so it was easy to narrow it down to those few. The instructor happened to be none other than Lt. Dembowski, the notorious screamer. He wanted blood.

After no one came forward, Dembowski intensified the search. My next flight was with Sandy, an introduction to basic instruments.

At the briefing Sandy asked. "You were one of the five solos out yesterday, weren't you?"

"Yes, sir."

"I'm not going to ask you if you were the one who joined up on Dembowski." I didn't say anything, but I knew Sandy knew.

"Actually, it was me." Sandy said with a devious smile.

I was shocked. "What do you mean?"

"I'll be telling Dembowski today. I was simply giving my student an advanced look at formation flying. Your friend Andy was with me. I'm sure he will remember it as I do."

"Sandy, you're the greatest. If I find out who the real culprit was, I'll sure let him know what a great American you are." We both laughed and exchanged high fives.

Dembowski knew Sandy was lying but was powerless to pursue it further. My next thought was: *What if I get Dembowski for an instructor?* I need to put that out of my mind.

UNDER THE HOOD

Basic instruments proved to be boring but necessary. Inevitably, our missions would take us into cloud cover. Your only survival is to believe in and fly on instruments completely. Disorientation can lead to stalls and spins and other bad things. Lt. Rosenblatt was my new instructor. He was a plough back from the fleet. He had one tour in Vietnam and was battle tested.

He was waiting for me in the briefing room. "Mr. Pinson, I'm Carl Rosenblatt. I keep hearing your name pop up. I feel like I know you. Why do you reckon that is?"

"I don't know. Luck keeps following me around, both good and bad."

Carl laughed. "Lt. Dembowski was blowing off steam in the instructors' lounge today. He says he knows the name of the student who joined on him Monday. Lt. Sanda apparently took the rap for him. I pity the guilty student who ever gets him for training."

I cringed but said nothing.

"The briefing today will be extensive on the use of instruments. Then we will do a 'Round Robin' around the operating area. You will stay on instruments and I will be the safety officer looking out. You will navigate using VOR's point-to-point. We'll go direct Crestview, direct Flomaton, direct Mobile, direct Saufley. It's a trainer so I will be constantly pointing out tips. I will handle all communications. You will tune the VORs. Any questions?"

"No, sir."

We did the same thing three straight days. I hated to not be able to look outside the cockpit. I couldn't wait till Friday and the weekend.

"Frank, have you thought about the weekend ahead?"

"Yeah. The girls are out of school, so I know they'll want to go to the beach."

"I presume they'll want to see us."

"I sure hope so. We spent the bucks. Maybe they'll be in for hamburgers this weekend."

One thing we both liked about the twins. They didn't play games—probably because of their teacher backgrounds.

When I called their house in Brewton, Mrs. Herring answered. "Hello, Peter. How are you?"

"Fine, Mrs. Herring. And you?"

"Great. I want to thank you for being so nice to my girls last weekend, especially taking them to church. I hope we get to meet you soon. Do you want to speak to Nan or Betsy?"

"Nan will be fine."

"What's up?" Nan cheerily said.

"You. Are you up for the beach this weekend?"

"Of course. I'm always up for the beach."

"Can I pick you up?"

"Sure. But Betsy will drive down so we can have a car. I presume Frank is coming down."

"Yes, he'll call Betsy later."

"Five o'clock Friday okay? That'll give you time to clear school."

I didn't have a good visualization of what the farm would be like. We overflew it on the way to New Orleans and I had glanced at the red brick house, but I was looking for the horses. The farm was more like a ranch. A white picket fence led me to the entrance, an arched gate adorned by a collection of deer horns, probably accumulated by Mr. Herring and Red. A gravel road wound down to a traditional large brick house with columns in front. I saw Pinta and Nina grazing out in the pasture.

Mrs. Herring answered the door. She was a beautiful lady, maybe more so than her daughters.

"Hello, Peter. You're so clean cut, just as I envisioned you. Come on in. Nan's just about ready. The girls are so excited about school being just about out for the summer. They love to camp out in the beach house. If they could get jobs down there, they would be out of here."

"You have a beautiful farm here. I've seen it from the air. I hope the airplanes don't scare the horses."

"No, they're fine as long as they don't land in the pasture."

Nan came bopping down in her usual afterschool

attire—jeans, sweatshirt, ball cap, and tennis shoes. "I'm ready as soon as I say goodbye to the horses."

We went out and walked over to the fence. The horses came running over to get some nose rubbing. "The brown one here is Pinta. She's mine. The pinto is Nina. I wish I could take them to the beach."

We jumped into the Corvette and headed south. "Peter, you're ridiculous."

"What do you mean?" I asked, startled.

"You're trying to put a snow job on my mom. I can't believe how nice she thinks you are."

"Well, wouldn't you want her to think that way?"

"Yeah, but you don't have to over-do it."

"Well, you're ridiculous, too!" I retorted.

"How so?" Nan acted surprised.

"She thinks I took you to church on Sunday."

"You did, don't you remember? We went by Saint Louis Cathedral on Church Street to get beignets in the French Quarter. I didn't say we went in." She grinned mischievously.

"Okay, okay, I give up."

On the road to the beach, we must pass the Saint Joe Paper Mill on US highway 90. I hate to go that way, but it was the only logical way to get to the beaches. When the wind is down, the smell is horrific.

As we approached the paper mill, I made the observation, "You know, the paper mill doesn't smell so bad today. I wonder why?"

We passed on by and I said, "Nan, what are you wearing?"

"Jungle Gardenia. Why?" She shot me a menacing look.

"Oh, nothing."

Betsy arrived at the Herring beach house soon after us. The girls couldn't wait and immediately hit the beach. Frank drove up awhile later and came in with a big smile on his face.

"What's up, partner?"

"I have a bit of news."

"Shoot."

"I've got orders to helicopter school. As soon as I get my instrument check next week, I'll be going to ground school at

Ellyson Field. Our Coast Guard pipeline doesn't require formation or carrier quals, so my fixed wing flying is over. It's exactly what I wanted. If I go into a career in the Coast Guard, it's the best way to go for promotion. Seaplanes are on the way out. Herkie pilots will never get a squadron. I like the idea of always being low level. Besides, I get to stay around the Pensacola area for awhile. Nothing wrong with seeing Betsy a bit longer. I'll be moving to Mainside BOQ after next week."

"Congratulations. I'll hate to lose you as a roommate. You've pulled me through basic instruments the last couple of weeks. Who's gonna get me through formation and carrier quals now?"

"Pal, you'll do okay on your own. Not many students come through here without a 'down' who have no prior flying experience. You have been lucky as hell so far, I'll admit, but you've got to quit joining up on instructors without their knowledge—particularly a screamer like Dembowski."

"Frank, you need to make a trip up to Brewton to see the farm. It's a beautiful place with animals and horses. Mrs. Herring is so nice. She thinks I'm wonderful. Sorry I couldn't put in a good plug for you."

"Thanks a lot, good buddy."

"Well, what's on tap for tonight?"

"Let's do a cookout and then go for a late-night swim."

"Okay, but can't we just cater it?"

"Heck, no. Let's just do hot dogs. We can't screw that up."

After the cookout, which went well, Nan said to Betsy, "You know Betsy, last weekend we were drinking champagne and eating caviar. This weekend it's hot dogs. Do you think we're being taken for granted?"

Betsy agreed. "Yep, Nan, next weekend it'll probably be some pizza joint going Dutch. Then we'll get ditched."

"Now wait, girls," I protested. "Y'all just don't get the big picture. We're still paying off the loan from last week. We'll go big next week."

"Promises, promises—from a Navy pilot. I just don't know, Nan." Betsy chortled.

The night was beautiful, a full moon, tide out, waves lapping gently on the sand—good night for a swim. Everyone got on swimsuits and started running for the beach. Nan and Betsy were first and when we caught up, we saw their swimsuits lying in the sand.

"Water's great, boys. Come on in."

After we got over the initial shock, we dived in. "Is this a tradition at the beach house?" I shouted.

"No, we're just starting it," one of them said.

"Here we go again," Frank hollered. "How're we gonna tell 'em apart in their birthday suits?"

"You'll just have to guess." One of them giggled. "We're both so sweet."

After splashing water at each other for awhile, the girls took off running for the house. We chased after them and caught up just as they were jumping into beach towels. They dressed differently today so we quickly solved the mystery.

"We're really as different as night and day. At least we think so. Nan is the troublemaker. I have to clean up her messes," Betsy said with a straight face.

"Yeah, but she was a terrible student and I always had to help her get through school," Nan countered. "Without me, she could never get a date!"

"Poor Red. How did he put up with you two?"

"He went to Auburn because he knew we were going to Bama."

"That makes perfect sense." I laughed.

"Frank," I whispered. "I think I've seen something to set them apart."

THE TATTOO

"All right, Peter, what's the great secret you found out? I didn't notice anything to tell them apart."

"Just as they were coming out of the ocean, I noticed Nan has a mermaid tattoo on her left cheek."

"Wow! You gotta be kidding! How did you know it was Nan?"

"I heard her say, 'Betsy, run for the house.' I saw her again right before they got to the beach towels."

"Have you said anything to either of them?"

"No, the time wasn't right. That's funny. Who would've thought?" I laughed.

"Are you sure Betsy didn't have one, also?"

"That, I don't know for sure," I said.

"Well, we have yet another mystery."

Saturday night was overcast and no moon shone through. It was very dark when we all went for another swim. Nan and Betsy led again, Nan hollering, "Last one in is a rotten egg," as she disappeared into a big wave.

Once again, bikinis were left in the foam.

Frank and I were alert as to whether Betsy had a matching tattoo. On the run back to the house, we both confirmed Nan's tattoo, a mermaid. Betsy was too quick, and we could not verify. Still a mystery.

We left the beach house Sunday afternoon without a solution. Maybe we'll know next weekend. Perhaps the girls will spill the beans.

"Frank, how'd the check ride go, today?"

"Okay, I passed."

After further discussion, I learned that he had aced it, like always. I finished my pre-check today and would get my check ride tomorrow at 0800 with Lt. Dembowski.

"Of all the instructors I had to get," I moaned. "He's gonna be on me the whole time. It'll be a miracle if I can pass the check. I know he knows I was the student pilot who joined up on him."

"Well, look at it like this. He may try to intimidate you, but on a check ride the check airman can't instruct; only act as your co-pilot, safety pilot, and check airman. Technically, they can't harass you."

"Technically, maybe, but this guy has a reputation. He's supposed to be a real screamer."

"Many 'downs' are caused by tuning in the wrong navaid. It is perfectly fine to ask the check airman to double check the ID (aural identification of the navigational aid) but be sure to direct the check airman as to which navaid you mean."

"I'll remember that. I'll try to keep him loaded up."

Morning came way too soon. I dreaded meeting up with Dembowski. I was in the briefing room at 0730, hoping to make a good impression. He came in shortly, coffee cup in hand.

"Good morning, sir," I cheerily said and offered him my hand.

"Morning," he grunted and reluctantly extended his own.

"Mr. Pinson, every instructor on the base knows who you are. I know more about you than you think."

I said nothing.

"Well, let's get on with the check. I'll ask you a few questions, then you'll show me how to file an instrument flight plan and read the weather briefings. We'll go to the airplane and you'll show me how to set up radio instruments for the flight. After takeoff, you're to keep your head in the cockpit and not look out again until right before our first landing. I'll call 'field in sight' if you're set up to make a safe landing.

"I'll be perfectly honest with you, Pinson. I don't expect you will pass this check. I give a lot of 'downs.' If at any point in the flight I think you deserve an 'unsat,' we will discontinue and come back to base."

With these unsettling remarks, I took the oral. Frank had gouged the hell out of me, so I was well prepared. He didn't stop the flight after the oral, so I assumed I passed that part. Checking the weather and filing the flight plan were easy enough. We went to the airplane and I set up the instruments for the flight. Lt. Dembowski had been silent for most of the pre-flight which further unnerved me, because I knew of his propensity to yell. I was still waiting for an outburst. I was about to pick up the radial for the Crestview VOR after takeoff when the first outburst came.

"You idiot! Give it more cut! You'll never catch the radial in time!"

I felt better now. At least I'll know what to expect. He's not supposed to be coaching, only grading. He obviously can't help himself. I joined the radial and after passing Crestview I started outbound for the procedure turn. I was about to make the 180 turn back when another outburst came.

"Hey, stupid, you've got to make a 45-degree bank or else you can't stay in the cleared zone. Don't you have a brain?"

I had already started the turn but apparently not as tight as he wanted. After turning inbound and capturing the radial, another outburst.

"Hey, dummy, get it down. You've only got a minute to get down to minimums. Where is your head?"

I almost laughed. Here it is *my* checkride, and he can't stop himself from screaming. I don't think I've done anything wrong to deserve a "down," at least not yet.

We were approaching minimums and I hadn't heard "field in sight" yet, so I executed the missed approach. Just as I added the power, he called "field in sight." Too late. I had added power and called the miss exactly when he called the field.

"Going to alternate," I declared.

"Okay, you're cleared direct to Lynne NDB, frequency 278, expect NDB approach to runway 16, Panama City Regional Airport. Maintain 3,000 feet."

He was trying to overload me which he absolutely did. I was trying to fly the airplane, clean it up for gear and flaps, tune in the NDB frequency, identify it, ask for weather at the airport, and prepare for the instrument approach.

I remembered Frank's advice. "When you have a co-pilot, you must use them to help you. Load them up with as much as they can take."

I rattled off things for Lt. Dembowski to do. "Identify the LYNNE frequency. After that get me the weather in Panama City." I had already started a turn toward the needle, which was pointing to LYNNE. Lt. Dembowski didn't expect to be asked to do all these things. Most students would have a 'down' by now. Frank had saved the day. I continued to load him up with everything I could think of. Double check this. Double check that. Brief me on the minimums. What's the missed approach heading? He was getting too flustered to scream. I was so far ahead of him all I had to do was fly the airplane. It was not a beautiful approach but Dembowski was so loaded up he may not have noticed. He finally called "field in sight" and I looked out and landed with a thud at Panama City International Airport.

"Damn, Ensign! I've never had a student do that to me before. Where did you learn that trick?"

"My roommate has an instrument rating already. That's what he was taught."

"Okay, we're going back directly to Whiting. I want you to tune the radios and do all the talking. We'll see how you do. Consider me not to be in the airplane this time."

I pre-tuned the radios on the ground and looked over the Whiting instrument approach procedure. I already knew it pretty well. I had the comm frequencies on my kneeboard.

We took off and things were going well until Pensacola Approach Control cleared us for the instrument approach to Whiting. Dembowski came unglued for no apparent reason. I was having trouble concentrating. I think he was worried he might have to pass me. I tried to tune him out and just shoot the approach. It was called a non-precision approach for good reason. (That is the official name of an approach without an electronic glide slope.)

As bad as the approach was, we arrived at the missed approach point and he called "field in sight." I looked out to see the beautiful runway straight ahead. A much better landing this time and I relaxed for a change as we taxied to the gate. I had no inkling if I passed or not.

"Shut her down, get the flight time off the meter and meet me in ops," he snarled while climbing out. He quickly disappeared from sight.

The plane captain installed the chocks and came over to me

with a grin. "He's a piece of work, isn't he?"

"I'll say. I sweated out five pounds."

I dreaded the debriefing. I was sure there would be more hollering.

"Well, Pinson. Let's go over the flight." After thirty minutes of nit picking, he finally came to a conclusion. "I'm going to pass you because you didn't do anything unsatisfactorily. There is a lot of room for improvement so try not to make the same mistakes again." There were no outbursts or hollering. He apparently randomly turns it on and off. Maybe he only screams in flight.

I rushed back to the BOQ to tell Frank I passed.

"Hey, that's great roomie! Let's go to happy hour to celebrate our graduation from instrument training."

We met Joe and Bax and Cal at the bar. Joe had passed his check, Cal had failed his, and Bax was scheduled for his check the next day.

Cal was obviously a little distraught, but he felt he made some correctable mistakes for the retake. "Man, I just got behind the power curve and wasn't set up properly for the approach to Mobile. I've got the retake with Dembowski tomorrow. What a break."

"Cal, I had him today and barely passed. Let's get together later and I'll tell you everything we did today. I think you'll be okay if you can tune out the screaming."

"Easy for you to say, you've already passed." We all laughed.

FORMATION

Frank and I were going in different directions. He was moving to Mainside Pensacola to start ground school for helicopters. I'd stay at Whiting to start formation and cross-country training. After that would come carrier quals. If the carrier quals were successful, I would move on to Corpus Christi, Texas, for multi-engine training and more carrier work.

"Frank, I can't believe we're splitting up. Who's gonna drag me through the program now?"

"Good buddy, you're on your own now. I don't know anything about carriers and don't want to. That's why I went Coast Guard."

"Reckon it's too late for me to switch over?"

"About as much chance as me going to the moon."

"I've got to move out today. Can you give me a hand with a few things?"

"Of course. Just leave your golf clubs with me. I'll get them to you later."

"No way. They're the first things outta here."

"What about this weekend? Are we going to double with the dynamite duo or try to split them up?"

"They're twenty-five years old so it's time to split them up—they shouldn't still be dressing alike." Frank laughed.

"I'll see if Nan will take me horseback riding and you can take Betsy for dinner at the Mustin Beach 'O' Club with all the big Navy brass."

"Okay, sounds like a plan."

Our class of twelve met for two full days of ground school on formation flying. Our instructor was Ltjg. Suter, a graduate of the Naval Academy. After initially getting his wings in Texas, he asked to plough back to Pensacola for instructor work. He was engaged to an admiral's daughter which may have facilitated the return.

"Gentlemen, the Navy prides itself in its formation flying. It is epitomized in the air work of the Blue Angels. That is the benchmark and what we want to achieve. Y'all are over the halfway mark to getting your wings. Formation presents a new challenge. You must rely on each other with your lives. It's a matter of trust. It's a microcosm of what you will be doing at the carrier."

Several of my gang were in the class. I'm thinking, *do I want to trust my life with these bozos?* I knew them all well by now, but I didn't know anything about their flying ability. Nor did they know about mine. We probably all embellished our airmanship at happy hour. I certainly did.

Lt. Suter laid out all the principles of flying formation. "The leader is the navigator, and everyone follows him in the order of the formation group. #4 flies off #3 who flies off #2 who flies off the leader. (Leader is #1 during training when you have an instructor in chase plane.) #2, #3, and #4 are fixated on the plane off to the left or right as is the case of the echelon.

"The leader must be in communication at all times with the group. Anticipation of power changes is necessary for smooth transitions. The leader must make smooth power changes and flight control changes. We will strive for three feet wingtip clearance. This separates us from the Air Force. Their definition of formation flying is two airplanes in the same direction on the same day." He laughed heartily.

"Is everybody with me? I had two DORs at this point in my last class."

No hands went up, so I guess we're all in. He made it sound easy, but I know it's not.

Bax, Joe, and Andy were in my four-plane group on our first flight together. Marine First Lieutenant Parker was our instructor in the chase plane. The instructor call sign is always "Boss."

"Okay, guys. Everybody give me a comm check before takeoff," Boss called out as we approached the threshold of runway 36.

Our call signs were #1, #2, #3, and #4. Parker was naturally Boss. We took off in single file and performed a running rendezvous to join up in a four-plane right echelon. Bax was #4 today. On rendezvous everyone has different power settings until join up. #4 had too much power and went flying by #3 and had to break away.

"Damn it, #4, where ya goin'?" Boss shouted out.

"Sorry, sir. I was carrying too much power."

"I'll say. Drop back and come in slowly. #1, you fly 270 degrees and we'll turn south at Silver Hill."

Our first day together was chaotic as you might imagine. Just getting all four together in the same direction was hilarious. Our debrief lasted an hour. I couldn't wait to get to happy hour to laugh with my mates. It was a toss-up to see who got yelled at the most. Nobody claimed the mantle, although I believe it went to Joe. It was no disgrace to be shamed.

"Boss" was Lt. Parker for our first four flights. We got better and better each flight and by the fourth flight we were clicking along until we had a mishap. #2 had an oil cap on the engine cowling work its way off. Black oil came streaming back onto the windscreens of #3 and #4. I was #4 this day. All of a sudden, I could hardly see #3. Boss could not see what happened from his port (left) chase position.

"Yikes," I yelled and pulled the power all the way back. #3, Joe, was in a bind. He could not see #2 clearly and didn't know where I was.

Joe hollered out, "I'm backing off #2. I can hardly see him."

I was way back by now. Boss got really excited. He had two students flying formation by themselves, one with an oil leak, and two students off somewhere flying blind.

"Everybody listen up! #1 and #2, you two break up and hang back VFR. You're on your own. #2, you find a field or runway anywhere, declare an emergency and get it on the ground ASAP! #3 and #4, you're going to file your own IFR flight plans back to Mainside Pensacola. Call Pensacola Radar on Freq #4. They should give you a squawk and vector. Hopefully a GCA approach. Do either of you know where you are?"

"No."

"Nope."

"Okay, both of you go into slow flight and go ahead and switch to Pensacola Approach. When I catch you, I'll ride wing on you till I catch the other. Steer 220 degrees which is the general direction of Mainside. I'll switch to frequency #4 also and monitor Pensacola Approach along with you two."

By the time I had switched over, Boss was already talking to Approach Control.

"Approach, this is Navy trainer 112. I have two student pilots with oil all over their windscreens. They'll be calling you for radar ident and requesting IFR approaches to Mainside, preferably GCA's (radar precision approaches). Can you work us in?"

"Yes, do you want to declare an emergency?"

"Yes, that would be very appropriate."

I was first to call in after Boss.

"Pensacola Approach Control, this is Navy trainer 160, level 3,000, heading 220, position unknown."

"Trainer 160, squawk emergency ident."

"Okay, 160, I got you on radar. Squawk 2134 now. Turn left heading 200, vectors for GCA to runway two five right. Maintain 2500 feet. Switch frequencies to your channel 5 for final controller."

I had never done a GCA approach before. We didn't do them in training. I knew the controller told you everything to do. I just had to follow instructions. The oil on the windscreen had mostly blown off. I thought I can see enough to land, but I'd stick on instruments for now.

"One six zero, this is your final controller, how do you hear?"

"One six zero, loud and clear," I responded.

Why do they have to call it "final controller?" I thought.

"One six zero, No further transmissions. Turn right 250, you're intercepting final. Descend to 1200 feet. You're intercepting glideslope."

I couldn't resist peeking out and saw the runway through the cloudy windscreen. I was having trouble staying on glideslope, and I could feel the tension in the controller's voice. I interrupted him and told him I could see the runway.

"Roger, 160. Take over visual and land. Winds are calm. Runway length is seventy-five hundred feet."

I decided to do an Air Force type landing and land long and float it down. I could see the crash trucks out of my peripheral vision with their flashing lights. It was one of my best landings ever. Maybe it's best I can't see out to land. I let out a big breath of air as I taxied off the runway.

I looked back up the runway just in time to see Joe turning final. I hope he was having more fun than me. I wondered what my friends on the USS Neptune were doing now?

I knew Joe would do a good job. He owned a small airplane, a Luscomb, while in college at Wyoming. He had lots of flight time coming in. His windscreen was like mine, a bit murky, and he landed long like me. I thought if I ever needed an excuse to DOR, it was now.

Joe and I found out later Boss had rounded up Bax and Cal and got them back to Whiting Field. Lt. Parker deserved a medal.

I called over to the Mainside BOQ to see if Frank was around. He answered the page and said, "Ensign Hammer speaking."

"Frank, Peter. I'm at Mainside."

"What for?"

"Long story."

"You okay?"

"Yeah."

"You didn't have anything to do with all those flashing lights on the runway, this afternoon, did you?"

"Yes."

"Figures. I'll be right over."

PHANTOM ACTIVITY

"Frank, I'm beginning to think I'm snakebit. Here I am flying along minding my own business and Bax's plane, #2, leaks oil all over my windscreen. What are the odds of that happening? The entire formation came apart and luckily nobody got hurt. I felt sorry for the instructor. He was babysitting three emergencies at the same time. We're scheduled for formation tomorrow with Lt. Dembowski. That should be interesting, assuming we have enough airplanes that are flyable. Bax is probably going to catch hell for that oil cap coming off. Hard to know if he tightened it properly."

The same four of us were on the schedule for the next day with Dembowski. We all talked about going to the sick bay instead.

Maybe a DOR would be better than flying formation with him as instructor. The briefing went as expected. He belittled all of us after the remarkable recoveries we made yesterday. He seemed to think we were not prepared.

I was assigned to be #1, the navigation leader. Joe, Bax, and Cal are #2, #3, and #4, in that order.

Just as we exited the briefing room, Lt. Sanda intercepted us and grabbed my arm. "You four come quickly with me."

We were shocked at the urgency of his actions. We complied and went with him as directed. Once we were in an enclosed room, three other instructors entered the room.

"Guys, we're hijacking your plane and hardhats. We are also taking over your names. Which of you is #1, #2, #3, and #4?"

"I'm #1 and Joe is #2, Bax #3, and Cal #4."

"We have approval from ComNavAirTra5 to impersonate you today as a 'tribute' to Lt. Dembowski. We have wired his radios to be recorded in all of his transmissions to us during the flight. He won't know he's being recorded. It will be broadcast to the tower, also. We will make his flight so miserable that he will have reason to become alcoholic. Maybe he will be the first instructor to ever DOR. I'm sorry you won't get to hear him first-hand, but I suppose this tape will be a classic of Naval Aviation history."

The instructors put on our helmets and quietly went to our respective planes and saluted the plane captains as if nothing was awry.

Dembowski came sauntering out none the wiser that he was being sabotaged. Lt. Sanda and the other three instructors were strapped in, ready to go. After the comm check, #3 says to Boss.

"I'm in terrible need to go to the head, Boss. Will that be okay?"

"Hell no. What do you think this is, nursery school? Suck it up, man."

#2 calls to Boss. "I forgot my kneeboard with the checklist on it. Would it be possible for the plane captain to bring it out for me?"

"#@%$ no, you idiot. Crank your @#$% engines up and let's get going."

The four instructors were taxiing out to runway 5 with Boss in trail. Suddenly #2 stops on the taxiway. "#2, what's the @#$% problem?"

"My brakes are dragging, and I can smell something."

"Are your @#$% parking brakes on?" Dembowski screams.

"Oops. Yes, sir."

"Well, get the @#$% off. What the @#$% wrong with you @#$% birds today?"

Boss tells everyone to switch to tower frequency for takeoff clearance. Boss requests takeoff clearance for the five airplanes.

Whiting Tower clears the flight of five for takeoff.

Boss sings out, "Roger, flight of five cleared for takeoff."

"#1: Roger."

"#2: Roger."

"#3: Roger."

Silence for thirty seconds.

Boss: "#4, @#$% it, answer up."

#4: "Are we cleared for takeoff?"

Boss: "#4, listen up you @#$%. Yes, tell the tower you're @#$% cleared."

#4: "#4 cleared for takeoff."

"Tower: "Expedite, takeoff immediately. I'm holding up landing traffic."

Boss: "Five on the roll. We'll be doing a left turn running rendezvous to the west."

Tower: "Roger, airspace is clear. You can switch to operational frequency when airborne."

Boss calls for check-in after everyone is airborne. "#1 is up. #2 is up."

Silence for 30 seconds.

Boss: "#3, where the @#$% are you? Answer up, @#$% it to hell."

Seconds later. "#3 checking in. Boss, I've lost sight of #2."

Boss: "Get your head out of your @#$. He should be at your two o'clock slightly higher."

#3: "Roger, I was looking at ten o'clock."

Boss: "Well, look at your watch if you can't tell what @#$% time it is. Do you have him yet?"

#3: "Yeah, I've got him now, but I think I'm gonna overshoot."

Boss: "Pull your @#$% power back and slide off. Don't hit the son-of-a @#$%."

#1: "Boss, do I keep the turn in?"

Boss: "Yeah, keep the turn in till we get these crazy @#$%'s all joined up. #4, where are you?"

#4: I'm joined up, but I don't know if I'm joined up on #2 or #3."

Boss: "@#$% it. How can you be so @#$% stupid? Just stay on him till we get this @#$% mess sorted out. Y'all are the worst @#$% students I've ever seen!"

#2: Boss, should I raise my flaps now?"

Boss: "@#$% right. No wonder #3 overshot you. Use your @#$% head. All right you @#$% meatheads, everyone keep turning to join up on someone. Maybe we'll get lucky before we all run out of @#$% gas."

As if by magic, the four instructors suddenly were in a perfect echelon formation.

Boss: "I don't know how you @#$% finally got joined up but I've had enough of you sons of @#$. You've all got 'downs.'

"We're going back in. #1, take us back to Whiting. We'll set up for carrier break and separation. Try not to get us all killed."

#1: "Aye, sir, turning to port."

Boss: "No, you @#$% idiot. Starboard."

As the formation now seemed to become a coordinated unit, Boss exclaimed, "How could you @#$% be so bad and now become so good? You're all @#$% head cases."

The formation was heading due east toward Whiting. All formations fly from the South Whiting Field complex. Suddenly, Boss hollered out.

"You @#$% idiots. You're headed for the North Field. Do not @#$% break over the North Field. Turn this formation south, #1. Don't you even know north from south? How in hell did you ever get out of grade school, much less Navy pre-flight? What a dumb @#$% you are."

#1 turned the formation south in perfect three feet wingtip separation.

Boss: "I want you to turn right and roll out on a 050 heading and when you pick up runway 5 on the South Field, South Field, South Field, set up for a carrier break and landing on runway 5, runway 5, runway 5. Can you @#$% loonies possibly do that? I'm recommending you all for SPDI boards after this fiasco."

The formation was perfect coming up for the break over runway 5. #1 called the break and rolled into a left 40-degree bank. Thirty seconds is the interval required to achieve proper separation. #2 suddenly broke immediately after #1.

Boss: "@#$% amighty, #2. What in @#$% are you doing? Have you @#$% crazy? I give ass up. I'm turning in my papers after this flight. I'm going back to the fleet where it's safe. I hope you idiots never see me again."

#3 and #4 also broke quickly. The four planes were all going downwind in a loose formation. Each extended downwind and turned final in perfect separation. Each made perfect landings.

Dembowski was livid. "I've never seen such incompetence. You @#$% are a disgrace to the human race, much less Naval aviation. You @#$% go to the briefing room and wait for me. I'm going to see Lieutenant Commander Housel about all of you."

We had been invited to the tower by ComNavTra5, Commander Housel, to listen in. Everyone was rolling on the floor as the instructors all taxied in. We all hustled down to the briefing room to await Lt. Dembowski.

Commander Housel and Lt. Dembowski entered the briefing room and saw the eight conspirators all grinning. His first reaction was, "What the @#$%?"

His frown slowly turned to a grin. "I guess you SOB's got me good. Surely you didn't get it on tape. If so, I'll buy all the copies."

"I don't think you'll have enough money." Commander Housel laughed.

THE HERRINGS

I arrived at the Herring farm at 0800. The whole family was home. This would be their last weekend together. School was out for the summer, so the girls would be moving to the beach house. Red had a weekend pass from the Marines and would be going back to Quantico Monday. It was my first chance to meet Red and Mr. Herring.

Nan met me at the front door.

"Nan, right?"

"Of course, silly. You know the difference by now."

"I know, but can I get a 'cheek check?'"

"I get it. You saw the mermaid tattoo at the beach. I'm so embarrassed."

"No, you're not."

"Okay, nobody's around. I hope the day will come when I don't have to verify myself to you."

"I actually like the verification."

"Bad boy." She laughed.

"I'll bet Betsy has one there as well."

"No, she doesn't. That's the only way you can tell us apart. Are you up for a ride today?"

"Yep, if Nina is in a good mood."

"She bucked my last boyfriend off. Betsy is about the only person she'll let ride her."

"I know you're kidding. Aren't you?"

"Only one way to find out. Let's go!"

"I think I'll bring along some carrots and sugar, just in case."

Red came walking in wearing his overalls. "I've got them saddled up for y'all. Nina is acting kind of strange today."

"Hi, Red. I'm Peter. We may have met on the football field a few years ago in a Tech-Auburn game. I was a backup. I got in when Auburn had Tech down by 30. One of the guys said you bit him in a pile up. I know that's not true, is it?"

"Absolutely untrue. I was always such a good sport."

"What's this about Nina acting strange?"

"She reacts that way when Nan brings a new boyfriend over. Happens all the time."

Nan shot him a menacing glare. "Let's go, Peter. Time to ride."

Nina turned out to be the most gentle horse I've ever seen. Being a novice rider, I certainly didn't need the challenge of a bucking bronco.

"I must be different from all of your other boyfriends. Look how she takes to a masterful rider like me."

"Don't be so sure. She's in the evaluation stage right now. She probably hasn't come to a decision yet. She'll let me know by the end of the ride whether you're a decent guy or not."

"Your other boyfriends must have been jerks if they all got bucked. They weren't Navy guys, were they?"

"No, you're the first Navy guy I've ever met."

"I'm sure."

"What was your week like? Just a bunch of boring flights?"

"Not exactly. I shot an emergency approach into Mainside Wednesday with oil on my windscreen. Could hardly see the runway. I got to visit Frank while there. He's living in the Mainside BOQ now. He gave me a ride back to Whiting. He's going to be training on helicopters, so he will stay in Pensacola for awhile. I wouldn't be surprised if he tries to get permanent duty here with the Coast Guard."

"He and Betsy are getting along very well. Their personalities are similar. She's not as nice as me. He's been driving to Brewton every other night."

"He didn't mention it to me."

"My favorite flight of the week I didn't fly. An instructor known as the 'Screamer' was taped on a flight where instructors substituted for students. The instructors screwed up everything possible and the Screamer had no idea his students were actually instructors. The tape is going to be priceless."

"Was it Lt. Dembowski?"

"Yes. I thought you didn't know any Navy guys."

"Now that I think about it, maybe I do know a couple."

After two hours of riding around the countryside, I could tell I was getting saddle sores. So far, Nina had not judged me to be a bad person.

We brought the horses in and took the saddles off.

"What has Nina determined about me? She didn't try to buck me like your other boyfriends."

"She has determined that you need to take me back to New Orleans so she can make further evaluations."

"That is one sharp horse. Wonder if she'll take a bribe?" I took out some squares of sugar and stuck them in her mouth. She seemed to smile in the affirmative.

Mr. Herring was cooking up some barbecue as we entered the farmhouse from the back.

"Wow, what a great smell!" I said complimenting Mr. Herring.

"Some people say I should go commercial. Too much competition down in these parts. How was your ride, Peter?"

"I'm a little sore, but determined Nina likes me."

"You must not have been bucked."

I looked over at Nan who was cracked up laughing.

Frank had arrived and it wasn't long before the girls recruited us to help them move their considerable belongings down to the beach house, their home away from home. Mr. Herring naturally owned a pickup truck which was easily filled, and he fixed up a huge serving of barbecue to take for a picnic at the beach.

The girls wanted to catch up on our futures in aviation. Turnover is a big part of the training process in Pensacola. Pilots come to Pensacola to train and leave. The turnovers depend on a lot of different variables—washing out, finishing up, getting killed, and further training in Mississippi and Texas. Betsy was especially interested in the pipeline for Frank.

"Frank, you're the first Coastie I've ever met. Your time in Pensacola seems shorter than most pilots. Why is that?"

"For starters, we don't go through carrier training because we have no need. Our mission is really interesting because we are so closely tied to the ocean. We need helicopters, cutter ships, small coastal boats, seaplanes, and ground stations along the coast. Our total time in Pensacola is about ten months. That's about what my total will be. If I had requested fixed-wing airplanes, I would be going to Texas next week. I'm lucky to get choppers."

"I'm glad you went choppers, Frank."

Right before my eyes, I was seeing something special between Betsy and Frank.

Nan asked, "What's your pipeline, Peter?"

"Quite different from Frank. I could've picked choppers after T-34s at Saufley. I didn't want choppers because our Navy chopper mission is flying around aircraft carriers picking up pilots who ditch at sea. Not very exciting. I chose to go multi-engine fixed wing because the duty stations are along beautiful coastal cities like Key West, Jacksonville, San Francisco, San Diego, and last, but not least, Hawaii. Who can pass up a chance to be based in Hawaii while you're still getting paid? I unfortunately have to leave this paradise of Pensacola in a few weeks to go to Texas for a few more months of training. My next few weeks are make or break. I start carrier qualification training next week. There are a lot of 'drops on request' before the actual carrier event. I've even thought about it myself. I've gone this far so I'm going to see it through."

"Can you stay here if you 'drop on request?'" Nan asked.

"Great question, but probably not. I'd probably go to a Navy workship to finish out my tour."

"Well, cheers to you both!" Betsy said. "Let's celebrate tonight for whatever comes along, be it hell or high water. I see no reason we can't have another celebration in New Orleans in the coming weeks."

"Cheers to that!" We clinked glasses.

After a sunset dinner of barbecue and champagne it was time for our ritualistic evening swim in the ocean. The girls led as always. Bikinis left in the surf. Girls break for the cabin with a head start. Tonight, they seemed slower than usual. Just as they jumped into the beach towels, we received a shock. Betsy had a mermaid tattoo on her right cheek! We had never considered that option.

Once everyone had dried off, I made a demand. "All right, girls, tell us all about the tattoos on opposite cheeks! That doesn't make sense. Why not the same cheek?"

"See, you boys are wired differently. While you are having different thoughts about us, it's very simple. Our dad actually approved it," Nan explained.

"You're kidding," Frank gasped.

"No, the reasoning was that if we were both in a car wreck and had to be identified, how would you do it?"

"Brilliant." I smiled. "The only downside I can see to this probably wouldn't apply to you girls."

"What would that downside be?" Nan asked curiously.

"What if one of you were to moon somebody? You could be identified."

Nan and Betsy both laughed. "We would never do that. You boys are definitely wired differently. I guess that's a good thing."

We clinked glasses again.

BINGO

The next week was filled with Field Carrier Landing Practice (FCLP) flights. Barron Field near Perdido Bay was the site selected by the Navy. The runways were set up exactly like the presentation on a US Navy aircraft carrier deck. The differences are aircraft carriers usually are headed directly into the wind. Also, there are no arresting cables at Barron. The landing technique is exactly like the real carrier. Carrier landings are substantially different from normal aircraft landings. The landing radial deck of an aircraft carrier is only five hundred feet long. That's slightly less than two football fields.

The object of the carrier landing is for the airplane to fly as slowly as possible with all of the drag items extended; flaps, landing gear, tail hook, and canopy open (as in the case of the T-28). The drag is offset by a higher power setting than normal to get a controlled descent rate and still maintain about 3 knots above stall speed. There is no margin for error. The LSO (Landing Signal Officer) is the man on the deck who talks the pilot down to the deck. He is a seasoned Navy pilot who is very experienced in conducting carrier landings and is entrusted with pilots' lives. He can look at an airplane coming in and, with the naked eye, determine the speed and sink rate with unbelievable accuracy. His recommendations are mandatory. He doesn't usually have to buy drinks at happy hour.

To supplement the LSO's guidance, there is a glideslope device consisting of lights and mirrors which give the pilot glideslope information. The object for the pilot is to keep the resultant "meatball" centered which tells him he is on the correct glideslope. There are four heavyduty cables lying across the deck designed to catch the tail hook and stop the airplane on the short 500-foot deck. The cables have some play so that the airplanes have some deceleration before the sudden full stop. The perfect landing should catch the number three cable.

The LSO will give the cut signal for the pilot to cut his power and essentially stall the aircraft over the #3 cable. It doesn't always happen that way.

Three other student pilots and I completed the FCLP

training and now were eligible for the carrier. It's the critical time in a Naval aviator's career to see if he has the right stuff. The DOR curve jumps sharply the week before the trip to the carrier. I had come this far and worked too hard to think of not finishing now. My friends Bax, Joe, and Andy are the other three.

We'll be leaving Pensacola next Monday in a five-plane formation to fly to Naval Station Mayport near Jacksonville. We'll overnight there and fly out at 0500 the next morning to rendezvous with our carrier at sea, the USS Intrepid, CVS-11. She'll be about one hundred miles at sea.

The Intrepid has a storied history. She was commissioned in 1943 soon after the Japanese attack on Pearl Harbor. During the war, she was hit by five Kamikaze planes. Her battle tally was 301 airplanes and 122 ships damaged or sunk.

The four of us will be led by Major Hooper, USMC, the operations department head for Whiting Field. Major Hooper is reputedly in consideration to fly with the Blue Angels. He will be the lead pilot over to Mayport and will lead us in a five-plane echelon out to the carrier the next morning.

Joe, Bax, Andy, and I met in the "O" Club the night before departure.

"Well, guys, this is it. Did y'all think we would get to this point?" Andy asked as he slugged down the first round.

"I honestly didn't. This wasn't my life plan. I was supposed to be a CPA. I don't know how I got sidetracked into this situation where I've got to go land an airplane on a 500-foot runway. I'm too dumb not to DOR," I said with a laugh.

Bax chimed in. "I almost DOR'd after that formation fire drill where we all got separated and two of you had to go into Mainside airport with oil all over your windscreens. I was #2 that day with the leaking oil. The low oil pressure and low oil quantity lights both came on about five miles out before I landed back at Whiting. The engine was coughing all the way down to the runway and quit as I touched down. I actually asked a yeoman for the DOR form."

"Joe, you're always so cool! You probably never thought about a DOR, did you?"

"Ha!" Joe bellowed. "I actually did DOR. I never told anybody about it. It was right after the Dilbert Dunker. I don't think any of you were in that swim class. The frogmen had to get me out twice before I finally passed. Lt. Williams talked me out of it. I had nightmares for weeks."

We all laughed at this confession time. It was nice to know we all had the same reservations about what lay ahead.

We met Major Hooper at 1200 in operations with our small overnight duffle bags. We were allowed only to bring a change of underwear and toiletries.

Major Hooper was a stern-looking dude who looked like he worked out with weights and ran five miles every day. It was said that he shot down two migs on the same day in North Vietnam.

"Men, congratulations for arriving at this stage of your training. You are about to do something that only Navy and Marine pilots do.

"None of you are nervous, are you?"

Our hands shot up.

He laughed. "It's perfectly normal. On my first one a Marine slipped up behind me and goosed me and I almost had a heart attack!

"I've checked the weather, and flight-planned us over to Mayport. Weather's good, so we won't have any problem staying formed up. We're filed VFR, but I'll be off frequency periodically to check in with air traffic control. It's a short flight, about fifty minutes. Be sure to check operation of your tail hooks. We don't do that normally. We'll do a running rendezvous to join up. I'll be #1, Bax #2, Cal #3, Andy #4, Peter #5. Peter you're tail end Charlie—sometimes I'll just call you Charlie. You're responsible for letting me know the formation is secure and tight. We'll be flying over in a loose formation and tighten it up to three feet about thirty miles out of Mayport. We must look sharp on our arrival there.

"The main difference in what we've been doing is I'll be #1 now and you'll be two through five. Everybody ready?"

We all nodded. Nobody was jumping for joy.

My head was swimming all the way to Mayport. The FCLP

training weeks went by so fast. So much to remember. And now tail end Charlie. I've got to keep the formation tight.

The flight to Mayport went by quickly. Before I knew it Major Hooper was calling out, "Charlie, are we tight?"

"Yes, sir. We're tight."

This was the most exciting moment of my life so far.

0330 came quickly. We were rousted out by the BOQ duty officer who cried out, "Up and at 'em, boys. Big day ahead!" He almost got hit in the head by a shoe.

There was very little moon, so the pre-flights were done in virtual darkness using flashlights. Major Hooper told us we would see the sun-up before we got to the Intrepid. We were instructed to fly out at twenty feet wing tip separation and join to three feet at the carrier. I wasn't crazy about doing the formation join-up in the dark. I remembered to check the tail hook operation for the first time.

We took off sequentially on runway 5 and immediately made left turns to begin the running rendezvous. The light in my kneeboard checklist wouldn't come on so I was doing my after-takeoff checklist from memory. Only three items are on it so that was easy. Gear up, throttle 36 inches, prop 2400, and accelerate to climb schedule.

I could see in the distance the flashing tail lights of #4 but I couldn't pick up the others yet. I set climb power and leveled off at 5,500 feet. I should be closing in shortly.

Major Hooper: "I have a 'Bingo,' men, ship's in sight! How's the join-up coming along? #2, you in place?"

#2: "Yes, sir, I'm at twenty feet as briefed."

Hooper: "#3?"

#3: "I have #2 in sight and closing."

Hooper: "#4?"

#4: "I have #3 in sight and beginning to close."

Hooper: "Charlie?"

"I have #4 in sight."

Hooper: "Okay, good. Everyone maintain 190 knots until I give the word to slow."

Cripes! I'm not closing. Only 150 knots. What the heck is going on? Andy's pulling away. I went to 35 inches MAP.

Hooper: "Charlie, you closed up yet?"

"Not quite, sir."

Hooper: "We're about forty miles out, now hurry up. Report when closed."

"Aye, sir."

I began to feel a rumbling. I had been steadily increasing power to catch up. I suddenly realized my cowl flaps were still open. They weren't a check list item. How stupid of me! I quickly went to max power and closed the cowls and accelerated to 220 knots. I was now closing like mad.

Hooper: "Charlie, you closed yet?"

"Yes, sir," I lied. I would be shortly.

Hooper: "We're 30 out now. I'm coming back to 25 inches."

I now had to slow this thing down for the join-up on Andy. I closed the throttle and threw out the speed brake just in time to see the startled look on Andy's face as I came shooting by him.

THE BOAT

This was not the textbook way to arrive at the carrier. Desirably, you're tucked in at three feet wing separation, slowing to 140 knots, readying to go into the landing checklist followed by the break checklist, each of which contains seven items. You would be stabilized at 1,500 feet, glancing out at the huge ship looming into view at your 10 o'clock position, just over your left wingtip. You would be thinking about your turn to go into the break thirty seconds after Andy made his break. Your heartbeat would be elevated but not racing.

None of these scenarios applied to me. My throttle had been going from full throttle to full back. I slowed to the point that Andy passed me back. I was not exactly tucked in but somehow fell into a loose formation close to Andy.

I glanced down at the landing checklist and finished item number 5, tail hook-optional. I remembered to leave it up since my first two landings are touch-and-go to get familiar with the tiny carrier runway. Item number 6 is canopy-open. I pulled the handle and the canopy opened and the cool fresh air of the ocean entered the cockpit. This cool, fresh air decided to blow my checklist off my kneeboard and right into the Atlantic Ocean. At this point I couldn't worry about trivialities like checklists. I was way too busy. Andy and I were past the 90 position and he would be breaking soon. The one checklist I had memorized cold was the break checklist which consisted of seven items. It started with a left 40-degree angle of bank 30 seconds following Andy's break.

Now it was all about doing the common sense items we normally do. I dropped the gear, stowed the speed brake, slowed to 120 knots, and set the prop to 2400. I counted the seven items as they fell into place. At the 45 position I somehow got the speed to the desired 100 knots after lowering the flaps to full.

The steadying voice of the LSO boomed out. "Trainer 5, I have you turning final. Your gear appears down and locked. Radio check."

"Loud and clear, sir."

"Roger, no more transmissions. You are slightly high and fast. Reduce power. You're 2 knots fast. Get on 83 knots."

I don't know how he could know all these things. It was like he was sitting next to me in the cockpit. Before I knew it, I was on final and got the cut signal. I slammed down hard onto the deck just as the LSO shouted.

"Get your power back on."

I slammed the throttle forward and away I went. The ocean was right beneath me as I cleared the short deck and climbed back to re-enter the pattern. My poor heart was beating for all it was worth. All thoughts of checklists no longer entered my mind. Just do what you think you need to do. My third landing was a "trap"—full stop with tail hook. I would need eight of these. After five pretty good full stop traps and takeoffs, I turned downwind readying for my sixth trap. I was approaching the abeam position and glanced down at my instruments. To my chagrin, a red sump light was staring at me. Dammit, I only needed two more traps and I'd be finished. I had to call the sump light to the LSO. A sump light gives an indication that metal shavings may have been magnetically picked up which could cause engine failure.

In response, the LSO ordered all other planes to climb 500 feet to clear the way for me.

"Trainer 5, you're #1 in the pattern. Go through your engine failure checklist and make your turn in when you're ready. Don't extend too far out."

What checklist? I muttered. Maybe it's time to bid back to the Neptune.

My focus was stretched to the limit. I just wanted to get back on the deck and get out and take a break. I've never worked so hard in my life. I made the turn to final and worked the speed to 100 at the 45. I turned final and the LSO boomed out. "Good job, Trainer 5. You're looking good. Speed is 85. You're on glideslope. Hold what you've got. A little low, add a little more power. Speed's good. Hold what you've got." I finally got the cut and snagged the #3 cable.

"Trainer 5, you get a 'Bravo Zulu' (Well Done). Pull out of the way and a tug will hook you up."

I climbed out of the T-28 and was taken to the wardroom. I learned a while later that all my buddies had finished their quals and were flying in formation back to Mayport. The LSO, Lieutenant Commander Whorley, came into the wardroom and sat down beside me.

"Mr. Pinson, you had quite a day. A sump light can be a harrowing experience. I've only had one in my career, but the engine actually seized on me. I was in the pattern with a student at Barron Field and we had plenty of airspeed and altitude. I have your grades for the day.

"Pattern entry-unsatisfactory. Someone pulled the tapes and said it was the most unusual entry in Naval aviation history. I'm anxious to see the tapes."

"I'll pass if you don't mind."

"Your touch-and-go landings weren't bad. Typical first time approaches. Your first five traps were okay. They were safe enough. About what we expect.

"Your sixth approach and landing was magnificent. By far the best of everybody today. It shows what you can do when the going gets tough. You followed the checklists nicely. I'm going to offset the unsatisfactory arrival because of your stellar approach and landing under stressful circumstances."

I didn't have the heart to tell him I had no checklists.

"You'll have to stay overnight with us on the carrier to get your final two landings. Operations are finished for today, but we'll get you first thing in the morning. Check with the chief steward and he'll find you a bunk for tonight."

Aircraft carriers don't sleep at night I found out. I heard strange sounds all night long. I still hadn't calmed down from all of the previous day's activities. I finally got to sleep and was aroused by a steward mate who informed me my solo launch would be at 0700 hours.

I was briefed by the operations officer as to what my period would consist of. My plane had been thoroughly inspected and found the sump light to be faulty. I would need two traps and finish up. The early sounds of the carrier were awesome. This was too easy. No early morning rendezvous in the dark. Lady luck was finally on my side. The two takeoffs and landings were right on the money. I was finished.

After debriefing, I was put on a COD (carrier on board delivery) airplane and flown to Pensacola. I arrived ahead of my three buddies who were coming back from Mayport. When they arrived at the "O" Club for celebrations, I was waiting for them.

When they saw me sitting there smiling, Andy turned to Joe and Bax. "You know, guys, Peter is always out of step with us."

Since school was out for the summer, the terrifying terrific twins were now hunkered down at the beach. I couldn't wait to call Nan to celebrate. She had probably known other Navy pilots who had hit the boat, but I hoped she would think mine was special.

"Nan, guess what?"

"You got a new car?"

"Of course not, dummy. You know what I did."

"I knew about it as soon as you did it."

"What!"

"My dad plays golf with Admiral Gay. He had the ship track your flight. The ship called him, and he called my dad. He says you made Naval history or something."

"I hope not. Are you free tonight?"

"I'm not free, but I'm cheap. Come on down. Frank's going to be here also. He's celebrating something as well."

"That's great—you can break out the champagne."

The girls prepared a big dinner for us. They don't cook, so they had it catered. Frank was there when I arrived. He had a big grin on his face.

"What's up, buddy? Why the grin?"

"I'll tell you later when it's time."

"Do you know where I've been the last couple of days?" I tried to appear humble, but it wasn't working.

"Of course, you hit the boat. I knew about it as soon as you did it."

"What!"

I looked over at Nan and Betsy who were grinning from ear to ear.

After the feast, I said. "Frank, Nan said you were celebrating something. What's up?"

Frank said, "Come over here, Betsy." They both stood up. "While you were out playing your little games on the boat, Betsy and I decided to get married."

After the initial shock was over, I gave them both a big hug.

"Well, maybe I can get my orders changed to stay here in helicopters as well—must be something in the water. But I doubt if it would be possible to change orders now." I laughed.

"Don't laugh," Betsy said. "Our dad plays regular golf with Admiral Gay. You never know."

EPILOGUE

Everything was moving at warp speed. Andy, Joe, Cal, Bax and I got orders to report to Corpus Christi, Texas, in one week for advanced training on the S2-F Tracker, a twin-engine airplane with fold up wings. These types of wings save valuable parking space on a carrier. Tiki will be training on the A-1 Skyraider, a single engine attack bomber.

I'm still getting over the carrier experience and trying to absorb the ecstasy. It's behind me now and time to move on to the next challenge to achieve the Navy "Wings of Gold." The "Needs of the Navy" trump all other considerations and the needs all point toward Vietnam. Helicopter training is not one of the needs for Navy pilots at present.

I was so excited to see the engagement of Frank and Betsy. That blindsided me but made me happy. I wasn't sure the redheads could be broken up. I hoped this wouldn't mess up our return to New Orleans. My drive to Corpus Christi would take me through New Orleans but it wouldn't be the same without the other three. I'm going to miss the beach house and all the "mysteries" we solved. Nan and I are going to the Mainside "O" Club for dinner before I leave. Maybe I'll have time to get one more ride on Nina, the horse who judges a person's character.

I may be leaving Pensacola but there is no doubt that it will not stay in the rearview mirror. All Navy flight training begins and ends here. One thing was for sure; as they say in Navy parlance— "A sailor never gets over the lure of a Mermaid."

ACKNOWLEDGEMENTS

As in any endeavor, the second project is easier than the first because of familiarity with the task. This is true in writing a second book about a similar subject. I am still indebted to my original helpers who got me started on the first project.

I joined a local novel writing group led by Mary Belk, a talented writer and teacher who has published books of her own. She also writes a weekly column in the local newspaper. Our class bonded and pushed each other to publish. One of the class members, Ora Maurer, has a book of her own coming out, and she has faithfully offered encouragement throughout the process. Our class consisted of me and "seven other women."

It's purely by accident that I joined another group of women writers in Atlanta. The group is called the Zona Rosa and was hosted by Rosemary Danielle, an acclaimed writer and teacher. I don't believe there were ever any men in the group before me, and maybe I made them a little uncomfortable. Rosemary invited the ladies down to the beach in Savannah for workshops, but my invitations must have been lost in the mail.

All of these people were invaluable assets in reviewing and recommending paths to follow in my two books. Another set of eyes always sees things you don't see, particularly those that are quite obvious.

My dear friend Janet Smith is an amazing editor as well as a French teacher. She retired from the Opelika School system as a language teacher after many years. She also worked as a proofreader for the Auburn Bulletin and Opelika-Auburn News.

Bill Womelsdorf, a friend and fraternity brother, provided some expert help in getting the work formatted and ready for publication.

A renowned local author, Ken Ringer, has been a great help in directing me to the right sources for publication and marketing. His book has been a local best seller and was pitched on the Paul Finebaum program.

Mary Belk continues to amaze me with her weekly articles in our local paper. She is truly a great writer and teacher. She is also a source of encouragement.

My son-in-law, Walter Thompson, made suggestions on the cover, and my sister-in-law, Frances Grandy was always a great help with use of Google Docs and Microsoft Word.

A big thank you goes to Tina Tatum, the publisher at Woodson Knowles Publishing Group for her expertise and advice.

I have a bunch of Navy pilot buddies who have shared stories of training "faux pas" in Pensacola but are too numerous to mention here. There were many other great stories about pilot training, and I wish I could have included them all.

I am grateful to my wife Cathy for allowing me the time to put these novels together. I have seen her shaking her head in wonder after reading some of the adventures of Ensign Pinson. I have to keep reminding her that this is only a novel, but I know she has her doubts.

APPENDIX I

Officer Ranks Navy and Coast Guard

Ensign	ENS	O-1
Lieutenant Junior Grade	LTJG	O-2
Lieutenant	LT	O-3
Lieutenant Commander	LCDR	O-4
Commanr	CDR	O-5
Captain	CAPT	O-6
RearAdmiral	ADMIRAL	O-7,8
Vice Admiral	ADMIRAL	O-9
Admiral	ADMIRAL	O-10
Fleet Admiral	ADMIRAL	O-11

Officer Ranks: Marine Corps

Second Lieutenant	2LT	O-1
First Lieutenant	1LT	O-2
Captain	CAPT	O-3
Major	MAJ	O-4
Lieutenant Colonel	LT COL	O-5
Colonel	COL	O-6
Brigadier General	B GEN	O-7
Major General	MAJ GEN	O-8
Lieutenant General	LT GEN	O-9
General	GEN	O-10

APPENDIX II

NAVAL ABBREVIATIONS

BOQ	Bachelor Officer Quarters
LT	Lieutenant
LTJG	Lieutenant Junior Grade
LCDR	Lieutenant Commander
CDR	Commander
BUPERS	Bureau of Personnel
OOD	Officer of the Deck (Ship)
OOD	Officer of the Day (Land)
NAS	Naval Air Station
UHF	Ultra High Frequency-Exterior radio
"O" CLUB	Officers' Club
COMNAVAIRLANT	Commander, Naval Air Forces, Atlantic Fleet
SECNAV	Secretary of the Navy
GCA	Radar Guided Instrument Approach
ILS	Instrument Landing System
ICS	Inner Cockpit Communication System
RDO	Runway Duty Officer
NDB	Navigational Radio
MESS	Chow Hall
PORT (side)	Left
STARBOARD (side)	Right
HEAD	Rest Room
SCUTTLEBUTT	Latest information
PDL	Pass Down the Line
MAP	Manifold Air Pressure
NDB	Directional Navaid
DOR	Drop on Request
NavCad	Naval Cadet
MarCad	Marine Cadet
The BOAT	Carrier
LSO	Landing Signal Officer (carrier)
FCLP	Field Carrier Landing Practice
GEEDUNK	Short Order Store

APPENDIX III

Navy / Military Time

1	AM	0100
2	AM	0200
3	AM	0300
4	AM	0400
5	AM	0500
6	AM	0600
7	AM	0700
8	AM	0800
9	AM	0900
10	AM	1000
11	AM	1100
12	AM	1200
1	PM	1300
2	PM	1400
3	PM	1500
4	PM	1600
5	PM	1700
6	PM	1800
7	PM	1900
8	PM	2000
9	PM	2100
10	PM	2200
11	PM	2300
12	PM	2400/0000

ABOUT THE AUTHOR

Ensign Pinson Goes to Flight School is a sequel to *All Back Two-Thirds*, another novel about humorous life in the Navy. The Navy is picked on more than the other services for good reason! "Mister Roberts" and "McHale's Navy" are just two long-living examples of naval humor.

Jim Dozier is a native of Columbus, Georgia, and a graduate of Columbus High School. He graduated from Auburn University in 1962 achieving ODK, Who's Who, president of Auburn's "A" Club, and won three SEC mile run championships. He served in the U S Navy for six years, earned the Navy pilot "Wings of Gold," and landed on the USS Intrepid, which was decommissioned in 1974 and is now berthed on the Hudson River as the centerpiece of the Intrepid Sea, Air & Space museum.

After six years in the Navy, thirty-one years with Delta Airlines, fifteen more years of general aviation flying, Jim finally retired from flying with over 20,000 hours of flight time. He has qualified in twenty-six different types of airplanes, from the Cherokee Arrow to Boeing 747s.

He currently lives in Auburn, Alabama, and is married to Cathy, a former flight attendant and Auburn graduate. They have three daughters and three grandchildren. Jim is a charter member of the "Wellreadneck Book Club," a diversified group of readers and authors in Auburn.

CPSIA information can be obtained
at www.ICGtesting.com
Printed in the USA
LVHW021520200123
737509LV00003B/741